SERGEANT CRUSOE

Luke Sharp is unaware that he has a double — Marco da Silva, the ruthless criminal gang leader known as 'Silver'. When a pair of vigilantes intent on taking their revenge against Silver shoot Luke by mistake, his life is changed dramatically. Convalescing at his grandfather's home, he agrees to transcribe the old man's wartime memoirs of his exploits in the South Pacific. However, Silver finds out about Luke, and attempts to coerce him into work as his double in crime . . .

LESLIE WILKIE

SERGEANT CRUSOE

Complete and Unabridged

LINFORD
Leicester

First published in Great Britain

First Linford Edition
published 2015

A catalogue record for this book is available
from the British Library.

ISBN 978–1–4448–2413–1

Published by
F. A. Thorpe (Publishing)
Anstey, Leicestershire

Set by Words & Graphics Ltd.
Anstey, Leicestershire
Printed and bound in Great Britain by
T. J. International Ltd., Padstow, Cornwall

This book is printed on acid-free paper

Dedicated to

Joan
Colette, Alison, Deborah
Dominic and Natalie
Ian and Peter
Billy, Louis and Joe.
And
The Cyclist, the Fisherman and the
Football Coach.

1

The first shot knocked me to my knees whilst the second should have killed me. I remember thinking just how warm the pavement felt against my cheek before two shadowy figures appeared above me. Then I distinctly heard what I thought was my epitaph.

'Aw shit, it's not him. Sorry mate.'

Then a different voice kept telling me to 'hang in there' as my systems began to shut down. I must have followed that advice because I woke four days later in a hospital bed with tubes seemingly coming out of every orifice and a mouth that felt like the inside of a sumo wrestler's jockstrap, figuratively speaking of course. I have never tasted a sweeter sip of water than the one I was given then by the policewoman sitting by my bed.

I must have slipped in and out of consciousness many times that day because at various times I registered the presence of nurses, a doctor and different policemen. I remember being asked 'what happened' several times and my repetition of that phrase I'd assumed was my epitaph. In the end they all left me in peace and the young policewoman resumed her seat by the bed. I remember her telling me that my assailants had a conscience because they had sent a bunch of roses addressed to the 'shot man' with a card that simply said 'sorry'. For some reason they didn't sign it.

My fortunate survival was due largely to the fact that an ambulance was turning into the street at the time the shots were fired. The driver and his medical partner were by my side in less than a minute. They kept me alive and got me into the hospital within seven minutes. I was apparently in the operating theatre fifteen minutes after the shooting. Oddly enough although there were fifteen people who saw the shooting not one of them could identify the gunmen. The two men were variously described as short and fat, tall and thin, black, white and Asian-looking. Their getaway car was a large black, grey or blue saloon with dark windows. The police found a dark green saloon car on fire two streets away. It had been stolen the day before from a supermarket car park.

When I woke the following day the policewoman had gone. In her place sat a guy in plain clothes eating a sandwich and drinking coffee from a plastic cup. I watched him for a couple of minutes before he realised that I'd come round. He looked in need of a shave and a few hours' sleep. When he realised that I was awake he put down the coffee and reached inside his jacket for something. I almost had heart failure but instead of the gun I was expecting him to produce he pulled out his wallet and waved his I.D. card in front of me.

'Cooper,' he spluttered through the remains of his sandwich. 'Cooper, detective sergeant.'

There was a piece of what looked like bacon stuck between his front teeth and he worked that loose with his little finger before continuing.

'Are you up to answering a few

questions?' he asked.

'I need a drink,' I replied.

'Liquor?'

'No, tea or coffee.'

'Hang on, I'll see what I can find,' he said, as he got to his feet.

He returned a few minutes later accompanied by a nurse who took my temperature before allowing me to take a few sips of the warm sweet tea that she'd brought with her. Then she asked the sergeant to wait outside while she checked all the various drips and drains that I was still attached to. Finally she allowed me a few more sips of the tea before telling me that the doctor would be with me shortly. She left and the sergeant returned and resumed his seat by the bed.

'Thanks,' I said.

'What for?'

'The tea.'

'Oh yes, it's been a long night. I'm not up to speed yet,' he replied as he rubbed the stubble on his chin.

'Well go and get some sleep. I'll still be here for a while.'

He smiled. 'I wish I could but I need some info from you first.'

'Okay.'

As he opened his notebook the sergeant groaned as he flipped over the pages and stopped at what I presumed was a clean one.

'God, I've still got that report to finish,' he said.

'Anything good?' I asked.

'Soliciting, no not you — I'd better start you off on a new sheet.' He flipped over the page then asked, 'Name?'

'Luke Sharp.'

'Address?'

'I'm staying at the New Oxford Hotel.'

'No you're not. They saw your picture in the paper and checked you out. We've got your suitcases at the station. I need your permanent address.'

'I haven't got one at the moment.'

'Hm, I'll make that no fixed abode.'

The doctor and his entourage walked in then and suggested that the sergeant waited outside again. Even before the door had closed behind him the nurses had lifted the covers from me and the doctor began his examination. That gave me the opportunity to look down at my body and apart from bandages my only covering appeared to be a pair of long white socks. There were two tubes leading out from my left side, one about halfway down my rib cage and the other much lower down. On my right side a drip was attached to the back of my hand. My chest was tightly bandaged whilst my stomach and my left shoulder carried plastered patches. I'd felt no pain before the examination but I was biting my lip by the time he'd finished. As he straightened up he looked at my face for the first time.

'Are you in pain?' he asked.

'Yes,' I groaned.

He must have known I would be because he merely nodded to one of the nurses and she gave me an injection.

'That should ease things,' he said. 'I'm your surgeon and I have to tell you that you are a very lucky man. Both bullets hit you in the chest but one was deflected up into your shoulder whilst the other finished up in your groin. Your ribcage is a bit of a mess, I had to wire you up in there and there was some damage to your plumbing but we got that sorted. You've lost a lot of blood but we should be able to get you out of here in a couple of weeks. Any questions?'

'Not at the moment,' I replied through gritted teeth.

'Good man.' He turned away then put his hand into his pocket and produced a small glass tube. He looked down at me again as he placed it on the bedside cabinet.

'A souvenir,' he said.

'What is it?'

'The bullets I took out of you.'

I was still lying looking at that tube when the sergeant was allowed back in. As he resumed his seat by the bed he asked if I was okay.

'Yes,' I replied. 'I was just wondering how two small objects like that could make such a mess of me.'

The policeman picked up the tube and shook it.

'Nasty little beasts,' he said. 'Now can we get back to my questions?'

'Yes, go ahead.'

'Why were you in that street?'

'I'd just been to my solicitor's. In fact I'd just walked out onto the street when I was shot.'

'Who did they mistake you for?'

'I don't know but I've just remembered that there was a bruiser in the hallway when I came down the stairs from the office.'

'A bruiser?'

'Yes, he was built like brick whatnot, broken nose, square head and square fists. He gave me a strange look when I passed him.'

'Would you recognise him again?'

'Of course.'

'Good, I'll get someone to bring in the mug-shots.'

'Well do it later. I'm nodding off again, sorry.'

The building that housed my solicitor had three floors. The ground floor held the offices of a group of lawyers who specialised in criminal cases. On the next floor up were my solicitors, completely separate from the group below and concentrating their efforts on lesser civil cases. The top floor held more offices, this time of a private enquiry agency. As a friend of mine once put it rather succinctly, 'all the sharks are in the same tank'. My shark had been tying up the loose ends of my divorce settlement.

I clearly remember picking out the photograph of the broken-nosed bruiser that afternoon but that was the last clear memory that I had for several days. Apparently my temperature suddenly shot up and I went into a weird world of broken dreams and nightmares for almost a week. When I eventually came round I felt like a limp wet rag. It was an effort to even attempt to lift my head off the pillow and I failed to correct the nurse when she said I must be feeling better. Shortly afterwards the doctor turned up, looked me over and declared that I could go home in a couple of days to recuperate. He really looked upset when I managed to mumble the fact that I didn't have one.

'One what?'

'A home, I haven't got a home?'

'Well you can't stop here, we need the bed.'

Until a few weeks earlier I had been living in what had been our marital home but it had been sold along with its contents in the divorce settlement. It was a fifty-fifty split despite the fact that my ex-wife had left me for a Canadian that she'd met at a cocktail party in London. All I was left with was two suitcases of clothes, three cardboard boxes of personal effects (stored in a friend's garage) and my half of the sale money. By the time the legal bills had been settled I had enough left to buy a caravan to live in if I needed a roof over my head. As it turned out I didn't need the caravan.

Apart from my ex-wife my only living relative was my maternal grandfather James Bullock. He was at the time seventy-seven years old and though perfectly sound in mind was getting a bit dodgy on his pins, as he put it. He lived in a quiet village in East Yorkshire supported by a twice weekly visit from the district nurse and weekly deliveries of frozen meals on wheels. He was approached,

10

without my knowledge, and asked if he could provide me with a bed for a couple of weeks. I think he must have been feeling lonely because he agreed on condition that the nurse paid more frequent visits to sort me out. That's how I ended up being driven by ambulance across the Yorkshire Wolds one sunny April morning.

On arrival at the bungalow I found a welcoming committee consisting of the local doctor, the nurse and a police constable. The constable stayed only long enough to assure me that he'd ride by regularly to check that I was okay. The doctor and nurse checked my dressings and assured me that everything was fine before departing themselves. Once they'd gone I felt shattered but my grandfather saw my plight and revived me with a truly glorious glass of cool beer. It was only later that I noticed that the diet sheet I'd been left made no mention of beer. In fact it was when I was studying that sheet that I realised that no one had thought about how I was going to collect or cook the food mentioned. At that time I was capable of walking only a few paces unaided and the one shop in the village was half a mile away. Apart from Grandfather's meals on wheels the only food in the house was a few dusty tins in his larder. I dined that night on baked beans and cream crackers. The date on the beans tin was indeterminate but the crackers were two years out of date. Two days later when the nurse finally realised my plight and arranged for a food delivery the dusty tins had been reduced to one solitary rusty individual without a label that looked suspiciously like the cat food tins we used to buy for our long defunct ginger tom, my ex-wife's moggy.

In response to the nurse's efforts to find me some nourishment the lady from the local shop arrived to ask just what it was I required. She looked quite shocked when she saw the state I was in and commented on it straight away.

'Shouldn't you still be in hospital?' she exclaimed.

'They needed the bed for somebody else,' I replied.

'That somebody must have been in a

bad way judging by you.'

I had managed to greet her at the front door but by the time I'd accompanied her into the lounge I was in a state of near collapse, seeing that she helped me back into an armchair. Once I was settled she held out her hand and introduced herself.

'I'm Sally Catchpole,' she said. 'My family runs the village shop. I'm told that you need some food delivering. What do you need?'

'Thank you for coming, I'm Luke, Luke Sharp and my needs are simple. I require food that I can stick into my grandfather's microwave and eat five minutes later.'

She looked at me in horror. 'You're never going to get fit again on ready meals. You need proper feeding.'

'The trouble is that I can't stand at the stove long enough to cook a proper meal,' I replied. 'I may be able to after a week or so. Anyway those meals can't be too bad because Grandfather lives on them all the time.'

'He doesn't need building up like you.'

She got to her feet and moved towards

the door. 'Joyce said that you had a diet sheet. Can I see it?' she said, turning back to face me.

'Joyce?'

'The nurse.'

'Yes, it's there on the table.'

She picked it up and read through it. 'Right,' she said. 'I'll be back in an hour. Cheerio.'

She actually returned within the hour and she brought with her a meal already cooked and piping hot. It was a simple repast of baked cod, creamed potatoes and peas but after my two days of beans and crackers it tasted exquisite. She sat with me while I cleared the plate. As I put down my knife and fork I looked across at her, smiled and then burped.

'Sorry,' I said.

'Don't be, the Chinese consider it polite to do just that after a meal to show their appreciation to the cook.'

'Did you cook it?'

'Yes.'

'Thank you, thank you, thank you — I was on the verge of starvation until you came along.'

'You could have had one of your grandfather's frozen meals,' she said.

'No, Jim is very careful with them. He checks them every day.'

'Jim?'

'My grandfather, he insists I call him Jim.'

'He must think a lot of you if you're using Christian names.'

'He's hardly spoken since I arrived. He offered me a beer when I got here, told me to call him Jim and has hardly spoken since.'

'Maybe he's shy.'

'I never thought of that, you may be right. I'll try talking to him again when we're alone this evening.'

She looked round. 'Where is he now?' she asked.

'In the garden shed, he spends a lot of time out there.'

'Why?'

'I don't know but I intend finding out as soon as I'm fit. If he won't talk to me in here I'll have to go and talk to him out there.'

'I still think he might be shy, he has

been alone here for some time.'

She picked up the plate and walked towards the door. In the doorway she looked back and smiled. 'You look better already,' she said. 'I'll bring you some cereal and bread and so on later then you'll be able to make your own breakfast.'

2

Sally Catchpole was a member of the village Women's Institute and I think she arranged a special meeting in the shop that day. As a result I received a cooked meal at lunchtime for the next ten days. Each day it was cooked and delivered by a different W.I. member and try as I might I found it impossible to remember all their names. I still remember the two Dorises because of the complete physical difference between them. Doris the younger was a plump, jolly fifty-year-old whilst her older friend must have been about seventy and was as thin as a rake and very shy. Ethel was covered in flour when she arrived. There was a smear of it on her face, more on her forearms and down the front of her pinafore. She said she was baking bread but she needn't have told me because the smell of fresh bread wafted around her like some exotic perfume. Then there was Betty, Janice,

Olive, Susan and Mary and others whose faces I remember but whose names defeat me. Even now when I greet them in the street I feel somewhat embarrassed because I can't always put the right name to the right face. However, without their assistance I am certain my recovery would have taken much longer than it did. Forget the 'Jam and Jerusalem' tag those ladies were brilliant as far as I was concerned.

I had to return to hospital for a day for a minor follow-up operation. There was a small splinter of bone causing me some discomfort but it was located and removed under local anaesthetic. That was the turning point in my recovery I think because when I got back I began to prepare my own meals. I passed on my thanks to the W.I. ladies via Sally at the shop and to each individual if I met them in the street. I cannot claim that my cooking was any better than theirs but at least I could concentrate on my favourites instead of taking pot luck with the ladies' choices.

Sergeant Cooper turned up the next

day bearing an unwanted gift. He brought me the two bullets that had caused me so much pain.

'I thought you'd like these back,' he said.

'When did you get hold of them?'

'I took them from beside your bed in the hospital. Forensics examined them but they haven't been able to find a match.'

'You've come a long way to deliver these,' I said as I took them from him.

'There's more,' he replied. Then he looked around before asking, 'Are you alone?'

'My grandfather's out in the garden shed, I can call him if you like.'

'No, it's you I want to talk to, do you mind if I sit down?'

'Sorry, please do, I wasn't thinking. Fancy a coffee?'

'Please.'

After I made the coffee we sat opposite each other. I waited for him to begin but he seemed reluctant to do so. Finally, after he'd drained the cup I'd given him he took an envelope from his pocket and passed it to me.

'Open it,' he said.

Inside it there was a black and white photograph, a photograph of me. I sat there open-mouthed at first because although it looked like me it wasn't me. The face was mine except for a small scar below the right eye but the hair definitely wasn't mine. It was jet black with a white streak above that right eye.

'Who . . . who?' I stammered.

'We believe that's the man who was the intended shooting victim.'

'Who is he?'

'His name is Marco Da Silva but he's commonly known as Silver.' He spelt out the names for me so I could see the difference. 'He's known to police forces in Yorkshire and Lancashire but he hasn't been convicted of anything yet.'

'What is he known for?'

'He's a leader, an organiser in all manner of criminal activity. He is even suspected of arranging a couple of hits on people who have opposed him.'

'Hits, as in murders?'

'Yes.'

'Why isn't he behind bars?'

'Mainly because he's a devious bugger. We have had him in court several times but our witnesses change their story or disappear.'

'So the people who shot me were after him.'

'We believe so.'

He brought the meeting to a conclusion then by getting to his feet and taking back the photograph.

'Are you planning on staying here?' he asked.

'Yes, for a while. I need to get myself fit, acquire a car and think about work.'

He stopped by the door and turned back towards me.

'What is your work?'

'My wife and I ran a corporate travel business but she got the client list as part of the divorce settlement. I'll have to think of something new.'

'I can't help you with the job, but if you need a car there's a Citroën dealer just up the road. I passed it on the way in.'

'Thanks.'

He nodded then walked across and opened his car door. Looking back over

21

his shoulder he said, 'Good luck and remember to watch your back.'

I watched him drive off then turned back into the room. His visit had been a surprise and the photograph a shock. However, that picture finally explained why I'd been shot. I'd been the mistaken target of a vigilante.

I was so preoccupied with his parting words that I failed to notice the shadowy figure of Jim standing in the corner.

'Are you in danger?' he asked.

His voice startled me but I was able to answer.

'I don't think so, Jim. That policeman seems to think I was shot in mistake for someone else.'

Jim nodded. 'I heard him. You might still be in danger from that Silver fellow. Come with me.'

He turned and led the way out to his shed. All I had seen of that place earlier had been an end-on view through the kitchen window so I was surprised how big it was inside. It was in two halves. The front section was a carpenter's workshop with a large bench on one side and a lathe on the other. Dozens of tools were arrayed in racks on the walls and a varied selection of timber was suspended from the rafters above. Jim led the way through a second door into a smaller room fitted out as an office. There was a desk with a large, old-fashioned reel-to-reel tape-recorder, a bookcase and a filing cabinet but Jim turned to a steel cabinet in one corner. It had a combination lock that he quickly opened. It was a gun cabinet holding, as far as I could see, a fine-looking rifle and a shotgun.

'Those two are licensed,' said Jim nodding towards the guns. Then he produced a cardboard box which he opened to reveal a revolver and ammunition.

'This one isn't, it belonged to Captain Fitzroy, my commanding officer during the war. If you are in danger you could always carry this, it's yours if you want it.'

'No, no thanks, I've never handled a gun. I've only got a vague idea how one works. I'd probably shoot myself in the foot if I took that.'

'Pity,' said Jim thoughtfully as he closed the box. He looked up suddenly and grinned.

'I could teach you,' he exclaimed.

'What happened to Captain Fitzroy?' I asked, in an effort to divert him.

'I buried him — it's all on those tapes. I need someone to transcribe them. Can you type?'

'Yes, that's one thing I can do. I'll have to get my computer from storage then I'll do it for you.'

'Great, you type that and I'll teach you to shoot.'

'First things first, Jim, I need a car in order to collect my things.'

'Okay, let's get that sorted then.'

He replaced the box then lovingly stroked the barrel of the rifle before locking the cabinet and leading the way back into the house.

As I followed him I couldn't understand what had happened. For weeks he'd hardly spoken to me and now all of a sudden I couldn't stop him talking. It was if the mention of Silver and the possibility of danger had fired him up. He'd certainly come alive again, there was a spring in the step of my ageing grandfather that I hadn't seen previously.

Back in the living-room Jim picked up the phone and dialled a number without having to refer to a directory.

'Harry,' he said, 'it's Jim, Jim Bullock, how are you?'

I couldn't hear the reply but Jim's response was preceded by a snort of derision.

'No, I'm not dead. I'm as fit as a fiddle. Has your lad still got the garage?'

The reply was obviously in the affirmative because Jim continued.

'No, not me, my grandson, yes I know he looked weaker than Martha's tea when he got here but he's got a bit more colour now. Aye, he needs a car. Okay, tomorrow, thanks, Harry.'

Two days later I was the owner of a Citroën BX, one of the last to come out of the factory in 1994. It had hydropneumatic suspension, barely five thousand miles on the clock and a very lively engine. The previous owner had used it once a week to drive the five miles from his home into the town of Driffield to collect his pension and shopping. So although it was almost five years old when I bought it, it was virtually brand new.

I collected the rest of my belongings the next day and had to lower the back seat to get the boxes in. Jim came with me for the ride and from the comments he made during the journey I assumed he hadn't been very far out of the village for some considerable time, possibly several years. He had a shoulder bag with him and when I suggested he put it in the back he said he preferred to keep it by his feet. I had no idea what was in it until we made one of the periodic toilet stops that Jim requested. On the one occasion that he left the bag in the car I couldn't resist having a peek at its contents. To my surprise I found Captain Fitzroy's fully loaded handgun wrapped in an old towel — Jim was riding shotgun! It made me wonder if I was in danger. Sergeant Cooper had advised me to watch my back and Jim seemed convinced that I needed protection. I on the other hand was of the opinion that lightning couldn't strike twice. Maybe it could, maybe I should worry. I decided then, rather reluctantly, to take up Jim's offer to teach me how to handle a gun.

3

Why is it that we, the younger generation, never realise until it's too late that we've not listened to our father's or grandparent's wartime experiences? Are we too interested in our own immediate needs to bother to listen to them or are they reluctant to say? I don't know the answer but I do know that I was humbled by what I heard on Jim's tapes. No, humbled isn't strong enough, at times I was close to tears. How could he have kept those things secret for so long? I knew he'd been a soldier but that was the limit of my knowledge until I switched on that old reel-to-reel recorder and the tape began to run.

James Bullock was born in York in 1922, the youngest of six children. His father was a labourer at the railway engine works and his mother helped out in a local bakery. Henry Bullock, James' father, had been injured during the

First World War and he died as a direct result of those injuries when James was four years old. His mother, Enid, died of influenza two years later. James was brought up by his eldest sister, Martha. He left school at the age of fourteen and immediately began an apprenticeship with an ageing local surveyor, Mr Stanley Withers.

One condition of the apprenticeship required Jim to move into accommodation provided by Mr Withers. This proved to be a room above a stable to the rear of the surveyor's home. The stable held a pony and trap which was the mode of transport favoured by the surveyor. Jim soon learnt that the pony was his first responsibility: he had to feed it, groom it and maintain both the harness and the trap. Mr Withers took the reins as they went to and fro between home and work.

In his spare time Jim was introduced into the intricacies of geometry and trigonometry. He was given problems to solve during the evening and was expected to have them completed by the following morning before he and his employer set off on the daily survey. It didn't take him long to realise the importance of these subjects when the serious work began. Their main task was to survey a large estate to the east of York, field by field and building by building. Months of work followed in all kinds of weather and Jim soon became adept at shouldering the theodolite along with the rest of the instruments and gradually understanding their use.

Mr Withers saved most of the building surveys for periods of inclement weather but they still had to brave poor conditions in the open at times. After about a year Jim began to suspect that his employer was ill when he found him one day struggling for breath and hanging onto a gatepost for support. He helped the old man back to the pony and trap and took him home leaving the days work incomplete. That day set a pattern for the next three months with Mr Withers taking to his bed for a few days then returning to work for some weeks. Jim had been his apprentice for fifteen months when the old man finally collapsed. He fell over in a field and by the time Jim reached him he was unconscious. Lifting him up Jim carried him to the nearest farmhouse but there was little that could be done for him there. By the time the doctor arrived the old man was barely alive. He died before they got him to hospital.

Jim's apprenticeship ceased with the death of his employer but he was retained in a caretaker role by the probate solicitor until the buildings and their contents were sold. He used that time to search for a new employer and to assess just what he'd learnt from Mr Withers. Not only had he handled and had begun to understand the use of instruments such as the theodolite but he had begun to appreciate how to transfer the field work to the drawing board. He had become adept in the use of drawing instruments such as a protractor, a T square and various set squares to produce survey drawings. Apart from that work he now knew how to handle a horse and how to maintain its associated equipment.

There was one other useful attribute the he had been taught — how to shoot.

Mr Withers had had a love of rabbit stew so when the pair where working in the fields he carried a light rifle in the cart. Early in Jim's apprenticeship he'd been instructed in the use of the firearm and he quickly became adept in its use. Rabbits and wood pigeons were regularly used to supplement the household diet. Mrs Raven, the housekeeper, encouraged Jim to bring as much as he could because she and her family shared in the free food as well. Even after his employer's death Jim was required to exercise the pony once or twice a week and on these excursions he took the rifle and returned with a rabbit or two to supplement his diet.

* * *

Jim left me alone while I listened to the first of his tapes but I found that I wanted to know more than the bare bones of the taped story. That night I took the opportunity to find out more by asking him about the gun. It was my way of getting past his initial reluctance to talk about himself and his lifestyle. The only time he'd really opened up to me had been when he felt that I was threatened and he had shown me his guns. I must admit though that I softened him up first with a couple of glasses of brandy after our evening meal — a meal that I cooked for both of us. Jim's meals on wheels offering lay frozen and forgotten that night.

'Was it difficult to learn how to shoot?' I asked.

'No, I found it quite easy. I know Mr Withers was amazed how quickly I picked it up. He showed me how to shoot at stationary targets but I was soon picking off rabbits on the run. It just came naturally to me.'

'Was it a rifle or a shotgun?'

'It was a point two-two rifle but I did get to use a shotgun. I was asked by one of the farmers to help him clear one rabbit warren and he leant me a shotgun. I found the gun heavy at first but simple to use.'

He paused as if thinking back over events in the past before continuing with a smile on his face.

'Actually it was the farmer's daughter who showed me how to use the shotgun, she taught me other things as well.'

I waited for him to continue and watched the smile broaden before he did so.

'She was a great girl, tremendous figure, great zest for life. She seduced me the first time — we made love behind a hedge. Later on we used the hay loft in the barn several times. It was a pity that it had to end.'

'Was that when Mr Withers died?'

'Oh, no, it was after that, just before the pony was sold. We made love one Friday night and afterwards she told me that it was over because she was getting married the next day. Great girl, she taught me a lot.'

'Did you see her again?'

'Only once — the next day, I was invited to the wedding. I even got to kiss the bride.'

'What was her name?'

'Vicky, Victoria to be precise, that husband of hers was a lucky man. I saw him some years later, after the war. He had two girls with him and they were younger versions of Vicky, beautiful, really beautiful.'

He sat quietly contemplating his past for some minutes before looking up at me again. He smiled. 'Sorry,' he said, 'I was thinking back.'

'Any regrets?'

'No, not about those days — plenty later.'

'May I use what you've told me about Victoria?'

He looked thoughtful again before replying.

'I don't suppose it will hurt anyone after all this time so type it up if you think it helps.'

'It helps me to put a proper timeline to what I'm typing.'

'Okay, put her in.'

That evening was the first of a number of similar evenings. I would listen to part of one of his tapes then talk its content over with him after our evening meal. Sometimes he would enlarge on the basic story immediately or our discussion would spark a memory or two that he'd overlooked and would bring up later. Occasionally I would find myself retyping a section several times over because he'd remember even more once he'd read the printed page.

My first shooting lesson was held in a meadow that had a great view over the Yorkshire Wolds. The field had recently been grazed by sheep so the grass had been eaten down almost to soil level. In one corner was a stand of trees fenced off to provide natural cover for wildlife in the area. The farmer was another of Jim's friends and had given us permission to use the field that day. We parked by the gated entrance.

Before we had put the guns in the car Jim had shown me how to check that they were unloaded and when we reached the field he made me recheck them. He erected a target on a fence post, merely a square of plywood with a couple of sheets of paper pinned on, before pacing out a shooting range. He then demonstrated how to load and aim the handgun.

'Forget the cowboys with their quick

draws and one-handed shooting,' he said, 'this thing needs two hands and a steady aim.'

He fired twice and both shots hit low on the target. He then handed me the weapon saying that there were four shots left. I missed with the first three and clipped the bottom of the board with the last. Although he'd warned me I was surprised by the shock my hands felt at each explosive discharge.

'Not bad for a first try,' said Jim. 'You'd have probably got him in the foot with that last effort.'

'Was this the kind of gun that I was hit by?' I asked.

'No, if they'd used this you wouldn't be here now. The weapon they used was of a lighter calibre.'

He reloaded and encouraged me to try again. Initially he had explained how the gun tended to kick upwards as it fired and I had fought to hold the weapon pointed down. This time I slackened my grip and managed to hit the target with three of the six shots. Jim then turned to the rifle and demonstrated how to fire it from a prone position. When my turn came he showed how to use the sights, how to hold the stock into my shoulder and how to gently squeeze the trigger. I found the rifle to be much easier to use than the handgun and began hitting the target immediately. That was when I began to enjoy myself and when Jim called a halt for the day.

'That's enough for today, we'll have another go tomorrow at a longer range,' he said. 'You'll find that your hands and shoulder will ache a bit so we'll stick to short sessions for now.'

My final lesson that day was gun cleaning. I passed at the second attempt.

4

When probate was finally settled and Jim's temporary home above the stable sold, he found himself with nowhere to live. He hadn't been able to find another job despite lowering his ambitions and applying for anything that was going including labouring work. His sister was married and had two young children so the room he'd occupied before was no longer available to him. During his time with the surveyor he had managed to put aside about ten shillings a week so he wasn't exactly destitute and was able to rent a room in a lodging house for a short while. The rent and his food ate away at his savings rapidly so in desperation he walked into an army recruiting office one day to volunteer for military service. He described his initial interview as somewhat bizarre. The only person in the office was a sergeant and he had both feet in a bowl of warm water. He looked up as Jim walked in.

'What can I do for you, lad?' he barked.

'I want to join the army.'

'Do you now,' he said as he lifted one foot out of the water and began to dry it. 'The army needs soldiers to look after their feet,' he continued. 'Do you look after yours?'

'Yes, sir.'

'No, it's yes Sergeant.'

'Yes, Sergeant.'

He then began to dry the second foot. 'Why?' he said.

'Why?' replied Jim, puzzled by the question.

'Why do you want to join the army?'

'I'd like to see the world.'

The sergeant began pulling on his boots and socks and as he did so he nodded at the bowl. 'Chuck that lot outside,' he said.

Jim emptied the water into the gutter in the street then returned to the office. The sergeant, now seated behind the desk, tapped a pencil against his teeth whilst studying Jim. Getting to his feet he walked round the desk and then round Jim.

'How tall are you?' he asked.

'Five feet nine,' Jim replied.

'Are you fit?'

'Yes I believe I am.'

'Could you march carrying a rifle and a pack when you're fully booted and spurred like me?'

'Yes.'

'Okay, well my officer isn't here today so you'll have to come back tomorrow. Be here at nine a.m. — be on time and look smart.'

'Yes, Sergeant.'

The following morning Jim was waiting in the street when the recruiting office opened its doors at nine o'clock. The same sergeant greeted him.

'Can you write, lad?' he said.

'Yes, Sergeant.'

'Okay, now sit over there and fill in this form.'

He handed Jim a foolscap sheet and pointed towards an empty desk. Ten minutes later Jim completed the form and sat rereading it, checking for any mistakes.

'Finished, lad?'

'Yes, Sergeant,' said Jim getting to his feet.

The sergeant took the form through to a back office and handed it over to his officer, Major Forthwright. The major studied it and made pencilled notations at intervals. By the details of Jim's curtailed apprenticeship he wrote 'Engineers?' then further down when the pony was mentioned he put 'Horseguards?' and finally when he came across the rifle and shotgun shooting he annotated the bottom of the sheet with the word 'Infantry?'. Eventually he put the form down, looked up at the sergeant and nodded.

'Looks like a good lad,' he said.

Two weeks later Jim was required to undergo a medical and when he passed was handed a travel warrant and directed to his training unit. He arrived there with three shillings in his pocket, one pound two and sixpence in his post office book and the rest of his worldly goods in a small kitbag. Initially he found living in a barrack room with nineteen other recruits a strange experience but he soon adapted.

The physical aspect of his surveying work had left him reasonably fit so he found he could cope easily with the squarebashing and exercise regimes unlike many of his fellows. Some of them looked as if they hadn't had a square meal for weeks and so it proved when he talked to them. Most of them had been out of regular work for months and were consequently out of condition. Jim and one or two others stood out from the rest because of this.

Once he had adjusted to the weight of a 303 rifle he excelled on the rifle range and it was this aspect of his training that he enjoyed the most. Whilst the rest of the recruits were struggling to come to terms with the rifle range Jim was in his element. Within two weeks he was regularly hitting the centre of the target so that the sergeant in charge of the range moved him to a smaller target at a longer range. He continued to do well. Before his basic training was finished he was selected to represent his barrack room against other recruits and he out-shot them all. That naturally accorded him a certain amount of status amongst his fellows and a note on his personal documents that read 'marksman, possible sniper.'

★ ★ ★

I was still working on Jim's basic training tape when the telephone interrupted me. Jim answered the phone and I couldn't help overhearing the one side of the conversation.

'Hello . . . oh it's you, Harry, what can I do for you?'

'When?'

'How odd? Okay hang on, I'll ask him.'

Jim then turned to me.

'Harry says that there's a big ugly bugger looking for you. He's been making enquiries at the garage.'

'How ugly?'

There was a pause while Jim conferred again with Harry before turning back to me.

'Harry's son says that he was built like a brick shithouse with a face that had been through a mangle.'

'That's Silver's man. I hope he didn't tell him that I was here.'

'No, he thought it best not to.'

'Thank him for me, Jim, and tell him he did the right thing. That man is trouble and I can do without that.'

Jim replaced the handset then turned to me again.

'Have you any idea what he wants?'

'I've never spoken to the man, I've only seen him once just before I was shot. I don't want to know what he wants because as far as I'm concerned he's trouble.'

'I think it's time we had some more shooting practice.'

'Look, Jim, I've no intention of shooting anyone.'

'Self defence — it's only for self defence. Come on, I'll get the guns.'

So for a second time I found myself lying in the meadow getting used to Jim's rifle once again. In an odd way I enjoyed it. It may be that I was lucky with my first two shots because they both hit the target and as a result Jim insisted that I moved further back. He moved me twice more before switching to the handgun again. For that I moved back closer to the target with little success. I did hit it once in the centre but my other five shots either clipped the edge or missed altogether. Jim laughed as I put down the weapon in disgust.

'Don't despair, lad, you're as good as me with that thing,' he said.

'But I thought you were a marksman,' I protested.

'Oh, I was but not with that thing, with this.' He held up the rifle as he spoke. 'Let's see if I can still do it,' he said.

He got me to change the target and while I was doing that he walked away across the meadow. Once I'd finished I hurried after him and found him clipping a telescopic sight to the rifle. To me the target now looked like a distant speck but Jim lined up the sights and fired a single shot. He grunted once then realigned the sights before firing again. He fired six times altogether and every shot hit the target. As far as I was concerned he hadn't lost his touch and he seemed quietly satisfied with the result.

Thinking back I'm sure that Jim thoroughly enjoyed those sessions out in that borrowed meadow. Although I'd been given the job of cleaning the guns that first time I never got that task again. Jim treated those weapons like babies when he took over the cleaning, taking great pride in removing even the slightest hint of dirt and lovingly oiling and shining them until they acquired a dull gleam. They looked precisely what they were when he'd finished — efficient killing machines.

It was two days later when I found myself inadvertently heading west on the road across the Wolds again, the same road we followed to the shooting meadow. I'd walked down to the shop to collect my copy of the Yorkshire Post, stopping now and then to exchange a few words with fellow villagers. Usually the topic was either my health or the weather. In the shop I had a chat with Sally Catchpole again about my health but also about Jim and his seeming reinvigoration since my arrival. I paid for my newspaper, tucked it under my arm and set off back up the street. It was about quarter to nine and the street was busy with mothers seeing their children off to school and it was quite common to see slow moving cars searching for a parking spot to drop the kids off. So when a car moved up alongside me I assumed that it was a mother doing just that, only it wasn't. I was suddenly grabbed by the arm and pushed sideways into the rear of a large black saloon. The man doing the pushing followed me in and forcibly held me down. A gun was thrust against my temple and a voice from above urged silence.

'Be quiet Mr Sharp, we're just going for a little ride, there's nothing to be afraid of.'

The car started to accelerate then suddenly braked to a halt.

'Fuck it,' muttered the driver.

'What's wrong?' asked the body holding me down.

'Lollipop man.'

'Go past him.'

'Can't, there's a copper across the road. Fucking peasants.'

I suppose I guessed it was Silver's man on top of me by his sheer bulk and it was confirmed when he allowed me to sit up as we turned onto the main road. The side and back windows of the car were tinted black but I could see forward through the windscreen so I caught a quick glimpse of the garage as we passed. From the view I had I could also see when we turned onto the York road, a road I was beginning to know quite well from our shooting trips. I was feeling furious but as the guy sitting beside me was about three times my size and was holding a gun there was little I could do other than seethe. I had begun to calm down slightly about fifteen minutes later as we were running at a fair speed along an empty road. Then a tractor and trailer suddenly pulled out in front of us and stopped, blocking both carriageways. As we screamed to a halt, accompanied by more ripe language from the driver, a second vehicle moved quickly out of a field entrance and closed up behind us.

'Now what?' exclaimed my captor.

The JCB behind us inched closer until I felt a slight bump as its bucket touched the rear wheels. Then nothing happened for a couple of minutes. Our driver got out and started shouting at the driver of the tractor who was sitting in the cab above him. Suddenly he jumped back into his seat and slammed the car door.

'I don't like this, Boss, he's holding a bloody shotgun,' he half shouted. Then he turned and pointed to the side. 'Look there's another one with a shotgun, oh Christ, that guy behind us has got one as well.'

'Ask them what they want.'

Our driver lowered his window and did as he was told, the answer he got surprised even me.

'Luke Sharp,' shouted the man at the side of the road. He lifted the shotgun menacingly as he did so.

My captor opened the door and motioned me out.

'On your way,' he said.

I scrambled clear and walked across to the man standing by the side of the road.

'Are you okay, Mr Sharp?' he asked.

'Yes,' I replied, holding out my hand and shaking his.

He smiled then held his hand in the air waving the tractor back into the field. As soon as he could the car driver moved forward shouting from his window as he did so.

'Fucking peasants.'

'Nice man,' said my companion.

'He has a nasty friend as well,' I replied.

We had to stand and wait then whilst the JCB trundled off the road and the half a dozen vehicles we'd held up drove on their way. As soon as the road was clear we crossed to the same field entrance the tractor had used and that was when I realised that it was actually the entrance to a farm. We walked together up the track following the two farm machines.

'Who should I be thanking?' I said.'

'Your grandfather.'

'Jim?'

'Yes, he rang Dad, that's him in the tractor, and asked for help and you know the rest.'

'It was like something out of a film.'

He grinned across at me. 'We timed it to perfection,' he said.

'Would you have used that?' I said pointing to the shotgun.

He broke it open to show me that it was empty.

'I'm not sure what would have happened if he'd called our bluff.'

'Well the driver was convinced they were loaded,' I replied.

Ten minutes later I'd met and shaken hands with the rest of my rescuers, Graham Fairbrother, the farmer, and his sons Bill and Brian. In the farmhouse kitchen I met Graham's wife Glynis and his daughter Denise. I was offered, and accepted, a second breakfast and I was still enjoying it when Jim arrived in my car. It was then that I learned how my rescue had been organised. Apparently one of my friends from the W.I. saw me being thrust into the car and dropping my newspaper as I did so. She popped into the shop and got them to ring Jim, who in turn rang the garage. The garage had a car being test driven and its driver reported which road we took and the rest as they say is history.

'Didn't you ring the police?' I asked.

'There was no time,' said Jim, 'by the time they'd have got organised you'd have been out of the county. Where were you going?'

'I've no idea.'

'Now I know why you've been using my top meadow,' said Graham.

'I think we'll be using it again,' replied Jim.

'Well let me know when and I'll keep the animals clear.'

'Why don't you call in for a cup of something next time,' said Glynis.

Both Jim and I thanked them all and agreed that we'd accept their offer. Brian, the son who'd walked with me, thanked us for the excitement. I'm not sure how he would have felt in my shoes though because I felt numb, as if it had happened around me but not to me. I had to let Jim drive home because I felt some form of delayed reaction — I couldn't stop my hands shaking for a while. Later I rang my friendly police sergeant, Cooper, and brought him up to date with our latest exploits, carefully downplaying the shot-gun part of the affair. Naturally he wanted to know why they wanted me but as I had no idea I couldn't help him. He did give me some advice though — buy a Doberman and take it with me when I go for my paper!

5

Jim's taped records were short on accurate dates because he lost all his papers during the war but he does remember that early in November 1938 he was supposed to be drafted to a Royal Engineers training unit but whilst still awaiting confirmation of that he was ordered to report to the admin office. Once there he was given over to the ministrations of a training officer who gave him a series of test papers to assess his ability. This took three days and at the end of it all he was interviewed by a Captain Fitzroy.

'Good morning, Bullock, do you know why you are here?'

'No sir, I have just finished some test papers but nobody said what they were for.'

'I wanted to know how far your knowledge went and you've done well. In trigonometry and geometry your work is good as it is in the basics of field survey work but your knowledge of army procedures is nil. You'll have to improve that as we travel.'

'Travel, sir?'

'Oh yes, we're going to Malaya to conduct some urgent survey work. You'll be part of a small troop sailing shortly.'

For Jim the next week flew past. He paid several visits to the medical section for inoculations for virtually every disease known to mankind, was issued with tropical kit in addition to his normal uniform and instructed on how and where to sew on the various insignia. He spent part of one morning in the camp cinema viewing a film on the dangers attached to the many and varied forms of sexual disease and the punishment accorded to those that became affected and left feeling slightly sick. One afternoon he was directed back to the training section where he learnt something of the geography of Malaya and Singapore and was handed a small pamphlet listing common Malay words and their English translation. On the Friday afternoon he was still struggling to fit all the gear he'd been issued with into his large kitbag when he was informed that he'd be leaving the next morning. He was regaled that evening by old stagers in the mess of the joys and horrors of travelling in a troopship. When he eventually got to sleep that night he was not looking forward to what lay ahead.

The following morning Jim was still eating breakfast when his transport arrived. He wasn't given time to finish eating by the corporal sent to collect him.

'Come on lad, get your arse into gear, we've a long way to go,' urged the corporal. 'Double along and get your kit.'

Ten minutes later Jim scrambled into the back of the lorry and joined two other soldiers. The corporal joined the driver in the cab. There was barely time for Jim to find a seat before the lorry pulled away. Once he was settled he introduced himself to his companions and discovered the lorry's destination.

'Southampton docks,' said the oldest of

the pair. 'I'm Fred and this is Dai. Are you on this Malaya lark as well?'

'Yes, we're supposed to be doing some survey work, aren't we?'

'So I'm told. Did you meet that Captain Fitzroy?'

'Yes, last week.'

'Is he in charge?'

'I've no idea. He made me do a series of test papers, geometry and the like before telling me where we were going.'

'We've missed the trooper,' said Dai suddenly.

'Well why are we going to Southampton then?'

'Dunno, but I'm told the troopship left last week.'

By the time they reached the docks they had collected a further six soldiers all of whom were connected in some way to survey work. En route they'd stopped at a roadside halt and collected sandwiches and tea for lunch from a Naafi truck that had been ordered to meet and feed them. It was dark when they reached the ship and they were directed to board via a gangway near the stern. They were met by a sergeant who lined them up on deck and gave them the news that they were not on a troopship but on a passenger liner of the P & O line.

'You've been allocated accommodation in the crew's quarters and you will not be allowed to wander round the ship,' he barked. 'Anyone found on the passenger decks will be on a charge, understood?'

'Yes, Sergeant,' chorused the troop.

'Right, well the corporal here will show you your billets and there'll be a meal laid on for you in the messroom in half an hour, any questions?'

'When do we sail, Sarge?' asked Dai.

'After breakfast tomorrow morning — if you've any last minute letters to write get them written and in the box tonight.'

Jim was allocated a lower bunk in a cabin that held four men. When all four were in there at the same time there was barely enough room for them to turn round. Their kit had to be stowed in an adjacent locker-room. The cabin across the alleyway from theirs was bigger but accommodated six, five troopers and the corporal. The sergeant had a separate single cabin in the ship's petty officers area. Jim was designated as his cabin's senior despite his relative youth. With him were Dai, Fred and a thin waif of a lad known as Simmo.

The alleyway between their cabins led straight out onto the poop deck through a heavy steel watertight door. A large steam winch dominated the poop and it was the racket created by that winch at work that woke them the following morning. The whole cabin resounded to its thunderous noise. Peering out through their one porthole Dai declared that the crew were singling up.

'What the hell does that mean?' Fred demanded.

'They're taking in some of the mooring ropes, getting ready to sail,' replied Dai, airing his knowledge of shipboard affairs gained from visits to Swansea docks with his stevedore father.

'Noisy buggers,' said Simmo.

Half an hour later the ship was eased away from the jetty by two tugs and their voyage began. About fifty or so people stood waving farewell to relatives and friends and two groups of dockworkers watched as the gap widened between ship and shore. The ship's siren blasted out a message and it was answered by one of the attendant tugs as the huge vessel began to turn its bow towards the lock gates and the open water beyond.

Shortly after they turned towards the sea a tannoy announcement called all passengers and crew to their lifeboat stations. Captain Fitzroy had already forewarned them about this so they each collected their lifejackets and made their way up to the boatdeck. Jim and his cabin companions found themselves allocated to the same lifeboat as about a dozen passengers and several crew members. Once they had all been shown how to don the lifejackets correctly Jim had time to look around the passengers allocated to their boat. There were four couples in various age groups, two children and two women. The children, a boy and a girl, were with a middle-aged couple who appeared to be their parents or guardians.

His attention was brought back to the present by the officer in charge explaining that boat drill would be a regular event throughout the voyage. He explained the signals that indicated boat and fire drill before releasing them.

In the sheltered waters between Southampton and the Isle of Wight the ship sailed in flat calm seas. Even when they turned out into the Channel there was little indication of what was to come. The following morning they reached Ushant and the ship's motion changed dramatically as they altered course and began the passage across the Bay of Biscay. A storm out in the Atlantic had left a legacy of a large lazy swell which bore down on the ship on the starboard beam causing her to roll quite dramatically at first but as she settled on her new course the rolling continued in a gentler, more controlled fashion. To the seasoned seafarers onboard this was no problem but for many of the passengers and soldiers there was first a feeling of queasiness quickly followed by a rush to toilets or beds. In Jim's cabin three of the bunks were occupied by green-faced individuals for the next two days. Jim took the advice of an old sailor who had seen him looking rather pale and advised him to stay on deck.

'If you are sick pick the leeward side and don't forget to eat. Bring your food out here and eat in the fresh air then you'll soon feel better,' he said.

Jim followed his advice and remained on deck throughout that day. To him the rolling swell looked alarming at first but he gradually learnt to ride with it instead of bracing himself against its movement. He tried to enter his cabin to sleep that night but the revolting smell of vomit forced him back on deck. Eventually the change of watch at midnight brought his old friend the seaman out on deck. Seeing Jim's plight he lead him up onto the passenger deck above and saw him settled in a reclining lounge chair.

'I'll be on a charge if I'm caught up here,' Jim protested.

'Don't worry nobody will know, I'll get my mate to give you a shake at six.'

Jim repeated those sleeping arrangements the following night although the weather was not particularly warm. He slept fully clothed wrapped in one blanket and was surprised to find that the seaman who woke him at six o'clock brought him a mug of tea.

'It's all part of the service,' said the sailor with a grin.

That day the ship reached Cape Finisterre and altered course again heading south towards the Portuguese coast and Cape St Vincent. Although the Atlantic swell was still causing the ship to roll most passengers had regained control of their stomachs and had begun to appear on deck and in the dining room. In Jim's cabin the three casualties of seasickness spent the most of that morning alternating between cleaning the cabin and making up for the meals they'd missed.

At lunchtime Captain Fitzroy, looking rather pale, called them all together on the poop and addressed them.

'From tomorrow,' he announced, 'we will all be assembling on the forecastle, that's the pointy bit at the front of this vessel, for exercises and drills before breakfast. Sergeant Browning will be in charge but I will be participating. Any questions?'

Simmo put up his hand. 'What do we wear, sir?'

'P.T. kit of course.'

'Aw gawd,' muttered Dai, 'it'll be bloody cold.'

There were no more questions after that so they were dismissed and, in a body, made for the messroom.

It was after the first exercise morning that the soldiers began to realise that their world was not confined to the cabins, messroom and poop. They had the freedom to roam the whole lower deck from forecastle to poop, had film shows two or three times a week and had a library and various board games for entertainment. They were in fact on something of a pleasure cruise especially as the weather began to warm up the further south they went.

Two days later they crowded the portside rail and watched as the ship passed through the Pillars of Hercules and into the Mediterranean Sea. They saw the signal light flashing from the Lloyds signal station on Gibraltar and the reply by Aldis lamp from the bridge wing.

'They wished us bon voyage,' said Dai.

'Could you read that?' asked Jim.

'Yeah, we did it in boy scouts. We used to go up in the hills and send messages to each other across the valley.'

'Could you teach me?'

'Sure, I'll write down the morse code for you and once you've learnt that we could practise with torches.'

That night Jim was out on the poop deck on his own and he could hear the strains of music from the passenger deck above. Looking round he checked that there was nobody watching before climbing the stairs and moving nearer to the sound of the music. At the top of the stairs he removed his boots and walked quietly across into the shadow of a lifeboat davit. From there the music sounded fine so he settled down to listen. He thought he was alone until a woman's voice asked. 'Are you alright?'

Jim jumped. 'Sorry ma'am, I came to listen to the music. I'd better go,' he said.

'No, stay and enjoy it. Come over and sit here in the shadow, no one will see you.'

Jim realised then where the voice was coming from and moved towards it before finally seeing the speaker. He recognised one of the women he'd seen at lifeboat drill. She indicated the seat beside her.

'Sit here,' she said.

'I'd better not,' said Jim, 'I'll be on a charge if I'm spotted.'

'Don't be silly, nobody's going to see you, sit and listen.'

He sat down but wasn't relaxed at first — he was ready to sprint for the stairs if anyone else appeared. Gradually though the music eased the tension and he began to appreciate it. Two tunes later they heard the bandleader announce a short interval and the woman asked if Jim had enjoyed what he'd heard.

'Yes, I've never heard anything like it before.'

'It's big band music, dance music

mainly from America.'

He looked across at her then and saw a young but rather plain face that was suddenly transformed into something rather pretty when she smiled.

'You're in the same lifeboat as me,' said Jim, 'so you must be Mrs Roberts or Mrs Monroe. There's a list of names on our cabin door.'

'Mrs Roberts, Sylvia Roberts,' she said holding out her hand.

Jim blushed as he shook her hand. 'I'm Jim, James Bullock.'

'Where are you going?' she asked.

'Malaya, we've got some survey work to do.'

When she asked if he was a surveyor Jim spent some minutes explaining how he'd gained his limited surveying knowledge and how he'd finished up in the army. By the time the music began again Jim had learned that she was en route to join her husband in Bombay. They were also calling each other by their first names. The band began again and Sylvia said, 'That's a waltz, do you dance?'

'No, I've never learnt any dance steps,' replied Jim.

'Will you try, with me?'

She got to her feet and held out her arms. 'Come on.'

They held each other at arm's length as Jim intoned the one, two, three routine and tried to waltz whilst watching his feet. Eventually they retired to their seats chuckling over their antics. Then Sylvia looked at her wristwatch.

'It's time I was in bed,' she said. 'Will I see you here tomorrow night?'

'I'd love to come again,' Jim replied.

'Okay, see you tomorrow if the coast is clear for you.'

'Goodnight and thank you, Sylvia.'

'Goodnight, Jim.'

After their physical exercises the following morning Captain Fitzroy called for all the soldiers to assemble in the messroom immediately after breakfast. Once they were all together he called for silence. His first words when he addressed them had an instant effect because officers were not supposed to use such language.

'During this morning's exercises I heard comments to the effect that Sergeant Browning was built like a brick shithouse whilst Simpson looked like a strip of wet bog paper.' He paused then as if considering what he'd said. The room was deathly quiet as if everyone there was shocked by his words and was waiting for the culprit to be named.

'What I want to make clear to you all is the necessity for this small troop to work together and comments like those do not help. We shall be working for some months in difficult tropical conditions and we shall have to depend on each other throughout that time. The sergeant's job is organisation and he's good at it, Simpson or Simmo is the best draughtsman I've seen for some time and when I look around I know each of you has abilities of various kinds, abilities that we need to sharpen if we are going to succeed in the task set for us. Have I made myself clear?'

A chorus of agreement was followed by Sergeant Browning getting to his feet and moving forward to take over. In his fist he held a sheet of paper which detailed duties for each individual for the rest of the morning. Jim found himself being instructed in the military aspects of surveying and the different terms used to that of civilian life. After that he and two others joined the captain to be initiated into the mysteries of using a sextant to take a noon sight. Simmo was working with two more on a drafting problem whilst the remainder were using a pair of torches to practise morse signalling.

After lunch there was a surprised look on several faces when it was announced that the ship's captain had given permission for rifle practice from the poop deck.

'But the ship's moving, sir,' said Dai.

'Do you expect your enemy to stand still for you in wartime, Davis?' asked Captain Fitzroy.

'No sir, but we've only ever used rifles on the range.'

Their targets were bottles tossed into the water from the stern and each man was allocated four rounds. They took up the firing position one after another and moved aside as soon as their rounds had been fired. Shots splashed far and wide with hardly a bottle being touched until Jim took his turn. His first shot took out the nearest bottle, the second the next and the third another. By the time he was ready to fire his final round the remaining bottles were almost out of sight. He stood with his legs apart and raised the rifle to his shoulder and waited till a bottle lifted on a wave in the distance then fired. The bottle disintegrated and there was a loud if ragged cheer from the boatdeck above them. Looking up Jim could see not only passengers but also a number of the ship's officers and crew. None of the soldiers had been aware of their audience until that moment.

Captain Fitzroy took Jim aside later and congratulated him on his fine shooting.

'I can see now why your documents indicate your marksmanship.'

'The odds were in my favour, sir, because I had time to assess the conditions before my turn came.'

'Have you ever used any other weapon?'

'Only a shotgun and a light rifle, sir.'

Fitzroy nodded. 'But you've fired at moving targets before.'

'Oh yes, sir, rabbits and pigeons.'

'Well done, Bullock, I'll see if I can arrange a more difficult target next time.'

6

Throughout the passage through the Mediterranean Captain Fitzroy kept up the regime of morning exercises and lessons. Jim and some of his compatriots improved not only their knowledge of military routines but found they were able to pass short messages in morse code, albeit very slowly. They did not have any further shooting practice. However, a new element was introduced — military history. The captain spoke of the importance of bases like Gibraltar and Malta, talked of Admiral Nelson's activities in the area particularly drawing their attention to the battle of the Nile. He also emphasised the importance of the Suez Canal in furthering trade throughout the Empire.

As the temperature improved more people began to appear on deck at night but despite this Jim's dance routines began to improve. His waltz progressed sufficiently for him to stop looking down at his feet and he began his first tentative steps at the slow foxtrot. Sylvia and he still favoured the two seats tucked away in the dark corner so that when other night time promenaders appeared on deck they stopped the dance lessons and sat and talked. They were not able to meet every night because Jim did not want to arouse the suspicions of his fellow soldiers but most nights the pair danced for a while and always at arm's length.

Although Jim was amongst the youngest of the ordinary soldiers on board he began unwittingly to assume a role of respect amongst them. Some would turn to him for advice if they had trouble understanding a particular point in a lesson whilst others respected him for his demonstrated ability with the rifle. Even men who had two or three years of service deferred to him at times and helped him with his understanding of the army's rules and regulations. Sergeant Browning and Captain Fitzroy both made note of how his presence had a unifying effect on the small group.

On the evening before their arrival at Port Said there were quite a number of people sampling the warmer evening air out on deck. Jim and Sylvia sat and chatted and for once the subject of Sylvia's husband was one of the main topics. Jim asked if her husband would be meeting her on arrival at Bombay and her reply startled him.

'I've no idea,' she replied.

'But surely he must be there.'

'I wrote to him and said when I would be arriving but I've had no reply.'

'When did you write?'

'Two months ago.'

'Oh.' Jim was at a loss what to say next.

'I was supposed to follow him out to India as soon as he had a place for us. He said it would take about three months to get it organised.'

'Has it been that long?'

He turned to look at her when she didn't answer and even in the dim light of the moon could see tears trickling down her face.

'I'm sorry,' he said, 'It's none of my business.'

She took out a small handkerchief and dabbed away the tears.

'He left England two years ago. I've written to him every week and had five replies in that time.'

'Is he a poor writer?'

There was a sound that was half sob and half strangled laughter from her before she eventually replied.

'He's a bloody civil servant,' she burst out. 'It's his job to write.'

Once again Jim had no idea just what to say in reply so he reached out and took her hand in his.

'Three years we've been married,' she continued, 'and now I've almost forgotten what he looks like.'

'What will you do if he's not there?'

'I'll catch the next boat back and see if I can divorce him.'

They sat in silence then for almost half an hour and she gripped Jim's hand throughout that period. Finally she tightened her grip even more fiercely before releasing her hold and standing.

'Thank you for listening, Jim.'

She turned and walked quickly back

into the accommodation. Jim waited until there was nobody watching and slid quietly back down the ladder to the poop. He leant on the stern rail for a while watching the wake stretching back towards the hidden horizon and thought about Sylvia's situation before finally shaking his head and sighing. There was nothing he could about it so he turned and made his way to his cabin and his bunk.

The following morning their usual exercise regime was cancelled. There was an air of excitement around as the ship moved into a mooring in the harbour of Port Said. Some passengers were due to leave whilst the ship waited to join the next convoy through the Suez Canal. There were already boats moving alongside, two containing officialdom in one form or another, whilst the remainder were bumboats full of merchandise for sale to eager and unwary buyers. Two sailors lowered a ladder and the officials scrambled aboard and as they did so more bumboats jockeyed for position knowing that they would soon be allowed to board as well.

Most of the soldiers were standing leaning on the port rail trying both to see what was going on whilst keeping clear of the mooring parties. Dai suddenly pointed to the statue at the end of the breakwater.

'Who's that?' he said.

'Buggered if I know,' said the soldier beside him.

'It's Ferdinand De Lesseps, the guy who built the canal,' said the sergeant.

'He used Irish navvies,' said somebody else.

'Don't be daft,' said another voice, 'if they can build pyramids they don't need the Irish.'

Suddenly there was a commotion by the accommodation ladder and a large launch was called in scattering the waiting bumboats. Stewards appeared from the passenger decks and carried several suitcases down to the boat. Shortly afterwards four passengers also boarded the boat and it pulled away and made for the shore. A ship's officer arrived and stood by the ladder beckoning the bumboats in. Eventually about a dozen Egyptians boarded, each carrying a large bundle of assorted goods over his shoulder. They were allowed to spread their goods on the forecastle and a mixture of passengers, soldiers and crew were soon eyeing and buying. A gilli-gilli man attracted a crowd as he performed various tricks and sleights of hand. He was particularly good at losing coins offered by his audience. He must have had a couple of dozen pockets because every time a coin disappeared he demonstrated that he couldn't have it by displaying an empty one. Instead of the coins he regularly produced an egg or a live chick. He took more cash from the gullible with the three card trick. While he was busy others were selling carpets, camel stools, hubble-bubble pipes and a multitude of other goods. At least two of the soldiers could be seen wandering around wearing a fez.

While all that was going on the last ships of the north-bound convoy were clearing the canal and heading off into the Mediterranean. Two hours after they boarded, the bumboat men were offloaded and the ship got underway again. They were the lead ship in the southern convoy. The soldiers and many of the passengers lined the rails as the ship moved into the canal and left the town behind. On the port side stretched the bare sandy reaches of the Sinai desert whilst the opposite bank could not have been more different. There the land was green with palm trees and irrigated farmland as far as the eye could see. Here and there camels and donkey carts vied with motor traffic on the road that ran parallel with the waterway.

When darkness fell they were still in the confines of the great waterway. A searchlight in the bow illuminated their route. Jim moved out on deck about an hour after he'd eaten his evening meal but there were too many passengers around for him to attempt to see Sylvia. Simmo was standing by the stern rail looking back along the water towards the ships astern of them. He turned as Jim moved beside him.

'I make it nineteen ships,' he said, 'all

of them heading away from home.'

'What's up,' asked Jim, 'you feeling homesick?'

'My old man's in hospital,' he replied holding up a piece of paper. 'I've just received a Marconigram, the captain brought it to me.'

'Is he bad?'

'Must be on his last legs, they'd never have got him in there otherwise. He was a nasty old bugger but I would have liked to say goodbye.'

'Will your mother be okay?'

'I never really knew her; she died when I was a kid. My sister sent the cable. She'll be alright.'

'Is she married?'

'Yes with two kids and a husband who's bringing in good money. I wrote to her just before we sailed. I sent a postcard for the kids.'

'Whose kids?' asked another voice.

'Oh it's you, Dai, my sister's kids. I try to send them something from wherever we go, sometimes it's only the stamp on the letter but it gives them an interest.'

'Have you sent a card from here?'

'No, the only ones I found were mucky ones.'

Dai laughed. 'That guy over there with the mooring boat has got some,' he said.

The two Egyptians sitting alongside their mooring looked up when he called.

'Hey Ali, what postcards have you got?'

'Dirty postcards?'

'No, camels or pyramids.'

Ali sauntered across and produced a bunch of postcards from his pocket. There were half a dozen sepia-coloured views of the pyramids with a camel strategically placed to one side held by a man in flowing Arab robes. Simmo paid sixpence for one.

'I got woman with camel,' whispered Ali producing a different set of cards. 'Pretty woman, no clothes, cost more.'

A shout from above interrupted them and Ali hurried back to his boat. Three seamen appeared and chivvied Ali along. The winch was brought into action and Ali and his boat were lowered towards the water.

'Looks as if we're through the canal,' Jim said looking towards the bow.

'There're lots of lights ahead.'

A few minutes later the canal pilot left the bridge and stepped from the accommodation ladder into a boat running alongside. With a shout and a wave the boat pulled clear and almost immediately the ship's engine note changed as the vessel began to increase speed.

'Where are we?' asked Dai peering over the side.

'In the Red Sea,' replied Jim.

'It looks black to me,' retorted Dai, 'just like the inside of my eyelids will be shortly. I'm for bed.'

Simmo and Jim followed him in.

7

As the weather became hotter and more humid Jim began to find that he concentrated less on his dancing and more on his partner. Sylvia's clothing had begun to reflect the weather conditions and therefore became lighter and revealed more of her figure. Two or three times he stumbled over his feet as he became distracted by the woman in his arms. They still maintained the same distance between them as they danced but the physical attraction increased.

It was the night before the ship arrived at the port of Aden that the inevitable happened. They were dancing in what had become their normal way when with no conscious movement on either part they were suddenly in each other's arms. They exchanged a tentative kiss then more feverish ones before Sylvia turned towards the accommodation and led Jim into her cabin. They made love with an intensity that left them both exhausted but deliriously happy. They talked, slept briefly then resumed their lovemaking at a gentler pace. Four hours later he slipped away and quietly moved across the boat deck.

He'd reached the poop deck believing that he was unobserved but Simmo was sitting out on the deck. Jim had to pass him to reach their cabin and as he attempted to do so Simmo gripped his arm.

'Christ, Jim, get a shower before anyone else smells her on you,' he said.

'Is it that obvious?'

'Be careful, Jim, there's more than one body around here wondering just where you get to at night.'

'You wouldn't say anything would you, Simmo?'

'Of course not, now get that bloody shower before someone else sees you.'

'Thanks, Simmo.'

Fortunately for Jim the morning exercises were cancelled because of the arrival in Aden. Most of the soldiers took to leaning on the rails to watch the entry into port. Their first impressions of the place were not complimentary and they openly said so.

'What a dump,' said Dai, 'just bare brown rock.'

'I wouldn't fancy being stationed here,' said another voice.

'You'd have no choice if you were posted here.'

'I think I'd go AWOL rather than take the posting.'

'We're taking on bunkers here.'

'What are bunkers?'

'Fuel oil for the engines.'

'Are we offloading anyone?'

'We must be the stewards are bringing out some suitcases.'

'I pity the poor sods landing here,' said Dai.

'Well they'll be able to get a good tan.'

'Wonder if we can get ashore.'

'What the hell for?'

'There might be a pub or even women.'

A passing sailor overhearing those comments responded.

'We'll be away in a couple of hours, no shore leave, sorry lads.'

Sergeant Browning joined them then. 'Good news, lads,' he said. 'We're having lifeboat drill as soon as we sail.'

The chorus of groans followed him as he made his way back into the accommodation.

Simmo commented to no one in particular that by the time they came to leave the ship he'd have learnt a new language.

'What new language?'

'Navalese, you know bulkheads instead of walls, deckheads instead of ceilings and decks instead of floors.'

'What about heads instead of loos?' said another voice.

'Or bunks instead of beds?' remarked another.

Jim had studiously avoided eye contact with Sylvia during boat drill because he was afraid of his emotions coming to the surface for all to see. However, as the drill finished and the assembly around their boat broke up he risked a sideways glance. Sylvia did the same thing and half smiled as she turned away. Later after boat drill was completely finished and everyone had returned to their normal places of work or play there was an announcement of the ship's estimated time of arrival in Bombay — noon in five days' time.

That night there was no thought of dancing. Sylvia took Jim's hand and led him straight to her cabin as soon as he arrived. Their lovemaking was gentle as though the initial urgency was over. They talked for a while before enjoying each other again. Neither mentioned the fact that circumstances would soon part them forever. The same happened for the next two nights but on their final night together things were different. That night they talked briefly, danced a waltz — their last waltz — then said their goodbyes out on the deck. The following day he watched as she made her way down the gangway and disappeared into the immigration building. She did not look back.

* * *

That evening after dinner I asked Jim if he'd ever seen Sylvia again. He smiled

88

before answering.

'Yes, just once in York.'

'Accidentally or pre-arranged?'

'Oh, it was a pure accident. It was just after the war, I was in York trying to sort out my affairs. We were staying in the same hotel.'

'Go on,' I prompted.

'I was sitting in the lounge enjoying a beer when she tapped me on the shoulder. 'May I have this dance?' she said. I was so startled I spilled my beer.'

He got to his feet and went over to the drinks cabinet and poured himself a small brandy before continuing.

'She never found her husband in Bombay and started divorce proceedings when she got home. Her solicitor discovered through civil service contacts that he was still in Bombay and living with a local woman. There was no problem with the divorce after that.'

He paused and sipped at his brandy. There was a smile on his face the like of which I'd never seen before.

'We had dinner, danced a foxtrot and a waltz then went to bed together, it just seemed so natural.'

'And,' I said, prompting him again.

'She told me afterwards while we were lying in bed that she'd remarried and was on her way to join her husband. He was an American flier. She was leaving for Southampton in the morning to catch a boat to New York.'

'Did you see her the next morning?'

'No, she checked out very early. I did hear from her though.'

'When?'

'About ten days later. She wrote a letter on the ship and posted it in New York. In it she said that meeting me had been one of the finest moments in her life and that I restored her faith in herself.'

'She was talking about your affair on the ship I presume.'

'Yes, she was beginning to doubt her physical attractions because her husband had abandoned her after only a year of marriage. Without being smug I believe I restored her faith in herself.'

He paused as if thinking over his next statement and that smile appeared before he spoke again.

'It must seem something of a casual affair but it wasn't, it was terrific and neither of us appeared to regret it. We were friends and lovers for a brief period in our lives.'

I looked across at him and although I knew he was in his seventies he suddenly seemed so much younger. It was if talking about Sylvia had rejuvenated him.

'Would you like to see her picture?' he said.

I nodded and he walked out and along to his bedroom returning a few minutes later carrying a photo frame. The picture inside was a pencil sketch showing the head and shoulders of a young woman with her hair blowing in the wind. She was smiling and that smile lit up her face. The paper was stained and creased but despite that I could see a tiny signature in one bottom corner. It read Simmo.

'Simmo gave it to me the day we left Bombay. He was a brilliant artist.'

'Was?'

'No, sorry if I gave the wrong impression, he is still alive and he still lives off the earnings of his artistry. He sends me a hand-drawn card every Christmas.'

'Do you meet up?'

'No, we talk occasionally on the phone but he now lives in New Zealand. He went out there shortly after the war. He never told anyone about Sylvia and me, he kept his word — a great friend and a great character.'

He peered into his empty glass before pouring us both another brandy. Taking a sip he suddenly smiled and looked across at me again.

'I'm glad you're here,' he said. 'I'm reliving my youth through you. Before you came I was rapidly turning into an old fossil, you've brought some interest back into my life.'

'But it's your life we've been discussing.'

'Yes and the best may be yet to come. I know this is all on the tapes but talking to you brings it to life again.'

'No, it isn't all on the tapes. You keep filling in gaps and adding new things when we talk it over. For instance you never mentioned that meeting in York on the tapes.'

'Have you listened to them all?'

'No, I'm trying to take them in sequence.'

'I think it may come up when I get back after the war. To be honest I can't remember.'

He picked up the photograph frame and went off into a world of his own again for a time as he gazed at her picture. After a while he began to hum quietly to himself and I recognised the music of one of the big bands and I realised that he was mentally back on the deck of the P & O liner. I got to my feet and walked quietly from the room and I don't think he noticed my going.

8

Captain Fitzroy held a meeting with his small troop the day after the ship sailed from Bombay. He told them that they would all be leaving the ship at the next port, Penang. There they would be collecting vehicles, survey equipment, drivers and camp aides. Their task was to survey several small airfields along the west coast of Malaya and to produce scale drawings of the airfields and the surrounding topography. The idea was that they would work their way down the west coast and eventually reach Singapore. He emphasised the fact that they would be working in areas of jungle where mosquitoes and other flying insects were a menace and snakes abounded. He finished with an exhortation to use their mosquito nets at night and to check their boots were empty before they put them on in the morning. In the question and answer session that followed Sergeant

Browning asked the first question.

'Am I to assume that we will be camping during this work, sir?'

'Yes, it looks as if we will be.'

'But surely if these are airfields there will be accommodation.'

'We may get more information about them in Penang but the info I was given in England suggested that there may only be a few huts because these places are little more than airstrips for use in an emergency.'

He produced a map of Malaya with the airfields clearly marked. The larger fields in regular use such as Alor Star, Sungei Patani and especially Butterworth were not their concern, the ones that they had to look at and survey had names like Jabi, Kuala Ketil and Sungei Bakap. There was a small field on Penang Island but as this was in regular use by a flying club its details were well known. They would be required to survey nine or ten minor fields as they made their way down the west coast of Malaya towards the island fortress of Singapore.

'What happens when we get to

95

Singapore, sir?' asked a voice.

'I don't know yet, I'll let you know as soon as I find out.'

Six days later they disembarked from their floating home and moved into temporary barracks in Penang. Captain Fitzroy had orders to report to the airfield at Butterworth so left his charges under the sergeant's watchful eye while he was away. On that first night ashore they were confined to barracks but that didn't prevent a number of them finding the opportunity to eye up the local women as they passed outside the wire. Others found their way to the camp canteen and enjoyed a beer or two whilst picking up local knowledge from the soldiers of the garrison.

They spent Christmas 1938 in Penang and were able to sample all the delights that the town could provide. There were drunken episodes and cases of late back from leave but nothing that caused the captain or his sergeant any real problems. By the time the festivities were over few of the men had any cash left so some were eager to get on the move whilst others were reluctant to do so because of connections they'd made with local girls. On the 28th December three trucks arrived from Butterworth, two for them and their equipment whilst the third was a mobile canteen complete with a Chinese cook and his assistant. All three trucks had Sikh drivers.

The only member of the party from England who had ever served in a tropical country before was Sergeant Browning and even he had never been to Malaya so virtually every day brought something new for them to learn. They did have a Malay guide but even he got lost at times. Most of the airstrips were close to small towns or villages accessed by dirt roads that at times were dry and dusty and at others awash with thick mud. On certain occasions they had to cross rivers by ford or by crude native ferries that were barely afloat when under the weight of one truck. They drove through rubber plantations, passed the occasional tin mine and were frequently held up on single track roads by bullock carts.

Many of them learned the hard way

about the local flora and fauna. They were bitten by mosquitoes and other flying insects, attacked by leeches and occasionally by snakes. Monkeys were a constant nuisance, venturing into their camps to steal anything left lying about. Every now and again on a river crossing they encountered crocodiles and on one notable occasion near the sea had one crawl into their camp. Lizards, millipedes, toads and butterflies and birds of fantastic colours were their constant companions. Their drivers and the guide talked of tigers and leopards and fortunately they never encountered either but they did see a tapir and a scaly anteater.

Their diet was supplemented by fruit and vegetables purchased at local markets. They learnt to recognise, and in some cases enjoy, fruits such as papaya, banana, lychees mango, guava and rambutan. The one fruit that none of them attempted to eat was the durian. Although it was described as the king of the fruits its revolting smell drove them all away. The Chinese cook added local foods such as yams, rice, noodles and breadfruit to the staple foodstuffs provided by the army and many of them enjoyed this variety. The local dish nasi lemak, rice steamed in coconut milk, became a particular favourite of some together with Indian-style bread. Then the Sikh drivers introduced them to various curry dishes and their menu expanded even further. There were of course those amongst them who wouldn't touch this 'foreign muck' but Jim was not one of them. He loved the variety and would often join the cook on his visits to the markets to learn more of what was available.

There were times when some if not all of the soldiers craved food that they'd loved at home. One frequent desire amongst two or three was a slice of bread and dripping. Another dreamt of a plate of tripe and onions whilst many requested fish and chips or Yorkshire puddings. Some of them refused to admit that food they craved from home was usually food they could only afford to buy on very rare occasions when they lived there.

On their visits to the airfields at Port

Swettenham and later at Batu Pahat the cook was able to buy fish fresh from the local fishermen. The addition of shrimp, prawn, crab and squid to their menu was once again welcomed as a pleasant change by the majority. Most of them avoided other delicacies that the cook bought and obviously enjoyed such as sea snails and sea cucumber.

Although they were operating as a detached unit they had to visit military bases as they made their way south down the peninsula. The main reason for the visits was to obtain petrol for the vehicles but those stopovers gave them the chance to replace other things such as cigarettes and tinned foods etc. They were also able to rest in reasonable comfort for a night or two and to enjoy luxuries such as showers. Most of them took the opportunity to get minor cuts and sores treated properly by base medical staff. However, when they stopped at Ipoh they left one man behind. Their corporal had been suffering with a fever and the doctor would not allow him to proceed despite his protests.

The airstrips that they surveyed varied wildly in condition. A couple that were used on a regular basis by flying clubs were well maintained but others were in a sorry state. One or two were so overgrown that they were practically useless, no aircraft could have landed because the vegetation had encroached over the runway. Others were maintained in a half-hearted fashion by locals who were apparently paid to do so in an equally half-hearted fashion by their estate managers. Most had no buildings other than those built of local materials and many of those were falling into disrepair. In one case a river had changed course and had cut a channel across the middle of the airstrip.

'I suppose this one is for flying boats,' said Dai as they stood beside the water.

'God help us if these are ever needed in earnest,' another voice muttered.

Captain Fitzroy overheard these remarks.

'That's why we are here,' he said. 'To make a report and get this lot put right.'

'We're not expected to put it right are we, sir?'

'Not today, laddie, not today.'

They were surveying the airfield at Tebrau, the last one before arriving at Singapore, when news reached them that their corporal, Jack Clitheroe, had died. The fever had intensified and nothing the medical staff had done was of any use. He had died two days earlier.

When the small survey party crossed the causeway onto Singapore Island three days later they had been on the move for eight months. It was the last day of August 1939 and their arrival did little to dispel the gloom that had settled over them when they heard the news of the corporal's death. The three vehicles were covered in thick dry mud and the men in them were in little better state. Their clothing was worn and patched and even their boots were in a sorry state. All of them were close to exhaustion and looking forward to a long rest period. None of them appreciated the greeting they received when they finally pulled up outside their allotted quarters. They were unloading their kit when an immaculately starched, blancoed and polished corporal marched across and snarled at them.

'Whose bloody army do you scruffy lot belong to then?'

Dai looked across at Fred. 'Will you hit him or shall I?' he said.

Then Captain Fitzroy appeared from behind a truck and marched straight up to the corporal, the anger in his voice evident to all.

'They're my bloody army, corporal, now sod off before I put you on a charge.'

Sergeant Browning walked across and took the now open-mouthed corporal by the arm and walked him away. Eventually when he was out of earshot of the others he spoke in a tone of suppressed anger.

'That troop of soldiers has been working in jungle conditions for the last eight months. They are extremely tired, their kit is worn out and they've just been told that their corporal is dead. Walk very carefully around us, corporal, very, very carefully. Now do as the captain told you and go away.'

The following day the drivers and cooks were leaving to return to Butterworth. Most of the troop was outside wishing them a safe journey and shaking their hands when the same corporal walked by and made a snide remark about native lovers. That night he was found lying behind the Naafi canteen. His jaw was badly broken, so badly that he could not speak for three weeks and could not eat solid food for a month. Three days after his 'accident' the news came through that war had been declared against Germany.

For the first week in camp in Singapore speculation was ripe that they'd probably be sent back to England but no such order came through. Instead they were re-issued with tropical kit to replace the tattered gear they'd worn for the past eight months or so. They then found themselves producing scale drawings of every one of the airfields that they'd surveyed. While they were busy with that task Captain Fitzroy was attempting to make sense of a series of signals passing between him, Butterworth and the War Office in England. One thing that happened as a result of one of the signals was the addition of personnel to the troop, two Royal Signals radio operators and three RASC drivers.

It was during that period that the camp commandant, Colonel Whitworth, issued a daily order requiring every unit in the camp to provide a marksman for an inter-unit shooting competition. The winner was to represent the army in a shoot off against the air force and navy. This apparently was an annual ritual and a war in Europe was not going to stop it. Jim was chosen and found himself competing against two Indians, an Australian, a Scot and a Geordie. He hadn't fired a shot since the passage out to Malaya.

On the day of the first competition Jim was accompanied by Sergeant Browning, Dai and Fred. Simmo and the others were still busy with the airfield drawings. When they got to the range Sergeant Browning was furious when he saw the marked-up blackboard listing the names and units of the competitors. Where the others had their names followed by their units such as Aust HQ, 1st Ind Div and Gordons, Jim's name was followed the term 'Odds and Sods'. The colour sergeant major standing by the board was smirking at his wit.

'Wipe that smile off his face if you can, Jim,' urged Sergeant Browning.

'I'll do my best but you know I haven't fired a round for months,' Jim replied.

They fired six shots each in the first round to get them used to the range. No one was eliminated in that first round. After that the lowest score was eliminated each round. The first to go was one of the Indian soldiers then in quick succession went the Geordie and the Gordon Highlander. The next round was so close that no one was eliminated so the shooting range was increased. Jim eventually won by one point. The smile was duly wiped from the colour sergeant's face.

Captain Fitzroy called his newly enlarged troop together the next day and, after congratulating Jim on his success with the rifle, brought them up to date with their next task. Apparently the commander of Butterworth had seen the results of their work and had as a result ordered several of the airfields to be brought back into an operational state. While they had been busy re-equipping and preparing the detailed drawings that improvement work was theoretically being carried out. Their task was to go back and redo some of the surveys to see just what improvements had been achieved.

Two days later the troop now equipped with its own three trucks, one fitted with radio, was preparing to leave when an order came down from the camp commander that they couldn't leave until the inter service shootout the following weekend. Captain Fitzroy was furious but there was little he could do — he certainly could not overrule a senior officer. He was overheard muttering about playing games instead of getting on with the war.

As the Navy was the senior service they were responsible for the organisation of the shooting match. However they did not have a shooting range, instead they built a range on their dockyard football pitch. Along each side of the pitch they arranged stands for the supporters of each force. Sergeant Browning was horrified about the safety aspect of the whole arrangement and said so in no uncertain terms to anyone who would listen. The actual shooting took less than an hour but the contest had music provided by bands of the three services and of course they all had to play so the whole thing lasted three hours. Jim came second to the RAF contestant, a sergeant, who had not only won it the previous year but also held an Olympic medal in the same type of event.

★　★　★

I couldn't resist asking Jim about the corporal who had been beaten up and the response I got surprised me.

'It wasn't our fellows that did him in. I asked each one individually and though they were delighted that he'd got his just deserts they all denied responsibility.'

'So no one admitted it.'

'There were rumours of course. The Aussies in the next block to us had had trouble with him so it may have been them.'

He paused for a while before nodding and smiling to himself.

'I remember what happened to him eventually, he asked for a transfer and they sent him up country, gave him a chance to sweat the starch from his shorts.'

'Hadn't he been up country before?'

'No, he'd been two years marching around that same parade ground upsetting newcomers like us. Mind you we were in a disgusting state when we first got there. My boots were so wet they had green mould on them.'

'What was Singapore like?'

'It was like Never Never Land after the jungle, wine, women and song as long as you could afford it.'

'And could you?'

'We had nearly nine months' pay to spend so you can imagine what went on. The strange thing was though that after we heard about the war in Europe all that seemed to intensify around us. You know the sort of thing I mean, if you ignore something it might go away so they did their best to do so.'

He was quiet for a while then before suddenly speaking rather forcibly.

'Silly buggers found out the hard way that trouble like that never goes away on its own.'

9

The day after the shooting final Jim was called before Captain Fitzroy. When he reached the office he found Sergeant Browning there as well as the captain.

'Well done yesterday, Bullock, but that's not only why you are here. As you know we've lost Corporal Clitheroe and the troop is increasing in size so we need a replacement. You are young and inexperienced but the troops treat you with respect. So I'd like to make you a corporal on an acting basis to see how you get on. How do you feel about it?'

Jim thought for a while before answering.

'There are several more experienced than me, sir, how would they feel?'

'Sergeant Browning has sounded them out and it appears they'd rather you had the job. Are you willing to take it on?'

'In that case I'll give it a go, sir.'

'Good, then from today you are acting

Corporal Bullock. Sergeant Browning will help you get started.'

'Thank you, sir.'

When the troop left the barracks later that morning in newly acquired trucks there were many differences from when they'd originally arrived. They now had new drivers, drivers who did not know the roads they were going to take and secondly they had lost the catering wagon and the Chinese cooks. In place of the cooks was a store of army rations for them to cook themselves. The food was stored in the third truck, the one that also carried the radio. Captain Fitzroy rode in the cab of the first truck, Sergeant Browning in the second and Jim in the third.

They drove across the causeway and left Singapore Island just after midday then continued on without stopping until they reached the first of the airfields at Tebrau. There they set up camp for the night and the problem of who was going to act as cook arose. The captain called for a volunteer but no one stepped forward. Then Dai asked if we would have funds for local food as we had done on the earlier trip. When the captain agreed that funds would be available Dai surprised them all by volunteering.

'I'd like to take it on, sir, providing I can try my hand at local foods,' he said.

'You have cooked before, have you?' the captain asked.

'Yes, sir, and I watched our Chinese cook. I like food,' he added.

That first night Dai had to manage with what the army had provided but was still able to produce a palatable meal.

The survey work began in earnest the following morning but because they were only assessing the improvements that had taken place it was easier. Nevertheless it took them four days to complete. By the time they reached the second airfield at Batu Pahat the drivers were beginning to appreciate the state of some of the dirt roads they had to contend with. None of them had previously driven in Malaya; they only had experience of the mainly tarmac roads of Singapore. They began to understand the difficulties their fellow soldiers had already faced.

Captain Fitzroy instituted a series of lessons amongst his men where troops exchanged information about their particular trades with their fellows. The idea was that soldiers should be able to temporarily fill in if any of their compatriots fell ill or was injured. Most of them had never driven a lorry or any other vehicle in their lives so the wide open spaces of an airfield runway were ideal places to learn.

The same applied to their newly acquired radio set, the operators were required not only to demonstrate its operation but to allow their fellows access to the controls. Some of them renewed their scant knowledge of morse code by listening to messages broadcast on a regular basis. They were shown how the radio could be disconnected from the fittings in the lorry and carried as backpacks for use in the field. One operator carried the radio whilst his partner carried a battery pack and a hand generator capable of recharging them.

Radio operators and drivers were required to carry out simple survey duties under the supervision of one or the other of the qualified surveyors and everyone was required to assist Dai at least one day a week. There were few grumbles because the variety of duties made their days more interesting. Captain Fitzroy's troop was rapidly becoming a tight-knit multi-skilled unit capable of handling whatever the jungle threw at them. They worked shoulder to shoulder to heave bogged-down lorries out of the mud, learnt how to change wheels and repair punctures and even climbed trees to rig aerials. They cursed together when the rain was torrential and sang together when the sun shone.

Christmas 1939 found them enjoying a well deserved rest period in Kuala Lumpur. It gave them time to clean themselves, their clothes and the vehicles as well as letting them enjoy the festive season in comfort. They did not have a turkey dinner on Christmas Day but instead enjoyed roast pork provided for them by courtesy of Jim's accurate use of a rifle.

The day before they reached Kuala

Lumpur their lead vehicle was waved down by a local villager who needed help. At first they couldn't make out just what he wanted but he eventually managed to make them understand that a wild animal was attacking his village. At first Captain Fitzroy was reluctant to help but, when the villager got down on his knees to plead, he relented. Jim, Dai and the captain, all armed with rifles, went cautiously with the now grateful villager along a jungle track. As they approached the village they heard a loud snorting, squealing and the sounds of a heavy body crashing through the undergrowth. Suddenly their guide, the villager, leapt aside with a shout of warning as a great black beast confronted them. It was a wild boar almost as big as a small horse with great curling tusks and wild red eyes. Jim dropped onto one knee and brought his rifle to his shoulder and as he did so the beast charged. He fired twice hitting it between the eyes but even though it must have died instantly its momentum carried it into and onto Jim. It took all four of the others to drag the great body off him.

While Jim was sitting recovering, the villagers dragged the beast into the village square. Helping Jim to his feet Dai and the others followed. They were shocked by the damage the boar had caused. Gardens were ripped up, two houses that had stood on stilts a few feet above ground level lay on their sides and three or four village dogs lay dying, their bloodied entrails evidence of their attempt to defend their masters.

'Christ, Jim,' said Dai. 'I thought you were a goner then.'

'So did I when the bloody thing kept coming,' replied Jim.

Captain Fitzroy had been studying the great bulk of the beast and he suddenly walked over to its head and examined it.

'The poor creature had toothache,' he said. 'Look at that tusk — it's grown into the side of its head by its left eye. It must have been in agony.'

He straightened up and looked around at the wrecked houses and at the villagers standing around as if in shock.

'Do you think we could help them put things to rights here, Bullock?'

Jim nodded. 'Yes, should I bring the lads, sir?'

'I'll go,' said Dai.

'Okay, tell Sergeant Browning to leave someone to guard the trucks.'

It took the combined might of the soldiers and a number of the male villagers to put the two houses back into an upright position. While that was going on the women had dragged the boar carcase to the far side of the village where it was being butchered. Three Chinese, two men and a woman, were busy cutting up the beast. A number of Indian women in saris were assisting.

'Where did the Indians and Chinese come from?' asked Simmo. 'I thought this was a Malay village.'

'It is a Malay village,' said the sergeant, 'but that lot are rubber tappers from the plantation houses beyond the village. I've sent Fred along to get us a share of the meat.'

'The Malays won't touch the meat, it's against their religion,' remarked Bill, one of the radio operators.

When they returned to the trucks Jim

was sitting cleaning his rifle and around his neck hung a garland of flowers. The villager who had pleaded for help originally had pointed him out to the village elder. While the others were busy with the houses Jim had been receiving his thanks and the thanks of two of the village women. To them Jim was their saviour because he'd shot the beast. Others returned bearing fruit or various sweetmeats, gifts from grateful villagers. One of the drivers later claimed that he'd received thanks of a more physical kind from one of the female rubber tappers in return for a pack of cigarettes. He was later to discover that she'd given him another painful unwanted gift.

Captain Fitzroy, Sergeant Browning and Acting Corporal Bullock served the Christmas dinner to the rest of the troop as was the normal army custom. The captain also presented each man a large bottle of Tiger beer. The pork proved to be sweet and tender which Dai claimed was the result of his culinary expertise despite the fact that most of the cooking had been done by barracks staff. After the meal they were free to explore the delights of the town for the rest of that day and for the next two days.

Throughout January 1940 they worked their way north visiting and checking airfields at Port Swettenham, Sitiawan, Ipoh and Taiping. One of the drivers had to be left at Ipoh to receive medical attention and after their visit to Taiping they went back to collect him. After that they moved north again checking three more airfields before arriving at Butterworth early in March. They remained at RAF Butterworth for over a month waiting for new orders and using the time for vehicle maintenance as well as rest and relaxation. Acting Corporal Bullock found himself working his way through exam papers to confirm his rank. Most of the troop adapted well to the tropical routine used at the base, working from early morning to noon then being allowed to relax. Many of them used the afternoons for swimming especially as the beaches were frequented by female base staff and families.

In April they were ordered to survey the airfields at Kuala Ketil and Jabi before returning once again to Butterworth. This took them further north almost to the border of Siam, not that most of them were aware of that fact. Anyway one area of jungle looks the same as another as one trooper was overheard to say as he used a cigarette to burn leeches off his leg. After the death of Corporal Clitheroe there wasn't a man who didn't sleep under a mosquito net or check his boots in the morning for unwelcome night-time intruders but men still became ill at times. On their return to Butterworth another of their number was hospitalised with a fever. The doctors were unsure whether it was malaria or dengue fever but it hardly mattered since the treatment appeared to be the same for both. Fortunately he had recovered sufficiently well enough to rejoin them as they turned south and headed for Singapore again in July.

★ ★ ★

I'd been typing so much about those airfields that I had begun to know the names off by heart but no mention had been made of the actual aircraft so I asked Jim about them one evening. The answer I got surprised me.

'The only military aircraft we saw were at Butterworth and there weren't many of them,' he said.

'Why did they need all those fields then?'

'The captain kept saying that there were a lot of new aircraft expected but we never saw them. We saw military aircraft in Singapore of course but only there and at Butterworth.'

'Of course, I was forgetting that the Battle of Britain was being raged then. They'd need the aircraft in England.'

'There was one airfield with a few biplanes and the captain did go up in one to look at it from the air but they were civvie aircraft. There were plenty of rumours about new aircraft coming but I never saw them.'

He was quiet for a few minutes, thinking back I suppose, then without warning he got to his feet and began walking backwards and forwards across the room.

'You just mentioned the Battle of Britain but out there we only got snippets of information. In fact if it hadn't been for the overseas service we'd have known nowt. Singapore just went on as normal.' He paused for breath but still continued to walk across the room.

'I was in the Naafi shop one day late in 1940 and there were two army officer's wives complaining bitterly that supplies from England were not getting through. Their main cause for complaint was the lack of marmalade. Can you imagine it,' he burst out. 'The country at war and they were moaning about bloody marmalade.'

'Were you in Singapore all of the rest of that year?'

'Yes, unfortunately we were stuck in barracks until the start of 1941. The only good thing about that period was the fact that my acting capacity was made permanent. It was most unusual because somehow I bypassed the lance corporal rank.'

He stopped wearing a groove in the carpet and sat down again.

'The worst thing about being in barracks is idle hands,' he said. 'You can only drill, maintain gear and exercise for so long. Eventually you start getting drinking problems and so on. We even had one of our blokes caught peeping into married quarter's windows one night. Brothels, men caught out of bounds, you name it we had it. I for one was damn glad to see the back of Singapore.'

'Can I take it then that you were as pure as driven snow?' I said.

'No, not really, I just didn't get caught.'

He got to his feet again and took his jacket from the hook by the door.

'Come on, all this talking is making me feel dry. The White Horse will be open and I fancy a beer.'

His mate Harry was in the bar when we got there so in no time at all we were talking cars, then darts and finally all the latest village gossip. You know the sort of thing — Charlie's left his missus, the Thompsons are having an extension built and who do you reckon will win on

Saturday! I was beginning to wonder how I was going to escape when Harry's wife turned up looking for a lift home. I think she had to drive him in the end, he'd had too many. We left at the same time and found ourselves wishing various members of the W.I. goodnight. I'm sure I spoke to three called Doris or was the third one Ethel — I'll get it right one day.

10

In early September I received a letter from the solicitor who had sorted out my divorce. My ex-wife and I had both known at the time of the divorce that certain areas of our business would take time to be finalised. Some of the business accounts we had dealt with were extremely slow to settle their bills and they had finally paid up and consequently my presence was needed in York to sign off the final settlement.

Jim wasn't interested in coming with me so I set off alone in the car. When I turned onto the Driffield bypass I happened to notice a car behind me. I'm not sure why I picked out that particular car; it just caught my eye for some reason. When I turned onto the York road I saw the car go off round the roundabout as if turning into the town. I was in no particular hurry so I wasn't pushing the car along merely cruising at about fifty-five. Anyway I was approaching Garrowby Hill when I noticed that car again behind me. I suddenly got the idea that he was following me.

Just over the brow of the hill is a small lay-by and I pulled over into it allowing the four or five cars behind me to carry on down. I turned off the engine and sat and enjoyed the view for ten minutes or so before setting off again. A few minutes later I passed a farm shop and café and lo and behold my suspicious car slid out of the car park and moved in behind me once again. It was then that I realised why it had caught my eye in the first place — the car gleamed as if newly washed and polished but both number plates were covered in mud. As far as I could tell there was no mud on the wheels.

About six or seven minutes later the vehicles ahead of me slowed and came to a stop. After two or three minutes we began to crawl forward again and as we did so I could see blue flashing lights ahead and a policeman standing in the road. I couldn't tell whether there was an accident or one of those vehicle safety checks that happen occasionally. We moved about three car lengths before stopping again and then I saw in my mirror a car doing a U-turn — it was 'muddy number plate'. Had the presence of the police upset him I wondered or was I getting paranoid? I didn't see him again until later that day.

The hold-up turned out to be a broken-down lorry and because the road was so narrow the police were controlling the traffic. It didn't hold me up for long and I was soon parked in York. I signed a couple of papers in the solicitor's office and came out of there slightly ahead financially which was a welcome surprise. I had lunch in a little café near the minster, bought a few odds and ends then set off for home. My paranoia came into play then and instead of returning by the same road I took the Scarborough turning and went miles out of my way, just in case. I could feel one of my bullet scars irritating me all the way home — paranoia?

When I eventually turned into Main Street there was the black car parked two doors away from the house. I pulled up behind it, got out and marched to the driver's door. It opened before I got there and a man I'd never seen before stepped out and handed me an envelope.

'I'm to wait for a reply,' he said.

Walking to the side of the road I tore open the envelope and read the short note inside. It read, — 'We should meet, Mr Sharp, such a meeting could be of mutual benefit — substantial benefit for you.' The signature was Da Silva.

I told the driver to wait and went inside the house, switched on my printer and copied the note. To the original I added the words 'no thank you' and signed it. I then put it into a new envelope and went out and handed it to the driver. He made no comment, merely took it and got back into the car and drove off. I parked my car in front of the house. Jim had obviously heard my arrival and came in from the shed. He gave me a long hard look then sat down and indicated the note in my hand.

'Trouble?' he asked.

I handed him the note without saying

anything. He read it then passed it back.

'Did you reply?'

'Yes, I told him no thank you.'

Then I told him how I had tried to avoid the black car, how I'd driven miles out of my way only to find the damn thing parked virtually on our doorstep.

'Was it that big ugly bugger?' asked Jim.

'No, I'd never seen this one before.'

'What are you going to do now?'

'I'll email a copy of this with my reply to Sergeant Cooper and then get back to work on your tapes.'

'Do you think he'll take no for an answer?'

'He'll have to, I've no intention of meeting him.'

★ ★ ★

The survey troop began January 1941 with a mission they had not expected. They were taken by patrol craft from the Singapore Naval Base to an island in the South China Sea called Tioman. Their task was to survey the beaches, possible landing sites and the whereabouts of possible underwater reefs. The patrol craft anchored offshore and landed them by boat on a beach that showed no sign of habitation. They were left with a boat and two seamen to man it, stores for a month and the radio.

None of them had any idea of how to survey for reefs so they left that until they had completed their other tasks. When the patrol craft returned at the end of the first month with more stores they had begun to experiment with reef surveys using a leadline and a measuring stick of their own design. It was easy enough to see the reefs because the seawater was crystal clear but measuring their extent and depth was a hit and miss affair. However by the end of the second month they had produced a diagram of a sort. They took their results back to Singapore and added their findings to a marine chart that was provided for them. Apparently the amended chart was viewed with great interest by the Navy.

Easter saw them back on airfield surveys but this time along the east coast starting with the field at Kluang. They gradually worked their way north again surveying at Kuantan, Gong Kedah, Machang and Kota Bharu. En route they used the facilities at various military camps and bases, encountering Indian, Australian and British troops. Once again they learned to barter at the local markets for fruit and vegetables to supplement their army rations, Dai became particularly adept at this. They were also able to obtain fresh fish on a regular basis.

The survey results were put together when they reached Kota Bharu and despatched to both RAF Butterworth and the UK through the army courier system. It was then early September 1941. They were ordered to stay in Kota Bharu to await orders. Their quarters were with a section of the Australian army and they soon discovered the Australian soldier's love of gambling. They would bet on virtually anything and somehow Jim found himself challenged to a shooting match by an Australian sniper. He was not particularly keen on the idea especially when he heard how much money was being laid in bets on both sides. However, he agreed to take part. After the first twenty shots they couldn't be separated so they had a further ten shots as a decider — they still couldn't be separated so they tossed a coin and Jim won. Jim's opponent, Duggie West, couldn't believe he'd been beaten by a pommie bastard but he took the result philosophically and bought Jim a couple of beers. Jim returned the favour and they talked shooting and army life together. From him Jim received a gift that he found extremely useful later. Duggie gave him a telescopic sight to fit to his rifle — he called it a sniper scope.

Their new orders arrived shortly after the contest and instead of being ordered back to Singapore as they expected they were given an island survey job again. Captain Fitzroy called the whole troop together to explain their task. He began by saying that he'd seen their enjoyment of the tropical sands and seas of the island of Tioman so he'd got them another couple of islands to enjoy.

'They are part of a group of islands

known as the Perhentians. We are only interested in two of them so we'll know them as 'little island' and big island'. They are out there in the South China Sea.'

'How far away, sir?' asked one of the drivers.

'About two hours by boat.'

'Will the drivers be needed out there?'

'Yes, you three and half a dozen others who will join us shortly will run the base camps while the rest of us are climbing.'

He went on to explain that the survey party and the radio operators were to climb to the highest point on both islands to assess their suitability for use as observation posts. The planned posts would be manned for the purpose of observing shipping movements and reporting these by radio to the shore.

'Will we be expected to man these posts, sir?' Jim asked.

'No, we are merely to assess the possibility of siting them there. We'll have the same sort of tropical rainforest to contend with but this time we'll be climbing through it. I'm told that we can expect monkeys, snakes and so on as well.'

'How do we get between the islands, sir?'

'We are being allocated two sea boats. They'll be towed out behind the ship that's taking us out to the first island. We'll use them to move round the coast as necessary and to move between the islands.'

'When do we leave?'

'As soon as the ship gets here, it's on its way from Singapore at the moment. There will be eight boat's crew as well as the two boats.'

'Eight boat's crew and six new men for the base camp — I make that thirty altogether. That will quite a strain on my cooking,' said Dai.

'You'll be on survey duty — two of the new men are cooks.'

'Are we getting a guide, sir?' asked Sergeant Browning.

'We've been allocated an interpreter but whether he'll be any good as a guide remains to be seen.'

It was the third of October 1941 when

they finally began to assemble aboard the ship that was to take them all out to the little island. As the captain had said the voyage out took little more than two hours but it took the rest of the daylight hours to unload their equipment and stores. The two seaboats, one larger than the other, had to make several trips between ship and shore to get all the personnel and their effects onto dry land. They dined on army rations and slept in tents pitched on the beach that first night. Many woke complaining of multiple sand-fly or mosquito bites the next morning.

Before any attempt was made to leave the beach the next morning the two radiomen were required to establish contact with Khota Bharu. They slung an aerial between two convenient trees and began transmitting. They tried medium frequencies first and failed miserably, there being too much static and atmospherics to hear a reply even if they themselves had been heard. On higher frequencies they heard morse signals, broadcast stations and various whistles, screams and howls but they still failed to contact the shore. It was decided that they needed to be higher up on the mountain. Eventually they packed up their kit and assembled it in backpacks ready for the climb.

While they were busy Captain Fitzroy and two others investigated the lower reaches of the mountain and found the undergrowth hard going. The only tracks appeared to be made by animals and were so narrow that even one man had to hack his way through the vegetation. There was no way that two men could walk side by side. As soon as they made their way into the undergrowth monkeys began screeching and howling at them whilst birds and fruit bats took off in flocks and added their screeches to the general cacophony. They stopped fighting their way through the rainforest at noon and turned back to the camp. Each man had taken turns at cutting their way with the bush knife but after fifteen minutes they'd had enough. By spelling themselves to fifteen minutes at a time they had made progress but it had proved hard going.

They made no attempt to resume the

climb that afternoon; instead the captain and Sergeant Browning went out by boat to examine the shoreline from a distance through binoculars. They eventually spotted what appeared to be an easier route two hundred yards to the left of their initial climb. Once back on the shore they walked along to examine their find and decided that it would be the better option.

The following morning the first serious attempt to climb began. The ten members of the survey group, the two radio operators and Captain Fitzroy made their way in single file to the spot selected the previous day. In addition to their rifles each man carried ration packs sufficient for four days and either survey equipment or radios. Three men carried bush knives. Once again each man took his turn with the lead cutting through the undergrowth for fifteen minutes or so before moving aside for the next man. The men left on the beach could only measure their progress when the climbers were visible through a thinner patch of vegetation.

The climbing team found that the

undergrowth thinned when the tree canopy above them was at its densest. However, as they were climbing through virgin tropical forest the ground beneath their feet was wet, slimy and strewn with fallen trees. Every man was attacked by leeches and flying insects as they stumbled along. After five hours of climbing they came out into sunshine onto a rocky ledge and a halt was called. Looking round at his exhausted troop the captain decided that enough was enough for that day. Dai went in search of dry wood in order to light a fire whilst the others were busy nursing aching feet, getting rid of leeches and cursing the man who came up with their latest task.

Dai reappeared a few minutes later with the news that he had found a cave that was both dry and roomy — he thought it would be the ideal spot to spend the night. As it rained virtually every day for an hour or so the thought of spending a night under cover without having to pitch tents on a mountainside was more than welcome. Sergeant Browning went with Dai to inspect it. He gave it his approval so they all moved their kit into it.

Once the two radiomen had freed themselves from the leeches that they had collected they set about setting up the radio again. While they were busy with that Dai took their rations and began turning them into a meal. Contact was established with Khota Bahru at the first attempt that time on a four megacycles frequency. The operators merely exchanged radio checks as there were no messages to be passed in either direction.

The following day the climb seemed easier although they still had to negotiate rainforest conditions. They found several caves similar to the one they had spent the night in though most were smaller. Monkeys followed their progress, swinging through the tree tops above them but not making the racket that they'd made on the first day. The birds and bats seemed to have accepted their presence as well. From time to time they could look back to the beach below and see the whole panorama of the islands they had passed on their way out. They reached the top on the third day. From there they had an even better view back towards the islands and the thin dark line on the horizon that they took to be the coast of the mainland. The view out to the South China Sea was partly obscured by the big island. Radio checks were exchanged once more.

★   ★   ★

Jim interrupted me at that point and I was pleased for the chance of a break so I took the cup of tea he offered and sat back for a while. I couldn't resist asking him about the leeches because his comment earlier about getting rid of them by burning them off with cigarettes intrigued me.

'How many of those things did you attract in a day?' I asked.

'It depended on the conditions we had to go through but on that first days climb we averaged about seven or eight each.'

'Did you have to use cigarettes?'

'Cigarettes or salt if you had it — the

real trouble was getting at the ones on your back; you needed a mate to clear them for you.'

He burst out laughing then.

'I wish I'd had a camera to record some the scenes. Can you imagine a dozen or so nearly naked men using lighted cigarettes to remove the little buggers from each other? They did get into some very embarrassing places at times.'

He put down his cup and stroked his chin.

'At first the ruddy things used to turn my stomach but eventually they just became an unfortunate part of the job. I found out by chance that swimming in the sea got rid of them. Unfortunately there isn't much seawater on a mountainside.'

11

The survey of the top of the mountain took no longer than a day. It mainly consisted of noting the position of relatively level areas for setting up equipment, the position of caves for shelter and the angles of view. Using a magnetic compass they were able to assess the angles of vista relative to magnetic north and estimated distance of clear view from various positions around the accessible area of the mountain top. The view to the east was partly obscured by the big island.

They began the descent at first light the following day and stopped to note any unusual or useful features that they had missed on the climb. Several caves were noted, most of them dry inside which proved extremely useful shelters when the daily downpours occurred. The biggest problem they had was with the wet ground. Most of them took at least one tumble when their feet slid from under them. These falls did cause injuries. Fred damaged a thigh muscle and struggled to complete the descent whilst one of the radio operators twisted his ankle. Both of them needed help from the rest.

When they finally reached the beach the captain decided to wait there for a few days in order to allow the battered bodies to recover. They all took the opportunity to swim from the beach but they always had one man with a rifle on shark watch. There were several sharks sighted but none of them caused any problem. During this rest period Simmo was given the task of producing sketches from the results they'd achieved on the mountain.

While the survey team had been climbing those on the beach had been busy in other ways. The cooks had been foraging for local foods to supplement their diet and had found most of the fruit and vegetables they'd earlier bought from roadside markets. The boat's crew had taken out one of the boats regularly to fish and the results they had were good. One interesting fact they discovered from the fishing expeditions was how the current between the islands changed twice daily with the tides. They estimated its strength at between one or two knots in a north/south or south/north direction when the tides changed. One other thing that had been noted was the caution displayed by the local native population: although they also fished in the area none of them would approach the soldiers. Their interpreter had virtually nothing to do.

Before any attempt was made to move across to the big island Captain Fitzroy took a trip across by boat to assess possible landing places. He had Jim and the interpreter with him. On that occasion they did make contact with the local population after they had found the ideal landing site. They went round the island deliberately seeking out the local headman because the site they had selected was uninhabited. When they eventually made contact they were advised that to the locals the beach was taboo but they couldn't or wouldn't explain why except to talk of devil voices.

They returned to their selected beach after talking to the headman and studied it further. The island was obviously much bigger than the small island and different in some ways. Whilst it still had the same dense rainforest there were areas where rocky outcrops predominated. In one part the rocks overhung the beach providing shade from the sun and shelter from the rain. The beach where they had landed was of smooth coral sand but at the far end rocks ran down to the sea. They were investigating that end when they heard what they took to be the 'devil voices'. A low moaning sound came from within the rocks making them both jump. It turned out to be air being pushed out through holes in the rock whenever a larger than normal wave washed in.

'If those are the devil voices then we've nothing to worry about,' said Jim.

'I wonder just what it sounds like when the sea is rough?' replied the captain.

'Spooky, especially at night,' Jim answered.

It took them three whole days to ferry all the men and stores between the two islands and a further two days to get the new camp organised. They had to pitch tents despite the shelter provided by the overhanging rocks. However, within the rocks they found several openings where stores, guns and ammunition could be placed in the dry. They even found some local artefacts in them to show that despite the so-called devil voices natives had been on the beach in the past.

It was the first week in November when they began the climb on the big island. They encountered the usual problems in the forested areas but even more when the reached the rocky outcrops. At first they came to a halt at a sheer rock face after working their way through the lower rainforest and when they edged their way to one end of it found a vertical drop. The rock face was coated in green slime and water constantly dripped from above on them. They turned back and eventually found at the other end a rocky ledge leading upwards. On one side was the rock face whilst at the other a drop of ten feet or so into the forest. That ledge led them back up into the rainforest. Half way up the ledge was a substantial cave that they utilised for sleeping in on that first night.

Four days of scrambling over rocks and slipping and sliding their way through rainforest eventually brought them to the top of the mountainous island. The view was tremendous. Even the small island hardly blocked an almost three-hundred-and-sixty degree panorama. It was the ideal place to position an observation post. From there the radio operators received an immediate response to their first transmission but once again only radio checks were exchanged.

They spent the rest of that day assessing the good and bad points of the site and despite its obvious advantages as a viewpoint it had drawbacks. One disadvantage was the lack of a regular water supply. Water would have to be carried up or a method devised to catch the rainwater that fell on a daily basis. Another problem was the lack of shelter. On the peak the sun beat down mercilessly on the bare rocks, the only shelter lay some two hundred feet below. They eventually withdrew to that shelter, a small cave, as night descended upon them.

The descent began the next day and once again they discovered aspects of advantage that they'd overlooked on the ascent. One cave they discovered, and slept in one night, went deep into the mountain and showed signs of human habitation. There were the remains of cooking fires, animal bones and even a broken arrow with a stone point. They also discovered when darkness fell that it was the home of thousands of bats. A great host of the creatures came from deep in the cave and exploded out into the darkness above their heads.

It was mid morning on the third day of the descent that they came to the ledge that they'd encountered on the way up. Jim was leading, Sergeant Browning was in the middle and the captain was bringing up the rear. The ledge was wet and slippery but the first three or four men were nearly safely down when there were shouts, the sounds of falling bodies and a terrible scream. Jim turned and scrambled back past the men behind him to find the captain on his knees peering over the edge. Seeing Jim, the captain pointed down.

'The sergeant's down there with one of the radio men.'

'Can you see them?'

'Yes, it's only about ten feet down but somebody's badly hurt judging by that scream.'

'I'll try to get down there, sir,' said Jim.

'No, wait.' He turned and looked back at the men behind him. 'Is that cave back there?'

'Yes, sir,' said a voice.

'Okay all of you back up and get into there.'

Back in the cave they took off their packs and rifles and Fred unpacked the medical kit that he carried.

'If we lower you down with the medical kit can you find out how bad they are, Fred?'

'Yes, sir.'

'We'll have to lower you from in here because that ledge is too slippery.'

Fred nodded. 'Okay,' he replied.

They made a loop in their one climbing rope for Fred to put his feet in then with him gripping the rope higher up they lowered him over the edge. He had the medical kit tucked in his shirt. He landed six or seven feet from the injured men and crawled over to them. They now lay side by side and the sergeant appeared to be unconscious. Those above saw him talk to the radioman and slide his pack clear. He then did the same to the sergeant after spending some time bent over him. He appeared to be examining the sergeant's leg. They saw him give both men an injection. Gathering both packs he tied them and the rifles to the rope and signalled for them to be pulled up. When the rope was lowered back to him he signalled to be pulled up again. Back in the cave he gave his assessment of the men's injuries.

'The sergeant's thigh is shattered: there are at least two breaks. As for the radioman he can't feel his legs; he's either damaged a nerve or . . . '

'Or broken his back,' finished the captain.

'I've given them both a morphine shot,' said Fred.

'Okay, we've got to get them out of there quickly. We need stretchers, any ideas?'

'We passed a stand of bamboo back up the slope,' said Simmo.

'Yes,' said Jim, 'if we can cut some of those down and tie the tents across them we should be able to make stretchers. Simmo take two of the lads and get half a dozen bamboos about as thick as your fist and around ten feet long.'

'Okay, Jim, we're on our way.' He got to his feet and waved to two of his mates to follow.

The captain turned to the other radio operator. 'We're going to need the ship out here. Can you get through to Khota Bharu?'

'No, sir, the radio's knackered,' he replied. He picked it up and shook it and they could all hear the sound of broken glass. 'My mate had it on his back when he fell.'

'Right, leave it there and leave your pack. Take your rifle and your water bottle and go down to the camp. Tell them we'll need the larger boat fuelled up and ready to go to Khota Bharu. You'd better eat something now before you go. Oh and tell four of them to come up here to give us a hand.'

He turned then to Jim.

'Can we use the tents as slings to lift them up?'

'They'll be strong enough but we'll need to make them rigid; that's why I want the bamboos.'

He nodded then turned to Fred.

'Can you splint the sergeant's leg while he's knocked out?'

'Yes, sir, I've been thinking about it. Can I use the tent poles?'

'Will they be long enough?'

'If I tie his legs together I can tie the poles alongside the damaged part.'

'Okay, gather what you need and we'll lower you down again.'

When Simmo and the others returned with the bamboos Fred was busy dealing with the sergeant. Both of the casualties were still unconscious although groans could be still heard coming from the sergeant. Working as quickly as they could Jim and the others began to produce a form of stretcher from the bamboo and tents. They used two ten-foot lengths for each stretcher with crosspieces tied between them about eight feet apart. Then they tied the tents across to form the part that would hold the casualties. Fortunately there was enough rope to attach to the four corners of the first stretcher. They tried it out in the cave using Simmo as weight on the tent material and when four of them lifted it with him in place it took his weight satisfactorily.

There was no way that Fred could lift the casualties on his own so when they lowered the first stretcher they lowered Simmo in it. Together he and Fred manoeuvred the sergeant as gently as they could onto the makeshift device and did their best to keep it straight as it was lifted from above. The lift was successful and the stretcher placed in the cave while they recovered Bill, the radio operator. By the time they'd got the second stretcher up and recovered Fred and Simmo it was late afternoon and none of them had eaten since breakfast. Because darkness was imminent they knew that they would have to spend the night there so they prepared a meal and resigned themselves to another night on the mountain.

Before it became completely dark the captain motioned Jim to join him outside.

'Do you think we'll get them off this ledge safely?' he asked Jim.

'We'll have to tie them onto the stretchers and inch them round bit by bit. I can see a man at the front facing the stretcher and lifting his end while inching backwards and there'll be a man behind him to make sure he doesn't fall. At the other end we'll have a rope attached for others to hang onto. We'll not be able to lift either stretcher until we've got them off this ledge.'

'I can't think of anything better so we'll try it your way,' agreed the captain.

Light was just brightening the sky the following morning when they were on the move. They left their packs, their rifles and the battered radio in the cave and began to inch the first of the casualties out onto the ledge. Both men were heavily sedated but groans were audible despite that. Jim took the first turn at inching backward with a rope round his waist held by the man behind him. At the other end a rope was attached to the crosspiece of the stretcher held so that it could be guided clear of the edge. It took almost half an hour to get the first casualty safely off the ledge. The second was easier but nevertheless took almost the same time.

Before they began the final descent the four men from the beach reached them. They were allocated positions on the stretchers, each stretcher needing four men, whilst three others moved ahead of them to cut a wider path. The whole party then set off stumbling and sliding their way downhill whilst desperately trying not to drop the stretchers. They had to change places frequently but they eventually reached the beach just after midday. The stretchers were immediately carried to the boat and loaded on board. Captain

Fitzroy talked quickly to the senior member of the boat's crew and emphasised the need to waste no time on the crossing. He detailed Simmo, the other radio operator, one driver and two of the beach crew to go with them.

'Get back as soon as you can Simpson, we need the ship to get all our gear loaded if possible, if not bring back this boat.'

'Rightho, sir, I'll do my best.'

With that the boat engine purred into action and the heavily laden boat made for the coast of Malaya in the far distance. It was then the third of December 1941.

12

Captain Fitzroy and Jim stood side by side watching the boat until it disappeared from view, hidden by the smaller island.

'You'll have to be my sergeant now, Bullock, Acting Sergeant Bullock, how does it feel?'

Before Jim could answer the captain turned and called the remaining men across to where he stood. When they gathered in a group before him he spoke briefly.

'I know some of you are not in my troop and will be leaving us as soon as we get back to Khota Bharu but until we get there Corporal Bullock here will be my acting sergeant. Any questions?'

'When are we leaving, sir?' asked one of the remaining boat crew.

'As soon as the ship that brought us here returns, probably in a day or two, it came up from Singapore last time.'

'Should we start packing?' asked Dai.

'We can certainly pack the survey gear but we've got to recover it first, most of it is still up the mountain.'

'So are our rifles,' said another voice.

'We'll organise something tomorrow but in the meantime some of us need food, we haven't eaten since breakfast and that was only a scratch meal.'

They had all grown used to torrential downpours that lasted for about an hour every day but that day the weather broke its normal pattern. The rain began as usual about four in the afternoon but never stopped. It was so heavy that it was impossible to see more than a few feet ahead and it just kept coming. They were all sheltering in the dry under the rocky overhang but the water streaming from the rocks above formed a solid curtain in front of them. It was so thick that it was impossible to see the sea. The boat's crew hauled their boat higher onto the beach and secured it by driving the anchor deep into the sand. Then the wind rose and drove the rain back under the overhang giving all of them a wet and miserable night.

When dawn broke its arrival was announced by a lightening in the all-over grey that surrounded them. The rain continued to pour and the sea became rougher. The moaning sound from the rocks increased in frequency and intensity.

'What's that racket?' asked one huddled figure.

'It's those rocks moaning.'

'I know how they bloody well feel,' said a third voice.

'That ship will never find us in this.'

'What if it comes and can't find us?'

'Then you won't get your Christmas pudding.'

'Shut up you miserable lot,' shouted Dai. 'Here you are in a tropical paradise and all you can do is moan.'

'Bollocks.'

'It's not us it's those bloody rocks.'

Jim got to his feet and walked out along the beach. He found the captain standing at the spot where the trail they had made came out onto the sand. Instead of a trail there was a river of mud pouring down the hillside.

'You won't get back up there today, Bullock,' shouted the captain.

'No sir,' agreed Jim. 'I was wondering if we should put a man on watch down by the water.'

'Good idea, it'll give them all chance to get a shower. I think one hour stints until the rain stops.'

It finally stopped as quickly as it started just before noon. One minute it was pouring down then the next it suddenly stopped as if someone had turned a tap off. Half an hour later the sand was strewn with clothing drying in the sun. Some of the men were wandering around in underpants whilst others went naked. The boat's crew were baling out the water that had half filled the boat and checking over the engine. They still had the boat pulled clear of the water because the sea was quite lively.

Captain Fitzroy and Jim walked along the beach to the route they'd cut through the rainforest and were dismayed to see that thick brown water was still running out onto the beach and causing a dark stain where it ran into the sea. The captain shook his head gloomily then turned to look out to sea.

'There is one consolation, Bullock, our two casualties should be receiving proper medical treatment now,' he said.

'I did wonder yesterday whether we should have sent our medic with them,' replied Jim.

'Yes, I toyed with that idea as well but we would have had no cover if we had. He gave them both morphine injections before they left and that should have been enough for that short passage.'

'It would have been a longer passage in the seaboat. It took two hours in the ship on the way out but the boat's crew reckon that the boat would have taken an hour longer at least.'

The captain nodded. 'I thought a bit longer because of the slower speed and the greater distance. The ship took us out to the small island not this one.'

'Well whatever, they should have got there before dark,' said Jim. 'I've been thinking about tomorrow,' he said changing the subject. 'If we go up for the gear in the morning we'll have to stop there overnight. Will you remain down here?'

'Yes, I've been going over it in my mind as well. If I stay with the four camp followers and the boat's crew we can load this gear here onto the ship while you're coming down. That way we won't delay the ship too long.'

'There is another thing, sir we may not be able to bring everything down because we'll be short on numbers.'

'Go through the four packs of the men who went in the boat and take out anything personal. Don't bother to bring clothing — that can always be replaced — but bring their personal items with you, leave the rest.'

'What about the radio?'

'Leave it and anything else you can't carry. Try and bring the survey gear.'

'Yes, sir.'

That afternoon one of the remaining drivers collapsed. He'd been complaining of a headache and feeling shivery earlier so Fred had given him aspirin but it obviously had not worked. By nightfall he had a raging fever with a temperature that had Fred worried.

'He's bad, sir,' he said, when the captain asked about him. 'He's another one that should be in hospital.'

'Do what you can for him and let's hope that the boat's here in the morning.'

The following morning the driver was no better so it was decided to leave Fred to look after him. Jim's already depleted squad was therefore even smaller. The one good thing was the fact that their route into the rainforest seemed to have dried out, or it appeared to have done so. In fact it was as wet as ever underfoot and to add to their misery water was constantly dripping from the trees above. Sometimes it was a case of two steps forward and one back as they slipped and slithered their way upwards. Every mosquito and flying, biting insect known to man came out to greet them and make their journey even more miserable. The only good thing was that they were not hampered with packs, rifles or survey equipment. They only carried their food and drink. Even so it was late in the afternoon before they reached the ledge that had caused so much trouble earlier. Every one of them took extra care as they edged their way round to the cave.

Dai soon had a fire blazing then, without anyone suggesting it, they began to strip and divest themselves of that day's collection of leeches. They quickly found that it wasn't only water that had fallen from the trees and down their necks. Afterwards they dressed again before eating a meal.

Before it was too dark to see what was what Jim tried to find the packs belonging to Sergeant Browning, Simmo and the two radio men. In their years of wandering through wet, humid, tropical conditions most of them had learned to carry their personal items such as photographs and letters in an oilskin wallet in an attempt to keep them dry. He soon unearthed the Sergeant's. When it came to Simmo's pack Jim found not only his personal wallet but a sketchbook full of pictures of the men around him and sketches of the mountain sites they had surveyed. Two sketches in particular made him do a double take, the first of

Sylvia, the girl on the ship, was similar to the one he had in his own wallet whilst the second showed a couple dancing on the moonlit boat deck. He smiled to himself at the memory and the thought that Simmo obviously knew more than he'd said. By the time he had collected the personal items from the radio operator's packs his own was beginning to fill and it was growing dark, too dark almost to continue.

They had light from the fire and they attempted to sort out what they would each carry the next day. From the start they could all see that it would be impossible to take everything so they attempted to prioritize. Each man put aside his own pack and rifle while Jim tried to sort through all the survey equipment to select the more important pieces for them to take. It was then that he came across Fred's personal pack. He'd forgotten all about Fred so he went through that one as well selecting what he thought he would like to have. In the growing dark he missed the second small medical kit lodged in the side pocket.

In the early dawn light they resumed sorting and Jim finally selected essentials that couldn't be left behind. He had to leave army rations, personal packs, some survey gear, a tent, the radio and its generator and despite his serious misgivings four rifles. He had all that gear carefully hidden in the back of the cave just in case they could come back for it. Then the small, heavily laden troop began the slippery descent once more.

They eventually stumbled out onto the beach in mid-afternoon to find that nothing had changed. There was no sign of the ship or the boat that had taken the casualties ashore. There were no ribald greetings from the men on the beach; instead they were quiet and subdued. The climbing troop looked round in puzzlement until they saw a newly dug grave and a wooden cross further along the beach. In answer to a quiet enquiry Fred looked up.

'It's Tim, the driver, I couldn't bring his temperature down. He died in his sleep last night.'

'What a bastard,' said a quiet voice. 'Another day or two and he'd have been in the base hospital.'

Jim knelt and opened his pack and passed over Fred's personal gear.

'Thanks, Jim, did you bring the other medical kit?'

'No, sorry, I never saw one, Fred.'

'It was in . . . no it doesn't matter now the poor sod's dead.'

'It's not your fault, Fred.'

Jim left him and reported to Captain Fitzroy. He detailed everything that they'd had to leave and everything that they'd brought down.

'Every man was heavily laden. We could never have carried more, sir.'

'Yes, I can see that, you've all done well. Sit down, Bullock and give me that list again. The men coming here might find it useful.'

The two men sat side by side and Jim waited while the captain took out his notebook. Selecting a new page he listed everything left in the cave that Jim could remember.

'I didn't like leaving those rifles and I'll

go back up tomorrow for them if you like.'

'No, go and get cleaned up then come and see me later. There's something we need to discuss.'

'Okay, sir.'

After he had divested himself of two days' accumulated dirt and his usual collection of leeches Jim washed the gear he'd been wearing and spread it on the beach to dry. He then sat and enjoyed the cooked meal that the shore party had produced. When he finished he looked around for the captain and saw him seated on the rocks at the far end of the beach. Walking along to join him Jim wondered just what it was that the captain wanted. As he neared him Jim could see that he was a very worried man.

'Thanks for coming, Bullock. I've got quite a bit to say.' He patted the rock beside himself. 'Have a seat.'

Jim sat and waited for the captain to begin.

'This morning after we buried the driver I overheard our interpreter telling the others that it was my fault that he'd died and that we'd had two men badly injured. We were warned that this beach was taboo, was dangerous.'

'Did they believe him,' asked Jim?

'There were mutterings that I didn't like. When men start believing in bad luck we're in trouble.' He stopped and seemed to be marshalling his thoughts before continuing.

'I've been keeping you in the dark about something and it is time that you know. Sergeant Browning knew and understood the need for these surveys. There is a possibility that we may soon have to fight the Japanese; they seem intent on expanding their hold on this area.'

'So we have been finding lookout points in case they do, have we, sir?'

The captain nodded. 'Yes, Bullock, and here we've found the ideal one. If we can put a small team with a radio up there then we'll know any shipping movements they make out at sea.'

'Yes, I can see that, sir but we've still got to get that information ashore.'

'I know — where is the ship? I'm

assuming that it was busy on another job and will be here soon. I can only give it two more days then we'll have to use the other boat. It isn't big enough for the men never mind the equipment but someone will have to go for help.'

'You go, sir. You've got the authority to get things moving ashore.'

'Thank you, Bullock; that is what I was going to suggest.'

Jim looked around. 'The rocks have stopped moaning,' he said.

'Don't you start, Bullock. I've got enough trouble squashing bad luck stories as it is. The sea's flat calm, there are no waves.'

'Sorry, sir,' replied Jim. 'I wasn't thinking.'

The captain got to his feet and placed his hand on Jim's shoulder. 'Come on, Bullock. Let's show them there aren't any bogeymen.'

13

On the afternoon of the 7th December Captain Fitzroy called the men together and informed them that he had come to the conclusion that something had gone wrong with the arrangements for the ship. He had therefore decided to take the remaining boat to Khota Bharu at first light in the morning. In addition to the boat crew and himself there was room for two of the camp crew, the remaining driver, the interpreter and one more. Those chosen would be able to take only their personal pack and rifle. They drew lots to decide who would go and from the troop it was an older soldier called Eric who was the lucky one.

Eric was, when given the chance, a regular visitor to brothels so when the boat pulled away the next morning there were various calls directed at him.

'Hey, Eric, mind you don't catch it again.'

'Give her one for me son.'

'You lucky bastard.'

These types of calls continued until the boat pulled well clear of the beach and headed off towards the distant shore. Those remaining on the beach were contemplating a second cup of tea when the sound of aircraft engines in a screaming dive caught their attention.

'Bloody RAF showoffs,' said one turning to see the planes.

'They're diving on the boat,' said another uncertainly.

'Jesus Christ they're bombing it,' screamed Dai.

'Take cover, for Christ's sake take cover,' shouted Jim as he dived onto the sand.

They all saw the bomb drop and the boat being blasted into pieces in the resulting explosion. As it did so a second plane followed in and machine-gunned the wreckage before turning away to rejoin its companion.

'Bastards, bastards, bastards,' screamed one of the men from his prone position on the sand.

'Japanese bastards,' shouted another voice.

'How do you know they were Japanese?'

'The markings — that red sun thing that they have on the wings, that's Japanese.'

'We must be at war,' said another voice, 'at war with the Japanese.'

'Why weren't we told?'

'Nobody told us,' exclaimed George, Eric's pal. 'Now the bastards have killed my mate.'

As the planes disappeared towards the coast they jumped to their feet and peered out at the smoking remains. There was a movement, an arm raised, as if someone was signalling for help.

'I'll go,' said Jim pulling off his boots and throwing them to one side. 'Dai cover me, there're bound to be sharks about. The rest of you get under cover. Those buggers might be back.'

Without waiting for any reply he waded out into the sea and began swimming. He could see that whoever it was waving appeared to be lying on part of the boat.

It took a real effort to reach the injured man because the current was taking him along almost as fast as Jim was swimming. He swam into an area of broken bodies and splintered wood and searched in desperation for other survivors but there were none. When he finally reached the casualty he attempted to push what appeared to be the bottom boards of the boat and the injured man back towards the beach but when he looked over his shoulder the beach was out of sight. The current had carried them both beyond it. The best Jim could do was to swim at an angle and push towards the island and hope to land in safety. There was blood on the timbers and blood leaking from the man curled in agony in front of him. Jim constantly scanned the sea hoping that he would not spot the telltale black, triangular fin that heralded a shark heading his way. He was almost out of energy when his feet touched sand and he was able crawl onto another tiny beach. He clung onto the boards with their injured body until he gained control of his ragged breathing and had sufficient strength to pull them from the water. As he did so the injured man who was now lying face down groaned and attempted to turn over. That was when Jim realised that he'd saved a badly injured Captain Fitzroy.

It wasn't until he'd eased the captain onto the sand that Jim realised just how badly injured the man was. There was a gaping hole in his chest that was as big as Jim's fist and an even bigger ragged exit hole in his back. Jim couldn't understand how he was still alive. The captain opened his eyes and focussed on Jim and tried to say something but he coughed up blood instead. Jim bent and cushioned the bloodstained head on his arm and wiped the blood away from his mouth on his own shirt. The captain looked and recognition showed in his eyes.

'Sorry, Jim,' he gasped. 'I've fucked things up, sorry lad.'

His head fell back and Jim thought at first that he'd died but there was a gasping, gurgling sound of air being drawn into what was left of the captain's lungs. Jim realised that there was nothing he could do so he eased his arm from beneath the bloodied head and got rather shakily to his feet. Looking around he could see that the beach he had landed on was no more than ten feet in length and only four or five feet deep. To his front lay the sea whilst behind him stood a sheer cliff face. His only way off the beach was by swimming and he was close to exhaustion. He noted that the tidal current would be against him in about an hour because the current had slackened and would soon reverse. He turned to look at the captain and saw that his eyes were open again. There was no attempt to speak this time so Jim sat beside the critically injured man and took his hand in his.

Jim must have fallen asleep because the sun had moved over them and the beach was in shadow when awareness returned. He looked down at the captain and realised that he was still holding his hand. He saw the bloodied lips move and he bent to listen. The words were said at a whisper and were drawn out but Jim clearly heard every one.

'Sergeant Bullock, you're in charge now.' There was a long pause as he painfully gasped for breath before he spoke again. 'Take care of my lads, Jim . . . pray for me.'

Jim lay beside him and cradled his head in the crook of his arm once more. The captain died half an hour later without speaking again. Jim slid his arm free and knelt reciting the Lord's Prayer over the body. He didn't quite finish because of the tears running uncontrollably down his face but felt he'd done his best. He lay down feeling completely spent and slept, albeit fitfully. The sun was colouring the early morning sky when he finally woke the next morning.

After splashing seawater on his face Jim turned to the grim task of burying the body. Using a length of driftwood he scraped away at the sand for almost an hour before reaching bedrock. The grave he had fashioned was barely three feet deep but it was all he could do. He then turned to the body and removed the oilskin packet containing the captain's wallet and notebook. It was sticky with blood but he laid it aside before removing the belt holding the officer's sidearm. He had to steel himself to drag the body into the makeshift grave. He covered it as best he could with the sand he'd scraped away before dragging over the bottom boards of the boat and laying them on top. Taking the oilskin packet he removed the wallet and notebook and the small pencil that went with it. He washed the oilskin cover in the sea and placed it in the sun to dry before examining the leather holster and belt of the sidearm. They too were coated in blood so he washed them as well. Finally he sat down and opened the notebook. Taking the pencil he selected the next clean page and listed the names and ranks of all those that had died in the bombing finishing with the fact that the captain was the only one with a grave.

Once the oilskin was dry he replaced the wallet and notebook and bound the packet as tight as possible before buttoning it into his back pocket. Before taking up the belt and holster he walked to the water's edge and tossed a piece of wood out into the water to check the direction of the current. He saw that it was flowing in his favour. Taking up the sidearm he fastened the belt so that the weapon itself sat in the small of his back then without a backward glance he walked into the sea and began to swim.

He had no idea how far he had to go so he swam at a steady pace to conserve his energy and to avoid causing too much disturbance in the water, disturbance that might attract the attention of sharks. Fifteen minutes after he started he became aware of an unusual sound, the steady throbbing noise of a ship's engine. No sooner had he become aware of the sound than a great grey shape surged round the headland ahead of him. From his position in the water the ship looked vast but it was in reality a smaller version of the British destroyers he'd seen in Singapore. On its side was the red circle of the Japanese flag. He was caught in the bow wave and thrown clear of the dangerous propellers but left struggling in the wake. It took him some considerable time to resume swimming in the steady style that he had adopted earlier. His encounter with the ship had actually resulted in him being dragged back towards his starting point.

A further hour passed before he rounded the headland that the ship had earlier come round. He was beginning to think that he wouldn't get back to the troop before dark when he suddenly recognised a rock formation ahead. It was one that he remembered from the morning swims he'd taken. He knew then that he was approaching their beach. When he eventually dragged himself ashore he was expecting to hear shouts of welcome but an eerie silence greeted him instead. He got unsteadily to his feet and called out but the silence remained. He then realised that their equipment was strewn untidily around the area and knew immediately that something was seriously wrong. Suddenly something else caught his eye — two huddled shapes lying some distance away near the driver's grave. He forced himself to walk towards them hoping that what he was seeing were two men asleep but somehow knowing that they were bodies. His worst fears were confirmed when he came upon the bullet-riddled body of Dai. He walked on and gazed in horror at the decapitated body of George, Eric's mate.

'Dear God, what happened here?' he said in a whisper.

He felt his legs beginning to tremble but he forced himself to stay erect. Then he turned and marched back to the food store under the overhang. He selected a water bottle and drank thirstily before walking out into the scattered equipment and taking up a trenching tool. Despite the fact that he'd been swimming for hours and hadn't eaten for over a day he dug a grave deep enough and wide enough for the two bodies. It was dark when he lifted first George and then Dai and laid them side by side. Before covering them with the excavated sand he searched their pockets for personal items. Then for a second time that day he recited the Lord's Prayer. This time he did it dry-eyed. He never made it back to the rest area under the overhang but collapsed by the grave, got to his knees and crawled half way towards it before finally succumbing. He slept where he lay.

The following morning he resumed his normal routine by swimming briefly in the sea before making a meal from the stores still sitting in their storage area. As he ate he looked around trying to assess if anything had actually been removed. Stores and equipment were scattered around the beach so it was hard to tell but he assumed some things had gone. As soon as he finished eating he began looking for weapons. He found his own rifle and three others so he then knew that some had been taken by the Japanese attackers. He never thought to question whether it was the Japanese, he had seen enough to convince him that it was.

Ignoring everything else for the time being he set to work to clean the rifles and the captain's sidearm. Once he was satisfied that they were clean he loaded them all and placed them in shelter in what he felt were strategic positions along the beach. He intended to have at least one weapon handy for when they returned as he was sure they would. His own boots lay where he'd kicked them off two days earlier so he collected them as he began the task of recovering the scattered stores and equipment. It took him the rest of the morning and half the afternoon to collect and store them all. He then made his second and final meal of the day.

Afterwards he took out the captain's notebook again and added two more names to the list of the dead and appended a short note detailing what state he'd found them in. Afterwards he sat thinking over the events of the last few days. He knew that he'd been shocked by the destruction of the boat and all those in it but since then he had functioned almost on automatic. He'd known as soon as he'd seen Captain Fitzroy's injuries that there was nothing he could do for him other than stay with him till he died. The same had applied when he'd seen the bodies of Dai and George. He had not been there to save them but he was determined to avenge their deaths. He looked again at the list and realised just how many deaths he had to avenge. Then almost as an afterthought he added the names of the missing men, those that he assumed had been taken prisoner.

14

The following morning when Jim was taking food for his breakfast he found the cook's stores list. It was in an exercise book inside a tin labelled biscuits. That tin also held the cook's matches and cigarettes. He had been meticulous in recording what army rations were still available in the store. His entry on the seventh of December concluded that there were sufficient dried and tinned stores for thirty men for two weeks remaining in his stock. Jim therefore assumed that if he lived on army rations alone then he had enough for some considerable time. He had however no intention of doing that because there were plenty of fish in the sea and ample fruit and vegetables available.

He was short of fresh water so after he'd eaten he took three water bottles to fill at the stream. When it rained the stream was a torrent but the rest of the time it maintained a steady trickle that descended from the mountain and came down by the moaning rocks. He filled the bottles and left them in the shade while he investigated a find that one of the cooks had mentioned a few days earlier. He, the cook, had been hunting for vegetables and had climbed the rocks to reach a patch that were out of reach from the beach. He came back and reported that he'd found a couple of dry caves that would be perfect for food storage. Nobody at the time bothered to investigate because they thought they'd be on their way to Khota Bharu in a couple of days.

Jim climbed about twenty feet to the first cave and it looked dry as the cook had reported but the interior sloped downwards. Jim assumed therefore that if it rained heavily rainwater could run into the cave. The second higher cave was larger and sloped gently upwards. He walked in remaining upright until he reached the back wall. There was clear evidence of earlier inhabitants shown by the remains of a fire and animal bones.

The bones looked like those of monkeys. He decided to move the food stores and his camp into that cave as it would give him much more cover in dry weather. It also gave an excellent view out to sea. Before he did so he investigated the rocky slopes above the caves and found that they went upward in a series of huge steps partly hidden by the forest vegetation. Where the water ran down the rocks were green and slimy but above the caves they looked reasonably dry. He wondered if he'd found a new route to the dangerous ledge by accident.

It took him the rest of the day to move the stores, ammunition and two weapons into his new home. Having found the store of matches he cooked a warm meal, the first he'd had for three days. He spent some time before sleeping pondering on the possibility of building a raft. There were a couple of tents that he could convert to a makeshift sail but anything he constructed would be out on the open beach in full view of enemy aircraft and shipping. He went to sleep still thinking of ways and means of making one.

The following morning he woke to the sound of many aircraft heading south towards Singapore. He decided that there must be an aircraft carrier in the area but then was surprised to see more joining them from the Khota Bharu area. He watched through the captain's binoculars thinking that they might be British aircraft but he soon identified the Japanese markings. If there were Japanese aircraft taking off from Khota Bharu, he reasoned, then British and allied forces must have been pushed back. He wished he knew just what was happening.

After breakfast he decided to investigate the rocky staircase above his new abode. He took his pack but it only held food for the day, a water bottle and his rifle slung across his back. He found the route hard going but much easier than fighting his way through the tropical forest. More than once he had to backtrack to find an easier path round a bigger than usual boulder but despite that he came up against a sheer cliff face after three hours of climbing. The same cliff face that had taken them nearly all day to find when they'd fought their way through the forest. Throughout the climb he'd had tropical forest on either side but it had never encroached on his rocky route. At times the trees had closed together over him making a green tunnel and on those occasions the rocks were wet and slippery in places but not too dangerous underfoot.

Making his way along the ledge below the cliff face he soon came to the section that had proved dangerous. Edging round with extreme care he came to the cave with all the abandoned equipment. He decided to remain there overnight and go through the abandoned stores more thoroughly to see if anything was of use to him. The first thing he uncovered was the radio and despite the fact that it was damaged he began to look it over. He removed both the transmitter/receiver and the battery unit from their back packs and connected them up as he'd seen the radio operators do. Switching on he could see some lights inside but there was no noise from the receiver and nothing on any of the meters on the front of the transmitter.

There was a handbook so he began to read in an effort to understand the inner workings of the set. He soon discovered that some of the radio valves were interchangeable between the transmitter and receiver. He knew they were made of glass and broken glass had been heard after the operator's fall. He switched off and decided to open the set up.

It took him almost an hour because he hadn't got a screwdriver and had to use a pocket knife on the screws. Using the handbook and its circuit diagram he could see that three of the transmitter valves were shattered as was one in the receiver. The casing in the area of the transmitter had been pushed in during the accident and he could see that more than the valves were damaged there. When he removed the damaged valve from the receiver he could clearly see an identification mark on it — CL14B. That same number was on one of the undamaged transmitter valves so he changed them over. Trembling with anticipation he switched on — nothing happened, no lights, no noise, nothing.

He switched off again and turned back to the handbook.

Before he was able to identify the problem dark descended and he had to eat a cold meal and think things over before sleeping. He thought he'd done nothing other than take off the cover and changed that one valve. Theoretically therefore if he put the cover back on it should work. Another thing that puzzled him was the generator thing that was used to charge the batteries. He thought that generators produced alternating current and if they did how could they charge batteries that used direct current? Eventually his brain decided that he'd better sleep on it.

His first task the following morning was to find something to eat and what he found was dried army rations in one of the abandoned packs. He managed to light a fire and using the contents of his water bottle and the army rations concocted a meal. After that he turned back to the radio handbook. Reading through the power supply details he found that he could isolate the transmitter by removing two fuses. Then he discovered why the power wouldn't come on with the cover off — there was a safety switch. He replaced the cover and switched on again and the noise of loud static flooded the cave. The sound delighted him but also stunned him — he couldn't believe what he'd done. Tuning along the waveband the static varied up and down in strength but there were no other signals. He couldn't understand why not. Reaching for the handbook again he suddenly realised what was missing — an aerial. There was plenty of aerial wire, he'd seen that somewhere but how could he erect it without a mast? That was when he remembered the stand of bamboo that they'd used for the stretchers. Some of the bamboo was still lying in the back of the cave. It took him about thirty minutes to rig a type of aerial, he had the bamboo sticking out from the cave at floor level but overhanging the ledge. That meant his makeshift aerial actually hung down to where the sergeant had fallen. As it did not touch the ground and was sufficiently high up the mountain to receive signals, he thought it would work.

He decided to stay in the cave another night to try for reception on the radio after dark. He switched off and went in search of water before making another meal from the army stores. While he was searching the packs for more food he found not only food but cigarettes and the small medicine kit. He placed that kit into his own pack. After he finished eating he sat impatiently waiting for full darkness because he thought that only then would he get a signal.

He almost shouted for joy when he heard that first signal. It was fading in and out and was in morse code but it was a signal! If ever there was a eureka moment for Jim that was it. He listened to that same signal for over an hour, it was continuously repeating the same thing and he thought it was the callsign of a station VNLN. By the light of his dying fire he found in the radio handbook that callsigns beginning with V could be Australian. He wanted to carry on listening but the radio lights began to dim indicating that the batteries needed recharging. He switched off and lay down absolutely delighted with what he'd achieved.

★   ★   ★

I'd been printing off Jim's story as I'd typed it and that afternoon my printer ran out of ink so I went into Driffield for more. Jim came with me mainly in his case for a change of scene. I still had his eureka moment in mind when we set off so I asked him about it.

'Were you right about that callsign VNLN?'

'Yes but it took me a long time to find out what station it was. It turned out to be an airforce station in Australia. I didn't find out until after the war.'

'That radio manual seems to have been very useful.'

'I read it from cover to cover several times and learnt all manner of things.'

'Such as?'

'Well for one thing that charging device

that the radio men kept calling a generator was in fact an alternator — you know just like the thing you have charging your car battery.'

'What kind of batteries did you have?'

'Bloody heavy ones, NiFe cells, nickel iron. The beauty of those was that they could withstand the harshest of treatment and still come up smiling.'

'How long did it take to charge them?'

'I don't think I ever fully charged them. I just turned the alternator for about an hour and that gave me radio reception for two or three days, bearing in mind of course that I never had it on for more than an hour or two at a time.'

'Why not?'

'I was trying to keep it going as long as possible because I'd no spares. I don't think anyone could understand the difference that link to the outside world meant to me.'

He went quiet then and I knew he was thinking back to the island so I let him sit in peace. I parked in the library car park and we strolled down the street to Sokell's where I bought a couple of printer inks and a local paper before crossing to Rafter's fruit shop. Jim came in with me and spotted some fresh figs and in the middle of that busy shop he started reminiscing again. He pointed to the figs and laughed.

'There was a big fig tree on the island and the monkeys used to beat me to the ripe ones every time,' he said. Then he spotted a display of papaya. 'They're great to eat if you sprinkle them with lemon when you first open them.'

We were getting in people's way so I quickly bought the bits and pieces I wanted and led him back to the car. He waved to someone on the other side of the street and had a brief chat with a couple of others so in the end our short foray into town took over an hour. I'd only paid for an hour's parking so I was relieved to see that I'd got away without a ticket.

When we got back there was a car that looked familiar parked outside the house. It turned out to contain the policeman, Sergeant Cooper. I invited him in and made coffee for the three of us. Cooper took his coffee and gently wafted the cup backwards and forwards under his nose before taking the first sip.

'You do make great coffee,' he said.

'Is that why you came?' I asked.

'Partly,' he said wafting his coffee cup again. 'I was on my way to Scarborough and thought I'd pop in for a natter.'

'Any particular topic?'

'Silver, you haven't been shooting at him, have you?'

'No of course not, did they get him?'

'No unfortunately, they had a go at him while he was in his new car. The damn thing's armour plated, it weighs a ton, built like a tank.'

'What happened?'

'Well whoever it was fired several shots but only managed to chip the paintwork and craze the windscreen.'

'Don't tell me the widescreen was armoured as well.'

'Yep, bulletproof.'

'Where did it happen?'

'On the M62, he didn't report it but several witnesses did so I was sent round to see him. He denied it at first then admitted it because he wanted to show off his new car.'

'Did you ask its petrol consumption?'

'Funny you should ask that because I did and he said it was inconsequential, less than that of one of his trucks. He slipped up there because we hadn't known about any trucks, gave us a new line to investigate.'

'Will you ever get him into court?'

'Oh we've done that several times but we've never got a conviction.'

'Keep trying.'

'Aye, we will.'

He glanced at his watch and put down his cup.

'I'll have to go, he said, 'got an appointment to keep in an hour. Thanks for the coffee.'

After he'd gone Jim suddenly decided that he'd put in his sixpennyworth.

'Somebody will have to do something about that man,' he said.

'Who, Sergeant Cooper?'

'No of course not, I mean that Silver fellow. I sometimes think that our legal system is too lenient on people like that.'

'Yes, somebody will do something one day.'

'Maybe they could do an Al Capone.'

'An Al Capone?'

'American gangster, they couldn't pin anything on him either but they managed to imprison him on tax evasion charges.'

'You should have mentioned that to Sergeant Cooper.'

'Maybe next time.'

15

After breakfast Jim studied the manual once again to make sure he would be connecting the alternator correctly to the batteries. There was no time indicated so when he began turning the alternator he planned to keep up the hand charging for at least an hour initially. It was harder work than he had thought so he split that first hour into fifteen-minute sessions with a five-minute break in between each session. After that he made himself a drink before continuing for another hour. By mid-morning his arms were aching so he decided to check by switching on the receiver and seeing how bright the lights were. Everything seemed okay so he left the radio on and began tuning along each band in succession. He heard a few more morse signals but they were all weak so he switched off and decided to leave it until the evening.

His food supplies were running low

and he toyed with the idea of carrying the radio down to the main cave where the rest of his supplies were but something told him to leave it where it was. He felt it was safe in its present place. In the end he decided to go down to the main cave and spend the night there. He could then return with sufficient food for a couple of weeks and listen to the radio on a regular basis. Setting off immediately he made good progress down the rocks and was back in what he now considered his main cave an hour before dark.

He was on his way back up at first light the following morning carrying a full pack, his rifle and a small amount of ammunition. He had in his mind a feeling that the rifles in the upper cave should be spread around in secure hiding places as he'd done with the ones on the beach so he was carrying ammunition to hide with them. He'd barely got started on the climb when he heard the sound he'd heard once before, the sound of the Japanese ship's engine. He looked back and saw it rounding the headland where he'd seen it the first time. A feeling of bitter hatred engulfed him as he viewed that bringer of death below him.

Shucking off his pack and his rifle he laid on the ground and watched as the vessel moved slowly into the bay. Clipping his sniper sight onto the rifle he focussed on the bridge. He could see three men there and they were peering at the shore through binoculars. Suddenly one of them started gesticulating at something he'd seen. Jim knew instantly that he was pointing at the graves. They, the Japanese, had left bodies on the beach and those bodies had since been buried so somebody had to be still alive.

Jim heard the faint sound of a buzzer echoing across the water and saw a burst of activity on the ship. Men were running to man guns whilst others appeared on deck carrying rifles and wearing helmets. A boat was lowered and a number of the armed men scrambled down a ladder to board it. The last man was obviously an officer because he had a sword strapped to his side. Jim immediately assumed that he was looking at the weapon used to decapitate George and brought his rifle to bear on that particular man.

As the boat pulled away from the ship's side Jim counted eight armed men in addition to the officer and two boat's crew. He waited until the boat motored halfway between the ship and shore before opening fire. His first shot hit the officer squarely in the chest and he collapsed back into the bottom of the boat. Jim shifted his sights then to the man on the tiller and shot him also in the chest. The boat began to turn in a circle and as it did so guns on the ship began to return fire. However, they were firing blindly and nothing came near Jim. He calmly continued to pick off the men in the boat. They were so tightly packed together that he couldn't miss hitting at least three more before the ship came in closer to shield the boat.

Jim could now hear bullet and shellfire bursting into the trees above and below him but he knew that the gunners hadn't spotted him. He was reloading when he saw the ship moving in and noted the men on the open bridge. Two were obviously officers and as he took aim on them he guessed that they were at the limit of or out of his range but despite that he fired twice and had the satisfaction of seeing one of them spinning round clutching at his shoulder. Then he too had to duck and take cover as a vicious stream of bullets whipped over him, showering him with broken branches and leaves. When he was able to look up again the ship had turned and was moving away sheltering the boat but it still continued its fusillade towards the island.

When the shooting finally stopped there was a deathly hush for two or three minutes. Then, almost as if someone had thrown a switch, the monkeys began screaming accompanied by every other wild creature on that side of the island. Jim on the other hand lay for some minutes trying to control both the trembling of his limbs and the urge to be physically sick. He'd done something that morning that he'd never done before, he'd killed men!

It took him a while to recover and when he finally got to his feet the ship had gone and he felt extremely tired. He was tempted to turn back but he knew now that they'd be hunting him down and the further he was from the shore the better. Height would give him time to see them coming. He dragged himself wearily upwards and reached the radio cave in the late afternoon. Although he was close to exhaustion he cleaned and reloaded his rifle before falling asleep with it by his side.

When he awoke he looked around in astonishment, it was full daylight and he had been used to rising at first light. Something had woken him and he lay listening before recognising the sound of many aircraft flying over the island. Crawling to the cave entrance he peered up to see a flight of about thirty planes heading south. It was obvious that they were not interested in him so he walked out onto the ledge and looked down over the beach. Everything was quiet so he lit a fire and made himself a meal. He used dry tinder for the fire to cut down on smoke and extinguished it as soon as he had eaten. He had no wish to advertise his presence by sending out telltale smoke signals.

That morning he cleaned and loaded the rifles that had been abandoned there. He had intended to hide them but decided to keep them by him for the time being. Later he spent some considerable time improving and concealing his radio aerial. He knew he should be able to receive signals from long distances and wanted to receive a news broadcast if possible. The fact that the Japanese appeared to have control of both the sea and the air worried him. He could not understand what had happened to our forces. If he could hear a news broadcast of some kind he would surely find out what was happening and he would also be able to discover the date. He had completely lost count of the days and date although he felt certain that the month was December.

Throughout the afternoon he kept an eye on the beach. He was sure that there would be some kind of retaliatory attack. Just what form it would take and when it would come was a mystery but it was keeping him alert and watchful. He felt he was safe at night providing there had been no landing during daylight hours. Before night fell he had his second meal of the day and once again he risked lighting a small cooking fire. In order to eke out the army supplies of tea he was allowing himself one cup in the morning and one at night. His sugar supplies were also low so he had sugar in the morning cup and none at tea time. Milk was available in condensed form in tins but it too was in short supply so he used that sparingly.

That night he finally located a broadcast station on the radio. It was an American forces programme that he first heard broadcasting music similar to that on the ship. The signal boomed in initially but as the night advanced it began to fade. The news broadcast when it came stunned him. He learnt of the attack on Pearl Harbour, a place he'd never heard of but was obviously an American naval base somewhere in the Pacific. Then almost as an afterthought there was the news that Japanese forces were advancing rapidly along the Malay peninsular towards Singapore. Penang was already in

Japanese hands. The date was the eighteenth of December. He marked the spot on the dial with a pencil before the signal faded altogether just before he switched off.

He sat in a daze for some time trying to understand what he'd heard. Was this the same war as that in Europe or a second one? Had the Japanese linked up with the Germans? Were the Americans now fighting on our side? What on earth was going to happen to him? It was obvious now that no help was going to come from Khota Bharu so he was on his own. He thought again about building a raft or boat of some kind but if he built one where would he go? In the end he gave up and turned in. Sleep came slowly but he did eventually drop off.

His first thought when he woke the next day was to check the beach for intruders, it looked clear. Then, after washing in rainwater, he made himself a meal and thought about the day ahead. He decided to spend an hour recharging the batteries before making a calendar. Although he had the date to start his calendar with he still had no idea of the day. Using charcoal from the fire he marked the date on the cave wall then marked two strokes, one for the eighteenth and one for the present day. His intention was to mark the days off in sevens to keep track of the weeks and months.

The battery charging and calendar took him part of the morning. Afterwards he set off on a search for fruit and vegetables in the rainforest. Every now and again he came across trees damaged by the cannon fire from the Japanese ship. One such tree was a papaya and it was laden with fruit. Although the trunk was partly cut through and the top had bent almost to ground level the fruit was fine so he collected as much as he could carry. He selected some ripe fruits and others that were green. Those green ones he could place out in the sun to ripen later. He could see that he was in competition with the monkeys because some fruits were already partially eaten. His arrival on the scene had obviously chased them away, they sat in the trees above him chattering and screeching, protesting at his intrusion into their territory. When he finally got back to the cave he had great difficulty removing a couple of the leeches that he'd inadvertently collected in the forest.

He followed a similar pattern for the next few days, charging the batteries when necessary, foraging for food and listening to the nightly news bulletin. The one change in his daily routine came when he found an Australian radio station to listen to. That station broadcast news of the rapid Japanese advance in Malaya and of the events in Europe and nothing that he heard was encouraging. There did not appear to be any good news at all. He spent Christmas day in the radio cave and heard Christmas carols on the radio in the evening. That night he avoided listening to the news broadcasts preferring instead the carols and church service from the Australian station.

The next morning he began the descent to the main stores cave carrying an empty pack and one of the spare rifles. His army food supplies were running low and he planned to spend a night in the lower cave before climbing back to the radio cave with fresh supplies. He also fancied a change of diet by catching a fish or two for his supper that night. Once down at the cave he abandoned his pack and collected his fishing line. Carrying the line and the rifle he made his way down to the beach. He was crossing the open sand when he heard aircraft and looked up to see two planes diving towards him. His frantic scramble back into cover took him as far as the lower cave, the one he'd not used because it sloped downwards. He'd barely reached the entrance when a tremendous explosion lifted him off his feet and filled the air with flying debris. He was flung far into the cave and rocks and soil poured into and over the cave entrance.

He lay shocked and deafened for some minutes before the dust settled and revealed the awful truth that the cave entrance was sealed. Getting shakily to his feet he stumbled towards the wall of debris that was sealing him in. He pulled at stones in despair only for more to run into the space he'd made. Eventually he gave up and went back and sat down trying to quell the shaking in his limbs and the ringing in his ears. He sat with his head in his hands for a while and when he eventually straightened up he realised that there was a dim light coming from further down the tunnel.

That light enabled him to see his hand when he held it in front of his face so he struggled to his feet again and made his way cautiously towards the faint glow. The tunnel narrowed and its roof lowered as he advanced so he was almost bent double feeling his way with his hands touching opposite sides of the cave when the floor disappeared. He scrabbled with his hands to try and hold on but his momentum was irreversibly downwards. The shock of hitting water was as surprising as it was welcome. He took in a mouthful of seawater and came to the surface again coughing and spitting. His feet touched sand and he found himself standing shoulder deep in a watery cave. Looking up he could see that he had fallen only about ten feet.

The cave was lit by a green glow that

came from below the water to one side. There were also small beams of light coming down through holes in the rock. It suddenly dawned on Jim just where he was — he was beneath the moaning rocks. He could see that opposite the underwater glow the water became shallower and eventually dried at a small strip of sand and rocks. He waded towards that strip and sat down still shaking from the shock of the fall.

When he had recovered sufficiently to stand without shaking he waded towards the underwater glow. The water was shoulder deep when he reached the rock face above the glow. Taking a deep breath he ducked beneath the water to investigate. He could see an entrance wide enough for him to get through so he returned to the surface and took another deep breath before diving through the opening and surfacing in the open sea. He got another shock then because ahead of him lay the same Japanese ship. Turning his head towards the beach he could see armed men swarming over it. He lay in the water watching for a few minutes before ducking back and returning to the watery cave.

Throughout the next few hours he remained in hiding only coming out briefly now and again to see if the ship had gone. Even after it left he stayed where he was until he was sure that no one was left on the beach. It was late in the afternoon when he finally emerged and scrambled up over the debris left by the bombs. He knew roughly where the main cave would be but all he could see at first was rubble. Above that debris he could see rocks that he'd climbed down earlier that day so he climbed up to them and studied the land below. An uprooted tree lay where he estimated the entrance to the main cave should be so he carefully climbed down to it. Peering down through the branches he looked directly into the cave. Heaving the tree to one side he started a small avalanche that partly cleared the entrance. Scrambling down into it he found that nothing there had been touched.

He thankfully fashioned himself a

scratch meal before lying down in an exhausted sleep.

The next day he was extremely careful when he first emerged from the cave. He moved cautiously down to the beach and remained hidden in the tree line until he was sure that there was no one else around. He was used to the normal chatter of the monkeys and the calls of the birds and everything sounded as it should be when he finally stepped out onto the beach. The graves lay undisturbed but further along lay a heap of broken and twisted equipment. Every piece of the survey equipment was smashed beyond recognition and amongst the pile were three broken rifles, rifles that he'd hidden earlier. He left the whole thing undisturbed and turned back towards the spot where he'd dropped his fishing line the day before.

Behind him he could hear the monkeys chattering and fighting amongst themselves. They too had come down to the beach as they had a habit of doing to search the beach for tasty morsels. One of them must have investigated the pile of damaged equipment because there was suddenly a loud blast from that area causing Jim to dive for cover. The monkeys disappeared in a screaming horde and Jim looked up carefully from his now prone position. A curl of smoke rose from the scattered pile and the remains of the inquisitive monkey lay amongst it.

'The bastards booby-trapped it,' Jim muttered to himself. 'Christ I'll have to walk on eggshells now because there are bound to be more.'

13

Twice more that day and once again during the evening there were explosions in the lower reaches of the forest as unfortunate creatures found Japanese booby traps. Jim left everything on the beach exactly as it was even to the extent of smoothing out his own tracks in the sand reasoning that if nothing was disturbed the Japanese would not land on their next patrol. He caught a sizeable fish that day, cleaned and gutted it by the water's edge and grilled it for his evening meal. All the army food stores were still safe in the cave so before it got dark he sorted out and packed supplies to take up to the radio cave. He was fairly confident that despite the hours the Japanese had spent on the island they would not have reached the ledge that led to that cave.

It took him twice as long as normal to climb the rocky route to the ledge and the radio cave. Although he thought that it was unlikely that the Japanese had found that route he checked and rechecked anything that looked in the least bit suspicious. The contents of the radio cave however were just as he'd left them. That night when he heard the news broadcast from the Australian station he was shocked to learn that Ipoh and Kampar were in Japanese hands and that the allied forces appeared to be falling back to the Slim River. Airfields that had been improved because of the visits of the survey troop were now proving to be very useful to the Japanese forces. Singapore was being heavily bombed on a daily basis and the allies appeared to have virtually no air defence. What, he wondered, had happened to the promised aircraft reinforcements?

Night after night through January and into February he listened to the broadcasts from Australia and occasionally from the American station and followed the remorseless march of the Japanese through Malaya. They reached the Slim River on January 7th, Kuala Lumpur on the 11th, Gemas on the 13th and on to

Johore Bahru at the end of the month. When Singapore finally surrendered on the 15th February he sat in shock unable to believe that the so-called impregnable fortress had succumbed. Whilst he had been concentrating on Malaya he was also aware that the Americans were fighting to defend the Philippines from that same enemy, the Japanese. He remembered then something that Captain Fitzroy had said a few days before he died. He said that the Germans had practised their blitzkrieg tactics in the Spanish Civil War and the Japanese had done something similar in China. If the Japanese could do in this area what the Germans had done in Europe then there would be little to stop them. Jim now knew what he meant.

He had settled into a routine of climbing down to the stores cave about once a fortnight and spending a day or two there. He liked to vary his diet by fishing from the beach and eating two or three meals of fish, vegetables and fruit. Some of the vegetables and fruit seemed to be available all year round but others appeared to be seasonal so he was starting a record of their availabilities. The monkeys were useful in helping him locate trees that were fruiting: he listened for their chatter and followed them to their latest find. However, they still managed to get to the ripe figs first. On the mornings when he was by the beach he watched what the monkeys ate when they came down to the seashore and ate what they did.

One idea that he seriously considered was making his way to the other side of the island either by swimming in relays or trying to climb over the mountain. He thought that he might be able to get help from the locals either by taking him by boat to a neutral island or country or indeed letting him have a boat. However, more than once he saw local fishing boats appearing to trade with the Japanese. The same ship came round the islands regularly on its patrol and Jim had seen it stop and take fish and fruit from local boats. It seemed that they were trading on a regular basis. The local fishermen would not come near the soldier's beach because of the taboo but they would still fish in view of it at times. In the end Jim decided to forget seeking help and settle for a solitary life until an opportunity arose to get away. He took care not to be seen by either the Japanese or the locals believing that the Japanese thought he was dead.

Early in May he was sleeping in the cave by the beach when he woke feeling uneasy. It was just breaking daylight but the weather felt oppressive, hot and humid. The sky had a peculiar purple tinge to it and heavy thunderous clouds were forming out to sea. Jim had intended to stay by the beach for another day but he did not like the look or feel of the weather so he packed up and headed for the radio cave. He had barely reached the ledge when the heavens opened — torrential rain and continuous thunder and lightning heralded a storm. He edged his way carefully along the ledge and reached the cave in safety. The wind reached a higher and higher pitch screaming round the mountain and driving rain into the cave entrance. Jim had to move the radio and other equipment deeper into the cave for shelter.

The storm lasted three days and Jim was appalled by its savagery and astounded by the brilliant lightning displays. At times throughout the day and night the cave was illuminated by sheet and fork lightning the like of which Jim had never previously experienced. The thunder that accompanied it was deafening, the floor of the cave trembling with its force. In fact there were occasions when he was not sure whether it was day or night because he lost complete track of time. He did not know it but he was experiencing his first typhoon. When the weather finally moderated enough for him to step outside he couldn't believe the damage that had been caused. Trees had been uprooted, snapped in two and thrown about willy-nilly. A torrent of mud-filled water was cascading down the mountainside making movement almost impossible and waves were pounding the beach.

Throughout the storm he hadn't been

able to use the radio and even when it finished he had to wait until he had re-erected his aerial. When he finally did get a signal again he learnt that the Japanese had succeeded in taking the Philippines overcoming the joint American and Filipino forces. General MacArthur and his staff had escaped to Australia.

* * *

I couldn't believe what I was typing particularly about the speed with which the whole of Malaya and Singapore had fallen into Japanese hands and I said as much to Jim.

'Neither could I,' he replied. 'Our troop had travelled from one end of the country to the other and seen all the thousands of troops, British, Australian and Indian and I couldn't believe that the Japanese could overpower them in such a short time.'

'Did you find out what happened later?'

'Yes to a certain extent. One of the main problems was lack of air power. The promised aircraft reinforcements never arrived. No, that's not strictly true because a number of Spitfires were shipped out and as I understand it they were still in crates in Singapore docks when the surrender came.'

'What happened to the Navy, didn't they have aircraft?'

'Two capital ships were sent out to Singapore and they should have had an aircraft carrier with them but it broke down and never got there. Therefore those capital ships, *Prince of Wales* and *Repulse*, were sitting targets for the Japanese aircraft. They were both sunk in the same attack.'

'What about the aircraft you saw at Butterworth and other places?'

'The general opinion of them before the war started was 'too slow, too old and too few'. They were no match for the modern battle-hardened aircraft squadrons that the Japanese could call on.'

'Surely the army could have held on longer than it did.'

'I talked to a number of surviving soldiers after the war and I couldn't believe some of the stories they told me. You must bear in mind that in Malaya and in India at the time there were independence movements and the Japanese promised these people that they would have their independence once the British had been kicked out.'

'So what are you saying?'

'That the whole campaign was a complex mess. I didn't know for instance that the Siamese army fought alongside the Japanese but they did.'

'Siam, that's Thailand now isn't it?'

'Yes, and there were units of the Indian army that fought well against the Japanese and others that changed sides and fought with them. There was a fifth column of great significance that led Japanese soldiers on foot on jungle trails to bypass allied defence lines and come up behind them. Some Malays fought with us, others against.'

He paused for a while before continuing.

'I spoke to two Scots who'd been part of that shambles and one of them said that at times they had to fight Japs behind them before they could retreat. An Australian said the same sort of thing — you thought you had a great defensive position only to find the enemy behind you. The Japs had tanks, we had armoured cars, but it was air power that was the biggest advantage they had.'

Pausing again he walked into the kitchen and returned carrying two glasses of beer. He handed me one and raised his glass in a silent salute before taking a mouthful from his glass.

'Burma was supposed to have been something of a similar shambles with Burmese independence people fighting first with the Japanese then after they realised what a mistake they'd made fighting to get them out again. You have to read the history of that war to try and understand what went on. It took a lot to stop them in Burma and in Papua New Guinea. But in both places their supply lines were overstretched. They could have been in India and in Australia but desperate defence by our troops and lack of supplies forced them back.'

'You said our troops then but who do you mean?'

'Well in Papua New Guinea they were primarily Australians brought back from fighting in North Africa to defend Australia. In Burma there were British, Indian, Gurkha and some American troops. There was also an aerial supply of arms to Chinese forces fighting against the Japanese.'

He paused again and sipped at his beer before taking up the story again.

'The Japanese murdered thousands of Chinese civilians in Malaya and Singapore. I once went to the war cemetery at Changi and I was shocked by what I saw there. Young nurses and doctors who were working with the wounded in military hospitals were slaughtered for no reason that I could see. Their names make grim reading along with all those of the soldiers, sailors and airmen. I don't know if the names of the civilians killed are recorded anywhere.'

'You went back after the war?'

'Yes, after your grandmother died I couldn't settle so I took a trip out there. I found a lot of people like me still trying to make sense of what went on many years after the war.'

'You said once that you met some of your men again.'

'Yes, it is on one of those tapes. You'll come to it eventually.'

He put down his empty glass and stood up. As he turned away and made for the door I could see tears glistening in his eyes.

'Too many memories,' he said. 'Goodnight.'

17

After the typhoon moved north Jim had to wait for almost a week before the flood of water came to a halt leaving the ledge and the rocky descent dry enough to use. He struggled at times as he climbed down because the storm had left trees and shrubbery uprooted and lying across his path. When he got down to the store cave some of the debris from the bombing had slid away revealing a larger opening once more but inside the cave there was evidence that the monkeys had been in there. Some of the packets of dried stores had been torn open and they clearly showed marks of the teeth that had ripped them apart. He presumed that the animals had used the cave for shelter during the storm because normally they never came near, preferring instead to live in the trees.

He gathered together all of the food that he could salvage and stored it in packs ready to take up to the radio cave before moving cautiously down to the seashore. The beach was strewn with debris including thirty or forty coconuts in their green outer shells. He took several of these and put them to one side where he could work on them out of sight of the beach. A number of tree branches lay over the graves and he lifted those clear and saw that the actual graves were undisturbed. However much of the equipment that the Japanese had destroyed had been washed away.

There was so much rubbish on the beach that he failed to notice the huddled form until he was almost on top of it. It was the partly decomposed body of what he thought was a British sailor. The remains of the uniform still attached to the body were dirty white with a dark blue edge to the collar of the shirt. There were no recognisable features because the body had obviously been in the water some time but Jim was of the opinion that the uniform indicated a British sailor. He was undecided what to do because he felt on the one hand that it was his duty to bury the poor man's remains but if he did so the Japanese would see the fresh grave. In the end the feeling of duty won.

He searched among the scattered debris and found the remnants of one of the tents that the Japanese had ripped apart and rolled the body onto it. Dragging it up the beach he laid it close to the other graves before setting to work to dig another grave. Eventually he completed the burial and recited the Lord's Prayer over yet another body. Back in the cave he added an unknown to the list in the captain's notebook.

The following morning he made a thorough search of the beach but found nothing other than driftwood and the debris left by the storm. He took several fronds from what had obviously been a coconut palm and laid them over the fresh grave to hide it from a casual glance from seaward before turning his attention to the coconuts. Using his bush knife he cut away the hard green outer shell as he had seen the market traders do to reveal the nut beneath. It took him most of the morning to shell ten coconuts and carry them to the cave. He knew he could store them for months and they would still be edible. Later down on the beach he opened another and drank the milk while he was fishing. That evening he dined on grilled fish and the flesh of the coconut.

During June and July that year there were several periods of strong winds and rain but nothing of the severity of the typhoon. During those periods, periods that sometimes lasted for days, he sheltered in the radio cave listening and occasionally dancing to the music broadcast by the American station. He became particularly found of the music of Glenn Miller and his big band. He heard some of the tunes so often that he found himself singing along with them at times. Then at other times he became moody and listless, muttering to himself and brooding about his dead and missing compatriots. In that mood he left the radio switched off and even lost track of the days and date. His calendar scrawled on the cave wall soon bore no relation to reality.

Early in August he woke one morning

with a splitting headache and a shivery feeling. He was at first loath to take any medication believing that the headache would wear off during the day. Then as the day advanced he found himself alternately shivering with cold and feeling hot and sweaty. In the end he opened the medicine box and took a couple of aspirin tablets. He waited for some improvement in the ache but things got steadily worse. In mid afternoon he made himself a hot meal, ate as much as he could then took more aspirin. Although it was still daylight he rolled himself up in blankets and attempted to sleep. Throughout the night he alternated between the states of sweating and shivering first throwing off the blankets then pulling them back over himself.

The following morning he attempted to make a meal but his hands were shaking, his head ached and his vision was blurred. He continued to alternate between the hot and cold states and eventually descended into a raging fever. For two more days he lay burning up before the fever gradually abated. When he was finally able to leave his bed he felt exhausted but forced himself to make a meal and a hot drink. He knew that he and his blankets stank of sweat but nevertheless he rolled back into his bed as soon as he had eaten. It took him two more days of that regime before he felt fit enough to consider climbing down to the beach. He did struggle on the way down but he eventually made a safe descent and carefully looked around before walking down to the sea. His blankets, his clothes and his body were then treated to a salt water wash. Moving then to the stream of fresh water running down the rocks he rinsed himself and the washing as best he could. When he laid his washing on the sand to dry he made sure that it was close enough to the cave to be scooped up in a hurry if necessary. He then wandered around naked waiting for his clothing to dry for the next hour.

He presumed that the fever he had fought his way through was malaria or something similar so when he returned to the radio cave two days later he hunted out the medicine pack. He knew there was a little booklet in there describing various illnesses and their suggested treatment and read through it from cover to cover. He found malaria and a treatment recommended to overcome it, a medicine called quinine but there was none of that in the pack. However, he had done the best he could with the aspirin which was the recommended alternative to counter fever. There were only twenty aspirin tablets left but on the other hand there were over fifty corn plasters which he thought would have been useful if he'd had any corns. He used one of the corn plasters to bookmark the page on fever.

Once he'd recharged the radio batteries he tuned to the Australian radio station in an effort to catch up on the news. He'd neglected the news from England for some weeks so he was surprised to learn of the landings in Sicily and the retreat of the Germans from that island. He'd been expecting more doom and gloom from the newscast so it came as a pleasant surprise to hear that the allies had finally had some more success against the Germans. He wanted to hear of success against the Japanese but that was not forthcoming. However, only a few days later he heard the announcement that allied forces had recaptured Lae and Salamua in New Guinea. He was delighted to hear that the Japanese were finally suffering defeats.

Two days later his radio stopped working. He had switched on to hear the news and all he got was a background hiss. He tuned along every band and got exactly the same, no signals only the background noise that indicated that there was electrical power. The first thing he checked was the aerial and that looked fine, then he turned to fuses although he knew that power must be there because of the background noise. Once again they were okay so he got out the handbook and read up on typical faults. He spent hours in a desperate search for something he could fix and found nothing. He switched on and off several times in the hope that whatever the fault was it might suddenly spring to life again but nothing happened. He removed and replaced all the valves but again the set remained dead. Eventually he came to the reluctant conclusion that he was beaten, the radio that had served him so well was finally beyond any repair that he was capable of. The feeling of hopelessness that came over him was almost unbearable, it felt as if he had lost a friend and he almost wept. His one link to the outside world was gone and he struggled to come to terms with that fact.

Two days later he decided to abandon the radio cave and make the permanent move down to the other cave. The loss of the radio was one reason but another was the shortage of food. The army rations had almost been used up so he thought it made sense to move to the lower cave to enable him to fish on a more regular basis. He went through all the packs that had been left behind once again removing anything that he felt would be useful before packing the remainder in the back of the cave once more. He had already raided those packs for clothing as his own had become more and more tattered and he put more clothing aside to take down. It took him three trips to move everything he felt would be useful down to the cave and settle there again.

Without the radio he gave up trying to maintain a calendar and set himself instead a daily routine that involved an early morning swim, a beachcombing session and a search for food. He alternated the food search between fishing one day and visiting the forest the next. The monkeys had become so used to his presence that they never bothered to run away when he appeared. In fact one day on his forest search he was handed a tasty morsel by a young one. In surprise Jim handed the larger fruit he held to the monkey and watched as it dashed away in what he assumed was delight. Birds and butterflies seemed to treat him as part of the furniture as well with one particular bird joining him on his fishing days and waiting patiently until he had caught and gutted his fish before eating the remains.

The Japanese patrol vessel was no longer making regular patrols around the islands; in fact for almost six weeks he never saw it at all. However, although the ship was not around aircraft activity appeared to have increased and on more than one occasion Jim saw what he thought were American aircraft. Then one day his thoughts were confirmed in a direct way.

That particular morning he was fishing from the beach when he heard what he thought was distant gunfire. Looking up into the sky he saw aircraft con trails looping around and in and out of each other. What he was looking at was an aircraft dogfight; although he had never heard that term he could see what was happening. One particular aircraft broke away and began to dive with smoke trailing from it. Another followed it down firing as it went. Both planes disappeared from view behind the island but he could still hear high revving engines coming towards him. He ran for cover carrying his rifle and as he dived behind a rock a Japanese fighter plane screamed low over the beach having overshot the plane it was attacking. Seconds later the crippled plane came in low trailing smoke and heading for the beach. It landed in a spray of foam at the water's edge and slowly slid up onto the sand. Almost instantly the cockpit canopy was thrown back and a man scrambled out onto the wing and bent to help another man from the seat behind him.

He was struggling to help the second man when the Japanese plane came back into view with all guns firing. Jim watched in horror as both men were flung back onto the sand by cannon fire. The plane turned out to sea and came back in at a much slower pace and as it did so the pilot slid back the canopy and laughed as he looked down at the men he had just killed. Jim eased his rifle forward and took aim at the Japanese pilot as the plane came at low level towards his position. He fired twice but knew instantly that the second shot was pointless because his first shot had hit home. The pilot slumped forward and the aircraft turned away as if to head back out to sea. However, the lower wing tip caught the surface of the water and the whole aircraft spun round and cartwheeled into the moaning rocks. There was a slight thud from inside the wreckage and before Jim registered the sound properly the whole thing exploded into flames. He was barely twenty feet away and had to bury his head beneath his arms as ammunition began to explode from within the wreckage. As he lay there a second Japanese aircraft flew over inspecting the wreckage from a distance before climbing and flying away.

Jim remained under cover until the burning Japanese plane stopped spitting out ammunition. He continued to search the sky for aircraft but as far as he could tell they had all gone. When he was finally satisfied that he was safe from both the ammunition and aircraft he picked up he rifle and made his way towards the American aircraft. Although it had been on fire when it force-landed the shallow water that it had come to rest in had doused the flames. As he got closer he could see that it was a twin-engine machine and both engines had suffered damage.

At first he could not see the two crew members because they had been thrown to the ground behind one wing. As soon

242

as he reached them he could see that there was nothing he could do for them other than to bury them. Although both bodies were shattered neither man had any damage to his face and Jim was immediately struck by their apparent youth. They looked to him as if they were just out of school. He pulled them both clear of the water's edge and laid them side by side on the sand. The bloody water had already attracted a shoal of small fish and a number of crabs eager to share in an unexpected feast. Jim kicked away the crabs and hurried back for his trenching tool in order to start on yet another grave.

Two hours later with the sweat glistening from his body he completed the burial. He had removed the identification tags from the bodies before he laid them side by side in their sandy grave. As he washed his bloodstained hands at the water's edge he was sobbing uncontrollably. To him it seemed that his task in the war was to act as a grave digger, a task he was beginning to hate. He glanced along the beach to the still smouldering wreckage of the Japanese aircraft and knew immediately that there would be nothing left of that pilot to bury, he'd been cremated. In fact there was little left of that aircraft other than part of the airframe and the engine block because the fire had been intense.

When he had recovered his control he studied the American wreck. Both engines had obviously been hit by cannon fire but most of the bodywork of the fuselage seemed intact. He decided to investigate the cockpit. After climbing up onto the wing he could see into both seating areas and he had no qualms about removing what he found there that he considered useful. He came away with a bar of chocolate, a pack of emergency rations, a pack containing a Very pistol and ammunition and a case holding several maps. The plane was fitted with a radio that he decided he would look at later because he felt there was a possibility that he could remove it and get it working. Later, inside the map case, he found a copy of a forces newspaper.

I could sense that Jim was reading over my shoulder as I typed that last sentence so I stopped for a short while.

'Did you learn anything from that newspaper?' I asked.

'It was that newspaper together with the maps that gave me my first real insight to what was happening around me. For a start I learned where Pearl Harbour was, I never knew before.'

I pointed higher up the page to the section where he'd shot the Japanese pilot.

'How did you manage to shoot that pilot?'

'He made it easy for me. For a start he'd slowed almost to a stalling speed with his canopy open to admire his own handiwork and he was flying towards me, I couldn't miss. I could have thrown a coconut at him with the same result. He never knew what hit him.'

'How did you feel afterwards?'

He thought for a while before answering and when he did he turned away so that I couldn't see his face.

'Savage delight at first . . . revenge for another of my men. Then when I had to bury the Americans the futility of it all really hit me. They were only kids. I know . . . I know I wasn't much older but by then I was feeling a great deal older. I was talking to myself, I was moody and miserable. In fact I was fed up of my own company. Much like I was when you arrived.'

He turned towards me then and suddenly grinned.

'You've been good for me you little bugger,' he declared with a grin. 'I think that deserves a beer.'

'Amen to that,' I replied.

18

From the newspaper that he had recovered Jim learnt that American forces had retaken Tarawa and Makin in the Gilbert Islands and Bougainville in the Solomon Islands. He already knew from what he'd heard on the radio that Lae in New Guinea had been recaptured by allied forces so he was delighted to learn that the Japanese were being driven back on more than one front. He had no idea how old the newspaper was but it looked relatively new and was dated late November. He couldn't remember the exact date.

While he was reading the newspaper he was demolishing and relishing the first chocolate bar that he had tasted for some years. It was melting as he ate and he finished eating with a sticky mess round his mouth and on his hand. He went down to the sea to wash and while he was doing that he realised that he could see shipping far out to sea. He hurried back to the cave for the binoculars but when he focussed on the ships he could not identify them. He waited hoping that they would come nearer but they were headed away and soon disappeared out of sight over the horizon.

The three maps that he had recovered were of the Pacific region, one was of the whole of the area whilst the others were more detailed charts of specific areas. The first of the more specific ones covered the South Pacific as far south as Australia whilst the other covered the Philippines and Japan. The Japanese-held areas were outlined in red so Jim was able to see how much progress the allies had made in first holding and then driving back the Japanese.

He eventually put down the maps and as he did so caught sight of the identification tags that he'd taken from the airmen. He picked them up and held them for a few minutes thinking that no one could identify the graves if he were killed and the tags lost. He began to ponder on the possibility of clearly marking all the graves. The Japanese ship had not been near for some weeks and when it had appeared it hadn't come close in so he decided to clearly identify every grave as soon as he could. There was ample driftwood on the beach that he could use so he set himself the task of collecting sufficient suitable wood for the task.

At dawn the following day he walked the full length of the beach selecting and collecting driftwood suitable for the markers. He found three short lengths still fastened together that appeared to have been part of a packing case and several other pieces, some smoothed by the sea. The problem of making indelible marks on the chosen timber was solved when he decided to burn the names into the wood. He had given up worrying that his fire would be seen and now regularly kept one smouldering most of the day. He examined the remains of the survey equipment that still lay on the beach and selected a piece with a wooden shaft and a stub of metal attached. He thought it had been part of a theodolite.

It took him three days to make the markers for all six graves. He heated the metal part of the theodolite remnant in the fire and used it to burn the names and ranks of the dead into the chosen pieces of timber. As he hammered the markers into the sand he made sure that they would not move by supporting them with rocks. When he had finished he brought the captain's notebook up to date once more. In addition he turned to the last clean page in Simmo's sketchbook and began a second list of all the events that he could remember adding names and approximate dates. He finished by thumbing through the sketchbook and admiring Simmo's handiwork once more. He dwelt for a long time on the sketches of Sylvia and himself that had been drawn on board the ship. He thought long and hard about the possibility of meeting Sylvia and Simmo again. He still could not understand why there had been no contact with Simmo after he left on the first boat. Surely that one must have reached the shore safely.

The radio on the American plane proved to be a disappointment. It took Jim almost two hours to remove the front panel using a knife as a screwdriver only to find a shambles. The front panel was in perfect order but a cannon shell or bullet had wrecked the interior. He checked for any valve that remained intact but there was only one and it was not only the wrong number of those in his radio it was also the wrong size.

He had only seen a Very pistol used once before when the control tower of one of the airfields used it to give an aeroplane the green to go so he decided to try out the one he had salvaged. There were six cartridges, two red, two green and two white so he selected one of the white ones for his trial shot. However, before he risked the shot he scanned the horizon for enemy shipping or aircraft. When he pulled the trigger he was surprised by the height that the flare reached. If he wanted to attract attention in the future he had the ideal means of doing so. In order to keep it safe he stored it in the rear of the cave in case another storm blew rain into the entrance.

A few days later while he was fishing from the beach he had a feeling that he was being watched. Looking around he could not see anything or anyone watching him so he got calmly to his feet and strolled back towards the cave. Something glinting in the water way out to sea caught his eye and he stopped and looked in that direction but whatever it was had disappeared. He went up to the cave for his binoculars and carefully scanned the sea from a greater height. When he eventually spotted the glint again it was moving and it took a while for him to realise that he was looking at a periscope. He toyed with the idea of using the Very pistol but rejected it because he had no idea whether the submarine would be Japanese or of the Allied forces. If he had been seen and it was a Japanese craft he presumed that they would pay him another visit. He therefore kept a low profile for the next few days.

The only activity he saw was aerial and too high for him to identify so he resumed his normal routine of fishing and hunting for food. He now kept a low fire smouldering day and night because his supply of matches had run out. If he did allow it to go out he then had to wait until sun up and focus the sun's rays through the binoculars onto dry tinder in order to relight it.

He had abandoned any attempt to maintain a calendar so he presumed it would be early in 1944 when the Japanese did eventually revisit him. This time they arrived in the form of a pair of planes fitted with floats. Both aircraft came in low over the beach and circled several times before one came in to land on the water. It motored to within a quarter of a mile of the beach and lay there rocking gently on the waves. Jim watched it through his binoculars and he could see two men aboard it searching the beach through their binoculars. The other aircraft in the meantime was circling overhead presumably keeping guard on its fellow. After about fifteen minutes the aircraft on the water turned out to sea and accelerated before taking off and rejoining its companion. Both aircraft then flew off towards the coast of Malaya.

A few weeks later he saw a convoy of ships passing within a couple of miles of the island. He saw smoke first well to the south and watched throughout the day as the ships grew nearer. He thought at one time that they were heading for his island then realised that they were merely passing. He identified four cargo ships, three of which looked like old coal burners, and an escort of three destroyers. It was not until the ships were almost abeam of him that he was able to spot the rising sun emblem of the Japanese forces. He had hoped to see British or American vessels and had prepared to use the Very pistol just in case. He returned it to its storage spot with a feeling of dejection.

Over the next couple of months he became used to seeing aircraft flying high over the island. They were too high for him to identify but he began to hope that some of them were friendly. When a flight of American aircraft did fly close enough for him to identify they were out of sight by the time he collected the Very pistol. It was after that incident that he began to build a beacon from driftwood that he could light in a hurry. He drained fuel from the wrecked aircraft and kept it in shelter near the beacon so he could light it in a hurry merely by bringing a burning timber down from his smouldering fire. By that time he had begun to believe that the Japanese would never return.

He had to endure two more storms that lasted for several days and after each he collected more driftwood to add to his beacon. After the second storm he had another bout of the malarial fever that he had suffered the previous year. He treated himself again with his dwindling supply of aspirin not knowing whether he was doing the right thing or not. He assumed that he must be doing something right because he emerged from that bout weak but alive. It took him nearly two weeks of eating and resting before he felt back to something like his normal self. His trouble was that he was beginning at times to lose sight of reality, mumbling to himself and wandering around naked and unwashed. Then at other times he would become disgusted by his state and wash, cut his hair and generally appear to smarten up for a few days. It was during one of his smarter sessions that he saw the submarine periscope again. That time he stood on the beach and waved not caring whether it was friend or foe. Nothing happened.

Some weeks later he watched as another convoy passed at a distance heading north. This time he saw what he assumed was an attack by submarines. One of the merchant ships exploded and sank in a very short time — he estimated that it took less than ten minutes for the ship to disappear beneath the waves after the initial explosion. The escorting vessels then started dropping depth charges. One of the escorts remained in view for some hours after the rest of the convoy had sailed on over the horizon. Every so often that vessel would drop more charges on its unseen enemy without any noticeable success. On that occasion the vessels were too far out for him to see their nationality but he assumed the attacking submarines were American.

That incident led him to believe that

the Americans were beginning to get the upper hand in the area and he started to hope that his ordeal would soon be over. He began a regime of cleaning and smartening himself and his equipment ready for the day of his rescue. He sorted through all the personal effects of the men who had died and packed them carefully into his own backpack. The revolver belonging to Captain Fitzroy lay at the bottom of that pack beneath the remainder of the personal effects of so many others, his own meagre bits and pieces lay on the top. He kept one uniform shirt and one pair of shorts clean ready for his departure, the shirt had belonged to Sergeant Browning but the shorts were his own. His rifle gleamed because he polished it daily. However, he could not control his hair or his beard. He would hack away at them on a regular basis with a knife but his razor had long ago collapsed and he could not keep his beard tidy.

It was early in September 1944 that his isolation ended though he did not at first get away from the island. He heard a strange noise shortly after sunset one night and carrying his rifle he crept down to the beach to investigate. Silhouetted against a rising moon he could see a dark shape lying off the beach. From its low profile he thought at first that he was looking at a small patrol boat but as watched he saw men emerge on the low deck and realised that he was looking at a submarine. He heard low commands and the sound of something splashing into the water. A few minutes later the faint sound of paddles being used came across the water and a small inflatable came into view with about five men on board. Jim waited until it was almost on the beach before calling out.

'If you are English or American call out now otherwise I'm opening fire.'

'Hold it you Pommie bastard, hold it, we're friends,' replied a hoarse voice.

'Okay, one of you come ashore without your guns and let me see.'

The boat grounded on the beach and one man stepped ashore with his arms in the air. Jim waited until he could see that he was clear of the boat before speaking.

'Identify yourself,' Jim ordered.

'I'm Major Jack Marshall, Australian Army.'

Jim got to his feet and walked towards the officer.

'Good evening, Major, I'm Acting Sergeant James Bullock, Royal Engineers.'

'What the hell are you doing here, Sergeant?'

'I've been stranded here for years, sir, fighting my own war against the Japanese.'

'How many of you are there?'

'I'm the only one still alive, sir.'

'Are there any Japanese here?'

'Only dead ones, sir.'

'I'm bringing two more men ashore. Have you somewhere for us to hole up overnight?'

'Yes, sir, but I want to get off this island.'

'I know that. The sub is coming back for us in a week's time; you'll be able to leave with us.'

The major turned and called to the others to land and spoke briefly to the seamen as they did so. Jim shouldered his rifle and helped carry equipment ashore before leading the way to the cave. Behind him he heard the submarine blowing tanks and submerging again. Once they reached the cave Jim put down the bundle he was carrying and turned to leave again. The major stepped in front of him.

'Where are you going, soldier?'

'Back to the beach, sir. I survive here by leaving no traces of my presence so I have to smooth out your footprints before daylight.'

'Okay.'

When Jim returned he was introduced to the other two members of the party, two Americans. The two were dressed in military clothing but wore no insignia. One said his name was Chip whilst the other answered to Sol. No surnames or ranks were mentioned. When the Australian explained that the three men were here to survey the mountain to see if a lookout post could be established Jim could not help bursting into almost hysterical laughter.

'What's wrong, son?' asked Sol as soon

as Jim got himself under control again.

'That's what my party came here for in 1942,' Jim explained.

'Do you mean that you've been up to the top?'

'Yes, in 1942, just before all hell broke loose here.'

'Can you guide us up there?'

'Sure, but it's rough going in places.'

'We expected that. How long will it take?'

'Three days up and three down providing all goes well.'

'Good, we'll start at first light.'

★　★　★

It was then that Silver reared his ugly head again. The telephone rang and I stopped typing to answer it. Jim came into the room as I picked up the handset. The voice on the other end responded to my 'hello' with a message for me.

'Tell Luke Sharp that his friends at the farm have been having trouble. It can be stopped if he agrees to a meeting.'

The speaker then hung up before I

could respond. I handed the phone to Jim explaining as I did so what had been said. He rang Graham at the farm, Glynis answered.

'Good afternoon, Glynis, I'm told you've been having problems, can I help?'

'Hello, Jim, how did you know? We had a barn fire last night, the old barn. One tractor was destroyed and the barn will have to be pulled down. There's not much left of it.'

'Is everyone safe?'

'Yes everyone is fine. They're out in the yard with the insurance man and the police. They think it is arson.'

'Ask Graham to give me a ring when he's free, Glynis.'

'Okay, Jim, will do.'

Jim put down the handset and as he did so he turned to me and spoke in a low voice full of suppressed anger.

'That bastard has to be stopped,' he hissed.

'I'll agree to his meeting,' I said.

'You're not meeting him alone.'

'Should I tell the police?'

'Possibly, but not these local people,

it'd better be your CID friend. No, on second thoughts let's sleep on it. The police may want to wire you and that could be dangerous.'

Jim took the car and went over to the farm the next morning while I tried to contact Sergeant Cooper. He wasn't in the office so I left a message asking him to contact me. Then I resumed typing, burying myself in Jim's past while trying to forget my present.

19

Jim found it hard to sleep that night. The thought of shortly being able to leave the island was unsettling. He wondered what would be in store for him when he finally got clear of the place. Added to that when he did fall asleep he found himself waking with a start when any of the others stirred. He was so used to the absolute quiet in the cave when he slept that the slightest unusual sound or movement had him reaching for his rifle as he woke. He did eventually get three of four hours of uninterrupted sleep before the first hint of dawn found him washing the sleep from his eyes in the sea.

Before he got back to the cave the aroma of freshly made coffee wafted down to him from the cave mouth. It was a smell that he had not been able to appreciate for some considerable time. As he entered the cave the three men glanced up at him as he spoke.

'If I were a Jap you three would be dead by now,' he said as he put down his rifle.

'We couldn't be seen,' said Sol.

'That's true,' said Jim, 'but I could smell that coffee down by the sea. It's a dead giveaway.'

'Can you smell anything else?' asked Chip.

Jim nodded. 'Yes,' he said. 'I can smell boot polish and a fancy soap. I could smell you coming at twenty feet.'

Major Marshall burst out laughing.

'What's the joke, Major?' asked Sol.

'He's dead right. I was told the same thing by a captured Jap in New Guinea,' the major replied. 'Our Aussie troops soon learned not to wash in enemy territory.'

Jim breakfasted on papaya and coconut whilst the others ate army rations. However, when he was offered a cup of the coffee Jim accepted and sipped it slowly as he savoured its taste and smell. When he finished he rinsed out the cup and handed it back and spoke as he did so.

'Thank you for the coffee but before we start climbing I'd like to get something clear. In agreeing to act as guide I'm moving away from my main source of food, the sea, so I will need to share yours. I can supply fruit as we go; can you supply the rest?'

'We've got plenty, Sergeant, you're welcome to join us,' said Sol.

'Thank you,' replied Jim.

Then he got to his feet, strapped on his water bottle and picked up his rifle. Turning to the others he said, 'The first part of the climb is over rocks, I'll let you know when we reach anything difficult. Have you brought bush knives? Because we'll need them later.'

The Americans nodded so Jim turned and began the climb leaving the others to follow. He climbed at his normal pace but had to pause at intervals to allow the others to catch up. His plan was to reach the ledge by midday but it took them longer. Before they moved off along the ledge Jim warned them about its dangers and pressed them all to take care.

'We had two men badly injured by

falling from this ledge so take care. If you need help then ask for it. We'll rest when we reach the next cave.'

When they eventually reached what he had long thought of as the radio cave the other three pulled off their packs and sat with their backs to the side wall.

'Christ, Sergeant, you set a fast pace,' gasped Chip.

'Well you three are hampered by those great big packs — do you really need all that stuff?'

'It's mainly food and ammo.'

'Then leave half of it here and we can pick it up on the way back. The going gets hard from here on.'

'What do you mean by hard?'

'There's dense rainforest from now on, wet, sweaty, stinking rainforest. Mossies, leeches and anything else that can fly and bite will be at you night and day and you'll have to struggle through mud and over dead trees so you'll finish up sleeping in wet gear.'

'Ugh, I hate leeches,' said Sol.

'Do any of you smoke?' asked Jim.

'Sure, do you want one?' asked Chip

producing a pack of Camel cigarettes.

'No thanks, but we'll need them later to get rid of the leeches.'

'How?'

'You burn their bums,' said the Australian.

Jim got to his feet, walked to the entrance and studied the sky. A mass of dark cloud was rolling in from the sea.

'It'll be raining shortly, the late afternoon downpour, so I suggest we stay here the night. I was hoping to have got further but we may as well start afresh in the morning,' he said. 'We'll sleep dry tonight.'

'That will give us time to sort our packs out,' replied Sol.

'We made the same mistake on our climb,' Jim said. 'We carried full survey gear, tents, guns and food, it was a real struggle. Our two radio men had a bloody great radio to carry as well.'

'Didn't you say one of them fell off that ledge?' Chip asked.

'Yes he was badly hurt and the radio was wrecked, what's left of the radio is in the back of this cave with all the other gear we had to abandon.'

The major got to his feet and walked to the back noting as he did so the aerial wire still slung from the roof. He examined the abandoned gear before returning to his seat.

'Just what did happen here, Sergeant?' he asked.

For the next few minutes Jim explained how the accident had happened and how they had subsequently lifted the injured men and made the bamboo stretchers for them.

'That was before I discovered the route that we used today so we had to cut our way back through the rainforest carrying two men on stretchers. It was bloody hard going,' he said. 'We needed the help of the beach party to get them down safely and we had to abandon that gear back there. We couldn't radio for help because the transmitter was smashed. I got the receiver going later but it eventually packed up.'

'I suppose that radio was your only link with the mainland,' said Sol.

Jim nodded. 'Yes we were supposed to

radio for the ship to pick us up but no radio, no pick up. We had two boats but they could only carry about half the men and virtually none of our equipment.'

'So what happened?'

'We sent the larger boat off with the casualties with orders for the ship to pick us up but it never came. In the end Captain Fitzroy set off in the other boat to fetch help but the Japs blew it out of the water.'

'Christ almighty,' exclaimed Sol. 'Then what happened?'

Jim went on to explain how he'd tried to save Captain Fitzroy and how when he got back to the beach he'd found the two bodies.

'There were more than two graves,' commented the major.

'Yes,' Jim agreed, 'the first was the driver who died of fever while we were on the mountain, then my two mates killed by the Japs and the fourth was a sailor whose body I found on the beach.'

'What about the ones at the other end of the beach?'

'Those are two American airmen, I saw

them murdered and I killed their murderer.'

'How?'

Jim explained how the Japanese pilot came back to view the men he'd shot and how he was shot in turn.

'You shot down a Zero with a rifle,' exclaimed Chip.

'If a Zero is a plane then yes, the pilot came in at slow speed with the canopy open. I couldn't miss, in fact I wasted a bullet on him because I fired twice but the first one killed him.'

Jim went on to explain how the plane then crashed into the moaning rocks and burned.

'Didn't the Japanese come to see what had happened to their pilot?' the major asked.

'A plane did fly over but it looked as if he'd made a mistake and flown too low over the sea. In any case they thought I was dead,' replied Jim.

'Why?'

Jim then related how he'd attacked the men from the warship and how the aircraft had attacked and bombed him in response and how the landing party that followed failed to find him.

'They destroyed all our survey gear and laid several booby traps in case I was still alive but an inquisitive monkey saved me from them. He was blown up by the first and I stayed clear of the others.'

'You've avenged your mates then,' the major said.

'I only got six in the boat and the pilot makes seven, I'm still owed some,' retorted Jim in a harsh tone.

'So am I,' replied the Australian with feeling. 'So am I.'

The four men set off at first light the next morning to continue the climb to the summit. Each man took his turn in the front swinging the bush knives when necessary and taking the easiest possible route. There was evidence in places of the route taken by Jim's original party but years of vegetation regrowth and several storms had combined to conceal most of it. The going was hard but the pace never slackened. Jim had said it would take three days up and three more down and he was determined to stick to that timetable if possible. By the time he called a halt that day the two Americans were flagging but the Australian major was coping quite well. They slept in wet, mud-caked clothing that night but they slept once more in a cave. The American's cigarettes came in extremely useful to remove their leeches.

They were on the move again at first light the next day and Jim continued to set a fast pace. As they got higher on the climb the vegetation began to thin allowing them to move faster. They began to encounter areas where the trees thinned so much that the sun managed to reach down to them. In the denser areas they never saw the sun but walked and stumbled along in a hot steamy atmosphere that sapped their energy and left them permanently soaked in sweat.

Shortly after midday they reached the cave that Jim remembered had held traces of human occupation and he realised that they were near the summit. He called a halt and they ate a snack meal.

'We're near the top now and I intend sleeping here tonight. You can leave your packs here if you like,' he said.

They did as he suggested so the last leg up to the summit was almost a gentle stroll. When they finally got there all three were delighted with the magnificent view.

'It's a perfect spot for lookouts,' said Sol.

'Coastwatchers, we call them coastwatchers,' said the Australian.

'Well whatever you call them this is the ideal spot for them. Any shipping movements they spot can be radioed in from here and they've got that cave for shelter at night,' Sol continued.

The Australian major walked around examining the mountain top before commenting again.

'As far as I can see,' he said, 'they would be short of water and escape routes. The only water up here would be rain and, as for escaping, that side of the mountain looks like a sheer drop. It would be difficult to get away if the Japs came the same way as us.'

'We'll put that in our report and let those higher up make the decision. It is a magnificent view though,' replied Sol.

'It is great,' Chip said, 'but we'll be soaked soon. Just look at that cloud coming in.'

The rain hit them before they returned to the cave so they spent another night in damp clothes.

Two days later they were all preparing for the final descent down the rocks when Jim asked for quiet.

'I don't like it,' he said. There's something wrong, something different.'

'What do you mean?' asked the Australian.

'The monkeys and birds are upset, they sound very different.'

'Could it be us upsetting them?'

'No it's something else. I think there may be someone on the beach.'

'Well we can't stay here.'

'Okay, we move but with care. The one good thing about this route down the rocks is that we cannot be seen unless there's someone directly below us. We should however be able to see through the trees when we get lower.'

The Australian turned to the Americans.

'Did you get all that?' he asked.

They both nodded.

'Okay, guns loaded, safety catches on, tread carefully, let's go, Jim.'

Jim noted the use of his first name and presumed that it meant that the Australian was feeling nervous.

They moved off down the rocky route taking care not to make any undue noise or dislodge any stones. Jim was convinced that something other than their presence was disturbing the local animal and birdlife. After about an hour he stopped and turned to the others.

'I can smell smoke,' he said. 'There must be someone on the beach.'

'Can you see anything yet?' asked Sol.

'No, but we should be able to see through the trees in a short while.'

They recommenced the descent with even more caution with Jim in the lead once more. About half an hour later he signalled a halt once again and pointed down through a gap in the trees. The Australian moved alongside him in order to peer through the same gap. Taking out his binoculars he focussed them on the beach. He could see a small vessel resting bow first on the sand.

'That's Japanese,' he said quietly. 'Those things are used for river and coastal patrols; there were some in New Guinea.'

'How many men do they carry?' asked Jim.

'Normally about eight to ten but they can carry more.'

The two Americans then moved down and took turns peering at the vessel.

'It looks like a small landing craft,' said Sol.

'That's just what it is,' agreed the Australian. 'They are ideal vessels for river and shallow water patrols because they are designed to be beached. You can see the bow door of that one is open.'

'The submarine is due to pick us up tomorrow night, but it won't come in with that thing there.'

'If it doesn't go by tomorrow morning we will have to move it,' muttered the Australian. Then turning to Jim he said, 'Can we get nearer without being seen?'

'Yes I think so.'

They had almost reached the large cave when a chorus of shouts rose from just below them on the beach. The four men scrambled into cover but they had not been seen.

'It's not us,' said Sol, 'they've spotted the submarine's periscope.' He held up his hand for silence. 'They look as if they're going to radio their navy,' he said.

'We've got to stop them,' exclaimed the Australian.

Without responding to him Jim led the way to the beach. They were almost there when a Japanese soldier stepped out of the trees buttoning up his trousers. He looked up in surprise and opened his mouth to shout a warning but he never stood a chance. Sol was the nearest to him and he swung his arm and gave the soldier a vicious one-handed blow to the throat. The Japanese dropped to the ground without uttering a sound.

'Dead?' queried the Australian.

Sol bent and checked the man's pulse and nodded in reply. Jim moved on at a crouch peering through the lower branches of the trees as he did so. As soon as he had a clear view of the beach he signalled the others to join him. He could see one soldier hurrying down the beach towards the vessel and several others looking out to sea. Jim indicated the man heading for the boat.

'Mine,' he said.

The Australian pointed at the others and said, 'Ours.'

'Ready?' whispered Jim.

He got three nods in reply before gently squeezing the trigger of his rifle. The soldier sagged to the sand within a few feet of the boat. His compatriots didn't seem to understand what had happened because they surged forward towards him without taking cover or responding. Two more collapsed into the sand before they realised that they were under fire. Only one man ran for cover and he dived behind Jim's timber beacon whilst the rest were being mown down. That lone survivor had a light machine gun of some kind and his first burst of fire whipped viciously around them. Chip cursed and clutched at his arm and rolled back into cover.

'The bastard nicked me,' he said.

Jim suddenly signalled the others. 'Keep his head down,' he said, 'I'll be back in a minute.'

He ran back to the cave returning a few minutes later with the Very pistol. Pointing to the beacon he said, 'Can you see that canister near the base of that timber?'

The Australian nodded.

'That's full of aviation fuel, if you put a couple of holes in it we'll have a bonfire,' he muttered holding up the Very pistol.

He loaded the pistol and waited until he was certain that plenty of fuel was running through the holes in the canister before standing and firing. The red flare hit the fuel and there was an instantaneous explosion and burst of fire. The hidden soldier ran out covered in flames and screaming. He was cut down before he'd taken more than a couple of running strides.

Sol was busy tending to the injured Chip so Jim looked across at the Australian.

'Cover me,' he said getting to his feet.

He checked and reloaded his rifle before moving cautiously along the upper edge of the beach checking for any survivors. Then, keeping the fallen Japanese between himself and the Australian, he checked each body in turn. He was nearing the boat when a sudden movement caused him to turn and fire. He dived to the sand and glanced up preparing to fire again when a monkey jumped from the boat and scampered off into the trees.

The Australian then hurried over to his side and indicated that the boat needed checking. Jim nodded and cautiously stepped on board. There wasn't much to search because the soldiers appeared to have used the open deck for sleeping. The wheelhouse and the engine compartment were empty of any hidden soldiers and Jim signalled the all clear to the others. The boat itself was filthy with empty food cans and bottles scattered anywhere and everywhere. A pair of tattered trousers hung from the back of the wheelhouse with a bucket holding more dirty washing standing below it. The only relatively clean thing on the whole boat was the radio. It was fastened to the bulkhead behind the wheelman's position.

Sol walked down the beach checking each of the bodies as he did so. The Australian looked up at his approach.

'How is he?' he asked nodding towards Chip.

'He'll live — the bullet went through without touching bone.' He turned and pointed to the scattered bodies. 'What do we do with this lot?'

'I suggest we drag them on board and sink the boat if we can.'

Jim turned and gripped the wrists of the first body and dragged it over the sand. The Australian Major and Sol followed his example and within twenty minutes they had all the dead men laid out on the deck. Jim walked back collecting their abandoned guns and slung them onto the deck as well. When they were sure that no trace of the Japanese presence remained they discussed what to do next. They talked first of taking it out into the bay and sinking it but decided against that because the bodies might wash back onto the beach. Burning was similarly thrown out because the flames and smoke might attract unwelcome attention. In the end they simply started the engine and lashed the wheel so that the boat would head far out into the South China Sea and keep going until the fuel ran out.

Jim went with it and stayed aboard until he was sure it was headed in the right direction. He then dived overboard and swam back to the beach. The others in the meantime had trailed foliage across the sand to eliminate all the footprints. By the time they had finished the burning beacon was no more than a pile of smouldering ashes and all trace of the Japanese had been wiped away.

★ ★ ★

When Jim came into the room I stopped typing and asked him who the two Americans were. Their lack of insignia puzzled me and the ability to kill with one blow was surprising. It was not what you would expect from a simple soldier.

'Oh, they were special forces, something like our SAS or commandos,' he said. 'The crew of the submarine treated them warily when we finally got onboard.'

'Why didn't the Japanese hear your first shot?'

'They were making too much noise themselves. They were shouting and pointing out to sea, the monkeys and birds were adding their own racket — it was bedlam.' He paused for a moment then said, 'They were on the grog, we picked up several saki bottles later. The silly buggers never stood a chance.'

He walked over to the window and stood there for some minutes before picking up the story again.

'They were such a scruffy lot that I wondered later if they were deserters. Either that or they were simply out for a jolly — some jolly.'

He shook his head, picked up the morning mail and wandered back out of the room leaving me to get on with his story.

20

Before the submarine arrived the following evening Jim took all the spare rifles and ammunition and dumped them in a hole he'd dug in the sand. He'd wrapped each item in the remnants of the tents just in case he needed to unearth them again. His own rifle and Captain Fitzroy's handgun were the only weapons he retained. He dressed in the solitary uniform that still looked in good shape and took only the one pack, the one he had prepared earlier with the private effects of the various missing and dead soldiers. He handed the identification tags belonging to the two American airmen to Sol.

It was dark when the submarine surfaced in response to a signal flashed by torchlight from the shore. Chip, with his injured arm in a sling, and Sol went out in the first boat whilst Jim and the Australian, Major Marshall, waited for its return. The date was November 3rd 1944 when Jim finally boarded the submarine and said goodbye to his island home. He could hardly believe he had spent just over two years there.

The crew of the submarine were naturally surprised to find that they had an extra passenger and word soon got around as to who he was. His unkempt hair and beard and the fact that he'd been stranded on the island for so long led to someone nicknaming him Sergeant Crusoe, a name that stuck with him for some time. When he heard it for the first time he thought it was quite apt so he was amused rather than upset by it. Later, after word got round that he'd shot down a Zero with his rifle, some referred to him as the Sniper sergeant. He wasn't too happy with that one.

He found it extremely hard to sleep on that vessel. The constant noise bothered him but his biggest problem was the proximity of so many men in such a confined space. Although he was grateful to have been rescued he was also extremely grateful to get off the submarine a week later. After years of living in the open and breathing fresh air the stifling atmosphere of the submarine's interior was almost unbearable for him.

When the submarine finally surfaced the fresh air passing through the inner hull was a blessing to Jim. Men had gone on deck through a forward hatch and through the conning tower so a welcome breeze helped to clear the fetid atmosphere. A series of commands and engine movements indicated that the vessel was preparing to moor alongside a jetty but just where the jetty was remained a mystery to Jim. Even when he and the rest of the crew were allowed on deck no one could tell him at first. Then the original crew appeared to be making way for new men from the shore and one of these took his position alongside Jim.

To Jim's untrained eye there appeared to be hundreds of ships of every kind anchored or moored within an atoll. He could see several islands, some with what appeared to be brand new buildings and others with the usual palm trees. Aircraft circled overhead whilst others landed or took off from different island runways. The trappings of war lay all around him. On board all the ships in the immediate area he could see gunners manning anti-aircraft guns and small craft weaved in and out of the ships in all directions. Eventually Jim turned to the new sailor standing beside him.

'Is this Pearl Harbour?' he asked.

'No, this is Ulithi Atoll, Pearl is a few hundred miles away. This place is much nearer to the Philippines and Japan,' he replied.

They were interrupted then by Major Marshall. He called to Jim to collect his kit and be ready to go ashore in a boat coming from one of the islands. Ten minutes later Jim, the Major and the two Americans, Sol and Chip, were taken by boat to a distant island. There they were met by two jeeps, one for the Americans and the other for Jim and the major. They were driven only a couple of hundred yards to buildings hidden beneath camouflage netting. Jim was put into care of a young soldier who led him to a building equipped as a barracks, but a barracks unlike anything Jim had ever seen.

He was allocated a bunk, directed to the showers and the adjacent kitchen, asked for his size in clothes and shoes and told to be prepared for a debriefing in about an hour. Before he had finished a very welcome shower another soldier appeared with shears and shaving kit and helped him remove all his excessive hair. Jim then took another shower before returning to his bunk to dress. Laid out on the bunk was a selection of American Army kit for him to wear. Once he was dressed he investigated the kitchen and was amazed to find a fully stocked kitchen with a refrigerator packed with delicacies. He was sampling a strawberry ice-cream when the original soldier returned. He grinned when he saw the new Jim.

'You'll have to ditch the ice-cream,' he said. 'You're wanted by your major.'

A few minutes later Jim found himself confronted by not just the major but another officer, an American. Major Marshall spoke first.

'You look better for the spring clean, Sergeant.'

'It feels better, sir.'

'Good, now Captain Mitchell here and I would like to hear your story again. Take a seat and tell us everything from the beginning.'

The three men sat facing each other and Captain Mitchell held a notebook in his lap. Jim spoke for nearly an hour, interrupted now and again by questions from one or the other of the officers. When he came to the events with the American aircraft and the Japanese Zero the captain took many notes, asking Jim several questions whilst doing so.

'Did you mark the graves, Sergeant?' asked Captain Mitchell.

'Yes sir, I took the names from the identification discs and put them on wooden stakes.'

'Where are the identification discs?'

'I gave them to the American officers, sir.'

'That is correct, Captain, I was there,' said the major.

'Good, well I think that is all for now,

Sergeant,' said the American captain. 'Thank you for your help. I'll get one of my men to show you around this place because you'll have to stay here until we can get you back to your people.' He then did a strange thing: he walked across to Jim and shook his hand.

'Thank you for looking after our fliers, Sergeant. I'll see that your humanity is rewarded.'

Jim stepped back, saluted and remained standing in shocked silence as the officers left the room. A few moments later the door opened again and Jim's soldier escort entered.

'C'mon, Sarge, I've got a Jeep outside, I've got to give you a tour of the place.'

'What's a Jeep?' asked Jim.

'An army car, that thing you rode in before.'

For the next hour Jim was driven round the small island having various buildings pointed out to him. He soon learnt that the three American forces had headquarters on the island. The number of high-ranking officers he saw was more than he'd seen in the whole of his time in the army. He also discovered that no one was required to salute. His escort took him into the PX, the American equivalent of the NAAFI and Jim left shaking his head in wonder at the vast array of goods available.

'I thought this was a war zone,' said Jim. 'I never expected a store like that here.'

His escort, who had persuaded Jim to call him Chuck, then proceeded to astound him even further by pointing to two of the ships in the anchorage. The largest apparently produced thousands of fresh bread loaves every day whilst its smaller companion was what he called the ice-cream ship. Adjacent islands had cinemas, a theatre, a chapel and countless other recreational facilities.

'How long has this place been here?' Jim asked.

'I think it's about three months, the Japs were here earlier this year. That jetty you came ashore on originally wasn't here two months ago. In fact none of the jetties that you can see were here. The Seabees did a good job.'

'Seabees?'

'Yeah, they're the guys who built all this.'

When they returned to the barracks Jim was surprised to find that his kit had gone but Chuck soon put his mind at rest by directing him to a room at the end of the hut.

'You've got your own place now, c'mon I'll show you.'

He led the way down to the room and pointed to the sign on the door.

'See, I told you they'd moved you,' he said, pointing to a newly printed sign pinned to the door.

The sign read, Acting Sergeant James Bullock and below it in large letters SERGEANT CRUSOE. The sign was beautifully painted on a sheet of white cardboard and the painter had added the silhouette of an aircraft. Chuck pointed to the silhouette.

'We don't get many people who can down a Zero with a rifle,' he said.

'How did you know that?' exclaimed Jim.

'Jungle telegraph,' said Chuck with a

grin. 'I had to show you round for an hour while this was done. You'll find all your kit in there. I'll pick you up at chow time.'

For the next two weeks Jim lived in almost a dream world. The food was plentiful, varied and of good quality although he did miss the fresh fruit he'd been able to pick for himself on his island. He went to the cinema several times, enjoyed concerts given by the very big bands he'd listened to on the radio and watched his fellow soldiers playing team games such as baseball. The Americans couldn't do enough for him even to the extent of giving him a pass enabling him acquire whatever he wanted from the PX. He had no money so he was grateful for the pass.

During that time there were several air alerts but the attacking aircraft did not appear to get through the American air defences. However, in the early hours of the 20th November he was woken by a series of explosions. He dressed quickly, grabbed his rifle and hurried outside. The explosions were coming from within the anchorage and shortly after taking up a position in a nearby slit trench a tremendous explosion signalled the end of a large tanker. Explosions continued to resound throughout the next couple of hours caused he later learnt by American depth charges. The tanker sank but continued to send up a column of flames and smoke throughout that day. He was told later that the attack was by small Japanese submarines.

That attack served to bring Jim back to earth. The Japanese were still the enemy and despite the vast armada that lay within the anchorage they had managed to bring the war extremely close. It reminded Jim of something he'd learnt at school — fireships sent in amongst anchored Spanish ships to 'singe the king of Spain's beard'. Was it Sir Francis Drake he wondered who had done that? He couldn't be certain but contented himself with the fact that he'd remembered the attack.

He spent Christmas Eve seated amongst a thousand American forces personnel at a carol concert. He found himself joining in the singing and feeling immensely moved by the tremendous chorus of voices around him. The feeling of comradeship staggered him, he was a foreigner but the Americans treated him as one of their own. Some men were reduced to tears at the finale whilst others walked quietly away their thoughts with family and friends thousands of miles away. Jim found himself thinking of Sylvia and wondering whether she found her husband again. His own family, his sister, was living in another world and another war. He had no idea if she was alive or not but he felt that she must be okay but he had no idea if he would see her again. That night he felt closer to both Sylvia and her.

Jim tried to contact the Australian major a few days after Christmas but he was told that he had left the island and was expected to return early in January. On the tenth of January Jim saw a submarine slide into the same berth as his had done earlier and an hour later a boat deposited the major on the island. He hurried away before Jim could speak to him but he acknowledged Jim's presence with a hand gesture that was half wave and half salute.

The following morning Jim was summoned and found himself in the presence of the major once again. The Australian wasted little time.

'I've news for you, Sergeant — you're on your way out of here. In a few days you and I will be boarding an aircraft to take us part of the way home, my home that is.'

'Do you mean Australia, sir?'

'Yes, but we can't go there in one hop, there will be an intermediate stop but I can't tell you where at the moment.'

'I've never been in an aircraft.'

'There's always a first time for everything. Now I want you to be ready to go at short notice so have your gear ready for the off.'

'Yes, sir. May I ask a question about money?'

'Money?'

'Well I haven't been paid for years, sir and it is a bit embarrassing living off the Americans.'

'I'm in the same boat, Sergeant. My

money stopped coming through six months ago. We may be able to sort something out at our intermediate stop. Are you short of anything now?'

'No, I'm okay, sir.'

'Fine, now on a different topic I'd like you to know that thanks to your efforts we have an observation post on the island and it has already alerted us of a Japanese convoy. I was on the submarine that successfully attacked it. Your men did not die in vain.'

'Thank you, sir. I wish I knew just what happened to our first boat.'

'We'll find out eventually, Sergeant. You've probably been posted missing believed dead yourself.'

'I never thought of that, sir.'

'Okay, that's all for now, just be ready for the off when I call you.'

Three days later he and his kit were collected and driven to a jetty where a boat was waiting to take him across to the island with the airfield. At the airfield he was hurried across to a large aircraft that was standing with its propellers already turning. He scrambled onboard with his rifle and his gear was thrown unceremoniously after him. A crew member directed him to a metal seat and showed him how to strap himself in. No sooner had he finished than the plane began to move. It rumbled slowly along at first then he felt it turn and stop. After that the engines began to make an increasing din before it suddenly surged forward at a tremendous rate.

Despite his seat belt being securely fastened Jim clung fiercely to the metal frame. He had no window to look through so the initial manoeuvres as the plane banked and turned were particularly unsettling. However, once the plane had climbed and levelled on course he felt his stomach begin to settle. He looked around for the Australian but could not see him. In fact the only men he could see were members of the crew. He appeared to be the only passenger.

After about twenty minutes in the air one of the crew came down from the cockpit and handed Jim a note. The engine noise made normal speech impossible.

'The major couldn't make it, Sarge so he left this note for you,' he shouted.

'Thank you, are we going to Australia?'

'Not on this flight, we're going to Fiji.'

'Fiji, where the hell is that?'

'Halfway to Australia.'

He patted Jim on the shoulder and turned back to the cockpit. Jim opened and read the note. It said, 'Sergeant, I have been delayed. Arrangements have been made for a driver to meet you and to drive you to Suva. There will be accommodation for you there. A passage by sea is being arranged.' The note was signed by the Major.

'A sea passage to where?' muttered Jim.

Shortly afterwards the same crewman returned and leant over towards Jim's ear, shouting again to overcome the noise.

'Are you Sergeant Crusoe?'

'Yes.'

'The captain wants to see you up front.'

'When?'

'Now, follow me.'

No sooner had Jim got to his feet than a large explosion shook the plane and it seemed to stagger in mid-flight. The crewman pushed him back into his seat telling him to fasten his seat belt as he did so. A second lesser bang occurred and the plane shuddered once again then began slowly turning. The engine noise noticeably diminished and to Jim the plane seemed to be flying at somewhat of an angle. Eventually the crewman returned and told him that the plane was in trouble and was returning to the island.

'We've got trouble with the engines,' he said. 'We've to return for repairs. Sorry but you won't be seeing Fiji on this trip.'

'Does the captain still want me up front?' asked Jim.

'No, he's got his hands full at the moment. He said to tell you that you should stay strapped in because we may have a bumpy landing.'

An hour later they came in to land back on the island. Despite the bumpy landing warning the eventual landing was remarkably smooth. When Jim dropped back onto the tarmac strip and collected his gear again he found the flight crew gathered under the starboard engines. For some reason one engine had exploded and pieces of it had damaged the propeller of its neighbour. The aircraft had returned with both of the starboard engines out of action. One of the pilots was later heard to say that they really did do as the song said, 'We came in on a wing and a prayer.'

Jim crossed back to his accommodation by boat once again. The room was still vacant and his name remained on the door. Chuck saw him arrive and walked over to stand leaning on the door post.

'What's up, don't you want to leave us?' he said.

'No, I came back for the fine company, the steak dinners and the movies. That was my first ride in an aeroplane and I can't say I was too impressed.'

'Word is you shouldn't have gone in the first place.'

'What do you mean?'

'Apparently this place is secret.'

'Secret! Bloody rubbish, the Japs know you're here so who are you keeping it secret from?'

'God knows, I don't, anyway you ain't going anywhere for the time being. You'd better see your major — he got a rocket for letting you go.'

Jim stowed his gear then went in search of Major Marshall. He never found him so he had something to eat and retired to his bed for an afternoon nap. The fact that he was practically the only man who was not actively engaged in preparing for what looked like a major assault made him feel out of place. Lying on his bed dozing or reading a book served as somewhat of an antidote to the activity outside.

He still had not shaken off his time on the island though because any sudden noise found him instantly awake and reaching for his rifle. This was a particular problem at night when patrolling sentries crunched past on the coral sand outside his room. More than once he had found himself crouching by the door with his rifle in his hand ready to shoot any intruder. By the time he was fully awake the adrenaline pumping through him, the raised blood pressure and breathing prevented anymore sleep that night. He had unloaded his rifle just in case he shot someone by accident. Nevertheless the rifle never left his bedside.

21

Jim stayed overnight at Graham's farm and returned home still fuming about the damage to the barn. The local police and the insurance inspector were certain that the barn fire was arson but whoever had done it hadn't left much evidence. The few traces that were left indicated a professional job rather than a casual attack by vandals. The insurance would cover the cost but Graham would lose financially because of the resultant rise in his premiums. Sergeant Cooper had not returned my call but shortly after Jim returned he knocked at the door.

'I got your message,' he said, 'I thought I'd pop over instead of phoning you back.

Jim and I then explained just what had gone on at the farm and on the subsequent telephone call from Da Silva.

'Have you agreed to meet him?' Cooper asked.

'Not yet, he hasn't suggested a date and time yet,' I replied.

'What will you do?'

'I'll have to meet him in order to stop the attacks on the farm but I'm not working for him. I'm not agreeing to anything he suggests.'

'Did he use the landline or your mobile?'

'The landline, he doesn't know my mobile number.'

'Would you object if I arranged for your phone to be linked to my office? I would like to be an observer at your meeting.'

I looked across at Jim and he nodded agreement.

'No objection,' I said.

'Good I'll get it sorted and I'll ring you on that phone when it's done. I want to hear Silver's proposal myself. Can you keep the calls to a minimum on that phone, use your mobile instead?'

'Okay, how long will it take to arrange?'

'It'll be done today.'

He got to his feet and turned towards the door then stopped and said, 'I want that bugger behind bars, the sooner the better.'

About three hours later he rang back to confirm that we were now linked to his desk by telephone and at his end every word would be recorded even if he wasn't there.

*   *   *

The last time Jim saw the Australian major was early in March 1945. He reappeared from one of his frequent sorties from the atoll and sent for Jim. The Major looked ill but said nothing about it. He merely told him that the British Army in England was now aware that he was still alive and billeted with the American forces in the Pacific.

'The War Office have authorised me to pay you an advance on your pay,' Major Marshall said.

'Thank you, sir,' replied Jim.

'You'll have to sign for it, there on the dotted line.'

Jim signed and was handed ten American dollars.

'I believe that's the equivalent of two weeks' pay, it's all they will let me pay you. I may be able to give you more some time later.'

'Is there any news of when I'll be able to leave here, sir?'

'I'm afraid not, for the time being you and I are stuck here.'

'Thank you, sir.'

Jim never saw him again.

On the night of the 11th March Jim was brought sharply awake by air raid sirens and the sounds of anti-aircraft guns. The noise was deafening as he raced to his allocated slit trench. By the time he reached it his rifle was fully loaded and the adrenaline was racing through him once again. A plane screamed down into the packed shipping and a massive explosion followed. A few seconds later another explosion erupted from one of the islands. Searchlights swept the sky and guns continued to fire for some time but there were no further explosions. There was a large fire burning out in the anchorage and a great deal of activity around it. Eventually things began to calm down and apart from the fire the area began to return to something like normal.

The early hints of the approaching dawn tinged the sky before the order came to stand down. In the first light of day Jim could see a pall of smoke rising from an aircraft carrier out in the anchorage. He could not see any sign of smoke from the explosion on the island and he soon found out why. Chuck walked up carrying his carbine over his shoulder and swinging his steel helmet in the other hand.

'Scuttlebutt says they were kamikazes, one hit the carrier and the other the baseball field. They think the one that hit the field mistook it for another carrier,' he said.

'Kami what?' exclaimed Jim.

'Kamikazes, they are suicide pilots. The pilot dives his plane into the target killing himself as he does so.'

'Is that what kamikaze means, suicide pilot?'

'One of the interpreters says it means divine wind but as far as I'm concerned it means suicide pilot.'

'Christ, what a way to fight a war.'

'It shows that they are getting desperate.'

'Are you really pushing them back?'

'Yes, we're back in the Philippines just as General MacArthur said we would be. This lot out here will probably be going to back up the troops that have already landed. Our aircraft have attacked Tokyo so it won't be long before we attack Japan itself.'

'What about the war in Europe?'

'The last time I heard anything our lot were driving towards Berlin. By the time you get home it'll all be over.'

'I'm beginning to wonder if I ever will get home. Will you be going with that armada when it sails?'

'Sure, I'll be on the headquarters ship.'

'What about me?'

'Come with us, nobody will notice. There'll be nothing left here when we go.'

'I'll have to see that Australian major to see if I can.'

'He's gone, medical casualty, left by air yesterday.'

'That's just my luck he'd made contact with the army people back home for me and now he's gone. I've lost the link.'

Chuck put his arm across Jim's shoulders and patted his back.

'Never mind, Sarge, I'll look after you. I'll book you a bunk on the ship.'

'What I need is a beer and a blonde,' said Jim.

'There're plenty of nurses on the hospital ship. Want me to get you a date?'

Jim burst out laughing.

'In your dreams,' he spluttered. 'Many thousands of soldiers, sailors and airmen and probably no more than a few hundred nurses, what chance have you and I got?'

'I'll tell you what,' said Chuck, 'I'll lend you my pin-ups.'

'No thanks. I want the real thing, no paper dolls for me, I'll wait for her whoever she is.'

'Well the offer's there if you change your mind.'

'Do you think I should ask that Captain Mitchell of yours about getting aboard the headquarters ship?'

'Yes, maybe we'd better. He may have other plans for you now that the Aussie's gone. I'll see him in the morning.' He looked at his watch before continuing. 'Chow time, are you coming?'

'Yes, let's go.'

Jim did not have to wait until the following day to see the captain; he was called to see him that afternoon. Chuck assured Jim that he had not arranged the meeting, he had not had time.

'It's nothing to do with me, Sarge. I've no idea what he wants.'

'Okay, maybe he wants me to look after the nurses while you buggers go off to war.'

'I don't think so, but if he does, ask him if I can help,' said Chuck.

When Jim entered the captain's office there were no polite preliminaries, the captain got straight down to business.

'Sergeant, you are not in my army so I can't order you but I need your help. The two men on the island are in some sort of trouble so I need to get replacements there. Will you agree to guide them?'

'Yes, sir, when?'

'There's a submarine leaving tonight, I want you on it.'

'Okay, sir, I'll get my gear together. What about provisions?'

'The replacements will have sufficient for you all.'

Jim was the last man to board the submarine that night and only Chuck and Captain Mitchell watched as the vessel moved away from its berth. Once below Jim was surprised to find two familiar faces, Sol and Chip.

'Are you the two replacements?' he asked.

'Yes, and before you ask, we requested your company,' said Sol.

'We like the way you operate,' Chip remarked, 'and Sol here would be lost in that forest without you.'

'How's the arm?' asked Jim.

Chip raised and flexed his arm as if to demonstrate its fitness. 'Fine,' he said.

The trio were then shown to their allocated bunks and began stowing their gear. Jim found that his bunk backed onto the torpedo compartment and the sight of those gleaming torpedoes made him secretly wish that there was a safer way of reaching the island. The thought of all that high explosive behind his head when he slept was not conducive to pleasant dreams. Nevertheless he slept well that night.

That sea passage was much shorter than the earlier one primarily because most of the time the submarine moved at a fast speed on the surface. Even during daylight hours they stayed on the surface most of the time. On the two occasions that they submerged they only stayed that way for a couple of hours. There was none of the hot, fetid atmosphere that Jim had hated on that first voyage.

The approach to the island was made submerged and frequent use was made of the periscope. As far as they could tell there were no Japanese present so the submarine surfaced at night and landed Jim and his companions by boat. Even though the periscope had not revealed a Japanese presence the three men hurried across the open sand into the shelter of the rocks before speaking.

'Can anybody see anything?' whispered Sol.

'Looks clear,' replied Chip.

'Jim?'

'It feels okay but I'll check the cave if you like.'

'Okay, we'll wait here till you signal,' agreed Sol.

'I'll make one short whistle if it's clear,' Jim replied as he got to his feet and moved off.

A few minutes later his whistle indicated the all clear and the others climbed to the cave entrance.

'It looks undisturbed,' said Jim shining his torch into the cave. 'I think I'll sleep just here in the entrance though just in case the Japs have been here and left a calling card or two. I can't see any booby-traps here.'

At first light Jim woke and made his customary trip to the water's edge. After a brief swim and a rinse under the fresh water he was joined by the others.

'It looks okay and it sounds that way too,' he said in answer to Sol's query.

'We've checked the cave and there are no booby-traps,' said Chip.

'Good, then after breakfast we'll start climbing. Have you any idea what could have gone wrong with the men up top?'

'No, they just haven't kept their radio skeds.'

By midday on the third day of the climb they were approaching the point where the sleeping cave was for the observers. They checked carefully before approaching the entrance and calling out. There was no reply. The cave itself looked in good order with the radio and the men's equipment and stores neatly laid out.

'I don't understand it; they should have heard us by now,' said Chip.

Sol took off his pack and checked his carbine. The others followed suit and the three of them moved on towards the summit. Before they broke out of the last of the trees Jim called a halt.

'Can you hear it?' he asked.

'Hear what?' said Sol.

'Those birds, I've never heard anything like that before.'

316

Chip moved cautiously on into the open and exclaimed in horror at what he could see. As the others moved alongside him there were confronted by a flock of large birds fighting over what remained of the corpses of the two men. Chip fired his carbine and the birds rose in a great black cloud screaming in protest. He made no attempt to move forward merely kneeling and studying the ground in front where the two bodies lay.

He pointed to holes blasted into the surrounding area.

'Cannon fire,' he said. 'Aircraft cannon fire. Why didn't they hear it coming?'

'There're the remains of a canvas awning out there,' muttered Sol. 'Do you think they were asleep?'

'God knows,' replied Chip. 'Come on let's bury the poor bastards.'

There wasn't a great deal left to bury because the birds had removed a lot of the flesh. Jim was physically sick when they gathered together the bloodied bits and pieces that had been two men. The grave they scraped out was barely big enough for one body but comfortably held the scant remains. They covered the makeshift grave with stones to keep off any scavengers. Shortly before they finished dark clouds filled the sky and rain poured down soaking and cleansing them all at the same time. As usual the rain only lasted about an hour so when they returned to the shelter of the cave they were able to change into dry clothing and lay their wet gear in the sun to dry.

'Do you think they were spotted by chance?' asked Jim.

'Possibly, is there a lot of air activity around here?' said Sol.

'Well you've seen the wrecks on the beach and there was once a visit by two aircraft with floats.'

'Float planes, where are they based?'

'It could be anywhere around here, there's plenty of water for them.'

'They may have been spotted by chance,' said Chip. 'But I think the wind has a part to play.'

'What do you mean?'

'The trade winds are quite strong up here in the open at times and they always blow in the same direction. Sounds carried by the wind could hide sounds from the other direction.'

'Especially if the planes glide in,' said Jim. 'When those float planes came in I saw them before I heard them.'

'We will have to be alert at all times,' Chip muttered, almost to himself.

Sol looked at his watch and moved over to the radio. He switched it on and picked up the handset.

'Time for the sked,' he said.

The transmission was short and promptly acknowledged giving any listener on the Japanese side little chance to take a directional bearing. In order to avoid the possibility that the transmissions made earlier by the now dead observers had been picked up new frequencies and schedule times had been arranged before they left the atoll.

Sol looked across at Jim. 'Now they know we're here your pick-up will be waiting for you in three days' time,' he said.

Jim nodded. 'Okay, I'll start back down at first light.'

22

I was under the impression that I had been discharged by the hospital so I was surprised to receive a letter directing me to the Alfred Bean hospital in Driffield. Apparently the surgeon who had originally operated on me wanted an x-ray to check on my inner progress. That was when I remembered him saying that he'd wired me up inside. Anyway I went for my x-ray yesterday and managed to get myself lost in Driffield. I'd followed Jim's directions but it was Thursday and he'd forgotten to remind me it was market day and of course the main shopping street is always closed that day.

Because of the road diversion around the market I lost my way and drove through the same car park twice before finding my way again. It was during that mix-up that I spotted the cars behind me. I was lost so going twice through the same car park was fine for me but I suddenly realised that other cars were doing the same. One of them I recognised as 'muddy number plate' but the other was new to me. It was a nondescript little Fiat, green in colour with two men inside.

When I got to the hospital the car park was virtually full but I managed to slot my car between two others and squeezed my way out of the door with some difficulty. I was on time for my appointment and for once in my life there was no one ahead of me. Fifteen minutes later I was back easing my way into my car again. 'Muddy number plate' pulled up across the back of me blocking my exit. The same driver got out and tapped on my window. He handed me a slip of paper with a telephone number on it.

'The boss says you're to ring that number tonight to agree time and place,' he said. 'If you don't you know what will happen.'

He didn't wait for my response.

It took me a while to edge out of my parking space and by the time I was clear he'd gone. As I was driving off I spotted the Fiat parked in a lay-by near the fire station. I couldn't be certain but I thought I saw the driver either taking my picture or examining me through binoculars. I had cars tight up behind me so I couldn't turn and confront him and by the time I was able to turn he'd gone. I think he must have nipped off down one of the side streets because I never saw him again.

As I drove back home I decided to ring my friendly police sergeant straight away and let him check on the number I'd been given before I made the evening call. I discussed it with Jim and he thought the same as me that it would probably be the number of a pay-as-you-go phone that would be thrown away as soon as I made the call. Nevertheless I rang the police and left it to them to decide whether it was worth following up. Then I put it out my mind while I got back to Jim's tapes.

★　★　★

Jim rendezvoused with the submarine three days later but he wasn't feeling too good. He had dizzy moments, a temperature and headaches. The submarine had a medic but he was not a doctor so he treated Jim with tablets that he hoped would bring down the temperature and advised Jim to sleep it off. Jim had no recollection of the next few days. He descended into a world of weird dreams, alternating between being freezing cold and boiling hot. He had vague recollections of being carried and manhandled in some way but when and by whom he had no idea.

He eventually woke ten days after boarding the submarine. In trying to lift his head he groaned at the effort and someone moved to his side and looked down at him.

'How do you feel, soldier?' said a male voice.

'Bloody awful,' muttered Jim. 'Where am I?'

'On a hospital ship.'

'How . . . how long?'

'We got you a week ago.'

'What's wrong?'

'You're on the mend now but you've

had a nasty bout of malaria.'

Jim tried to say something else but slipped back into unconsciousness again. When he next woke the man had gone and he was able to edge up in the bed and look around. He could see that he was in a ward of about twenty beds and most of them were empty. A tube ran from the back of his hand up to a bottle of clear liquid suspended from a metal frame above him. His groping hand found the metal frame of the bed and he tried to use it to pull himself upright but failed. However, that movement had been spotted and another figure in white appeared above him. This time he had a pleasant surprise — the figure was female. Her voice was low and husky.

'It is nice to see you awake at last, Sergeant.'

'Thank you, nurse, it's very nice to see you.'

'You must be feeling better.'

'I feel rough but it's good to be alive. I'm hungry, any chance of something to eat?'

'I'll see what the doctor says, he's due here shortly.

She lowered the bed rail and helped him into a sitting position and as she did so the doctor came down the ward towards them.

'He says he's hungry, doctor,' said the nurse.

'Okay, nurse, feed the man and let's get him back on his feet. We'll need that bed in a couple of days when we reach Manila.'

'Manila!' exclaimed Jim.

'Yes, the war has moved on in the last week. Now, let me check your pulse and your temperature.'

He tucked the thermometer under Jim's tongue and took his wrist to check his pulse. Releasing the wrist he picked up the chart from the end of the bed and made a note. He raised an eyebrow when he inspected the temperature reading and looked down at Jim.

'Is this your first bout of malaria, soldier?' he said.

'It's the first that had been called that but I've had other attacks. I only had aspirin to treat myself with.'

'Where was your medic?'

'He was dead, sir.'

'I see. Where were you when you first had one of these attacks?'

'On an island off the coast of Malaya.'

'Is that why they call you Sergeant Crusoe?' He pointed above Jim's head to the sign that had been attached to his door at the atoll.

Jim craned his head round and looked up at the sign.

'I can't get away from that name,' he said.

'Right, Sergeant Crusoe, I'm not happy with your temperature so you'll have to stay where you are for now. You can start back on normal food and drink but take it easy, you're not fit yet.'

'Yes, sir.'

Then turning to the nurse he told her to remove the drip and start the patient on a recovery diet. Then he nodded to Jim and walked briskly away. The nurse then left and returned shortly afterwards with a metal dish, cotton wool and a plaster strip. She removed the drip connection from the back of Jim's hand then used cotton wool and plaster to stop the bleeding. As she worked she talked.

'Your friend Chuck told me all about you,' she said. 'We don't get too many English sharpshooters in here.'

'He told me he was going to get me a date with a nurse but I didn't think I'd have to go this far to get one.'

'From what I was told you've done enough to deserve more than one date.'

'Good Lord, what did he say?'

She stood up then and picked up the dish again.

'My boyfriend's a flyer,' she said turning away and walking off down the ward.

'I'll be back in a minute with some food,' she called.

A few minutes later when she returned he was fast asleep again, she smiled and turned away, leaving him to carry on sleeping.

Two days later he was back on his feet. He still felt weak and unsteady but he was definitely on the way to full recovery. The ward was filling up with injured soldiers, sailors and airmen. As soon as the ship anchored a steady stream of ill and injured began to be ferried out to her. Jim was beginning to feel in the way and the doctor agreed with him.

'We'll have to get you back to your unit, Sergeant,' he said when he paid his ward rounds.

'I'm it, sir. The rest are either dead or captured.'

'I see, well we need the bed so we'll have to find you somewhere else to go.'

Half an hour later one of the male ward orderlies walked up to his bed and lifted down the Sergeant Crusoe sign.

'C'mon, Sarge,' he drawled, 'you're bunking in with me for a while. The Doc needs your bed. Grab your gear.'

'Where is it?'

'It's in a locker at the end of the ward. We'll pick it up as we go.'

When the locker was opened and Jim lifted out his pack and his rifle the orderly exclaimed in surprise.

'Lordy, Lordy, Lordy — you're not supposed to have guns on here. This is a hospital ship.'

'Well I won't tell anyone if you won't.'

'Wait there,' said the orderly. 'I'll find something to hide it in.'

He returned a few minutes later with a hospital dressing gown and wrapped it round the rifle.

'That'll do for now,' he said. 'Now follow me.'

Jim followed him as he led the way down two decks and finally opened the door of a cabin. There were four bunks but only one was obviously in use; the others had bedding neatly piled on top.

'Help yourself,' said the orderly pointing to the bunks on the opposite side of the cabin to his. 'Use either of those bunks and lockers.'

'Thanks, by the way what do I call you?'

'Everybody calls me Ellis; it's short for Elliott. Now before I get back to work the showers and bathrooms are at the end of the corridor to the right and the messroom's the other way. It's twenty-four hour messing so if you're hungry just wander along and grab a plate.'

He opened the door and stepped out

into the corridor then looked back round the door and said, 'There's a library and other stuff next to the messroom if you're interested.'

Jim stowed his gear and tested out the bunk before investigating the bathrooms, messroom and library. He then looked for a way out onto the deck. He found a cross passage with watertight doors that he could open. When he stepped out onto the deck the heat and humidity hit him like a wall. He hadn't realised that the ship had some form of cooling that kept the wards and cabins at an acceptable temperature. In no time at all his shirt was soaked in sweat so he did not stay outside too long. He could see that they were anchored in a bay with many other ships around them. It appeared to him that many of the ships from the atoll had moved to that anchorage.

Moving back to the library he found a selection of forces newspapers and tried to bring himself back up to date with the events in both the European sector and the Pacific one. Having been in virtual isolation for three years or so he was so far out of date that most of the places and battles mentioned were a mystery to him. He was surprised to learn that the British were driving the Japanese forces back in Burma largely because he had no idea that the Japanese were there in the first place. While he had been fighting his own little war it was obvious to him from what he was reading that great events had taken place world wide. He sat back and closed his eyes and slept almost at once, the papers he had been reading slid from his hands to the floor.

For the next four days he did little more than eat, read and sleep with the occasional chat to whoever happened to be in the library-cum-restroom at the same time as him. He found by chance that mail could be sent from the ship so he wrote a letter to his sister and hoped that it would somehow find her through one route or another. He considered writing to the British army but he had no idea who to write to. The Australian major had made contact for him but that contact was now lost so he had no idea just what to do. Just when he was wondering what to do with himself his roommate made a suggestion.

'How are you feeling now, Sarge?' he asked.

'Fit and raring to go,' Jim replied.

'Go where?'

'I've no idea.'

'Would you like to help with the patients?'

'I wouldn't know what to do but I am willing to help if you think I can do anything useful.'

'Can you write?'

'Yes.'

'There are several patients who want letters writing to their folks but we haven't time to do it. If I ask the senior nursing officer if you're allowed in the wards would you do the writing?'

'Okay, Ellis, I'd be glad to do something useful.'

Two days later Jim found himself collecting paper, envelopes and pens from the ship's padre. He was then escorted to a ward full of convalescent soldiers and marines. Some were fit enough to sit up in bed whilst others were laid prone. The padre gave Jim a list of the men who required his help then excused himself by saying, 'I'm sorry that I have to leave you to it, Sergeant, but I've got my hands full elsewhere. I'll try to catch up with you later.'

Jim nodded and turned towards the first of the men on his list. He did not know the nature of the injuries of the patients but the first man lay prone with his eyes heavily bandaged. Jim sat down in the chair positioned by the bed. The name on his list simply said Todd.

'Good morning, Todd. I'm Jim. I understand you want a letter written, I'm here to help you with it.'

'You're a Limey,' said Todd.

'Yes, I'm English and a soldier like you. Who would like me to write to?'

'My mother and my girl, tell them I'm blind and no bloody use to anyone anymore. Tell Sue to find another man.'

'One letter or two? Your mother may be able to break the news gently to Sue if we just write one.'

'Okay, one letter to my folks, Ma will see Sue if you ask her to.'

He gave Jim the address and Jim went back to the library to compose the letter. Before he left the ward however, he checked with the ward nurse that Todd was indeed blind. She told him that Todd would be returning to a military hospital in the USA for further treatment on his eyes and that there was some hope that sight could be restored in one eye.

'Does he know this?' Jim asked.

'Yes, he was told yesterday.'

'He's just told me to tell his family that he's blind.'

'Don't tell them that for goodness sake, give them some hope.'

Jim sat writing and rewriting the letter until he felt it was about right. He took it back to the ward and read it to Todd. He wrote:-

Dear Mrs Sullivan,

My name is Jim Bullock, I'm a British soldier and Todd has asked to write to you because he cannot do so at the moment. He has been injured and his eyes are damaged, that's why I'm writing for him. He is safe on board a

hospital ship and will soon be trans-
ferred to a military hospital back in the
States for further treatment. He sends
his love to you and to Sue. Please let
Sue see this letter. I cannot tell you just
where we are but you will probably
know from news reports.

    Yours truly,
    James Bullock, Sergeant.

Todd reached out and gripped Jim's
hand.

'Thank you, Jim, I'm glad you changed
it for me.' He then called out to anyone
else who was listening. 'Hey, you guys,
Jim here might be a Limey but he writes
great letters.'

Jim wrote six more letters on a similar
theme for other injured soldiers on that
ward. None of the others had eye injuries
but hand and arm wounds prevented
them writing their own letters. There was
one exception, a young soldier called Josh
who asked Jim to take two letters from his
locker. Both were addressed to Josh but
were unopened.

'Please read them to me, Jim, I never

learned how to read. When I was in my unit my pal read them for me.'

Jim not only read them but wrote the replies. Todd was in the next bed and heard everything that Jim said and when the letter writing was over asked Jim if he would read to him.

'What do you want me to read?' said Jim.

'Would you find a book and read some each day?'

'Any kind of book?'

'Maybe you could find a detective story, something other than war stories.'

'Okay, I'll have a look in the library.'

Before visiting the library he asked the senior ward nurse if there was any objection to him reading to Todd on a daily basis and she was happy to let him carry on.

'What kind of books does he want?' she asked.

'He said detective stories.'

'There's a new one in the library called *Farewell my Lovely*. I've just finished it and put it back there. I think the author was called Chandler.'

Ten minutes later Jim seated himself beside Todd's bed and began to read. He'd hardly finished the first page when a soldier further down the ward shouted that he couldn't hear. The senior nurse heard what was said and asked Jim to wait while she came back. A number of the patients were now sitting beside their beds so the nurse returned with two others and they were all pushing wheel-chairs. A short time later those patients who wanted to hear Jim read were seated in a circle around him either in wheelchairs or in beds. He started again and read continuously for half an hour and only stopped when a doctor arrived to conduct his rounds.

After the doctor had gone, the book and its references to places back in the US that some of the men knew was the topic of conversation for some time. Jim read again for the next three days until he finished the book. Those sessions were such a success that on the final day even the doctor waited until Jim finished before beginning his rounds.

23

Four days after the Okinawa landings the hospital ship turned for home with every ward crammed with injured soldiers and marines. Jim went with her. His writing and reading regime continued although the amount of letter writing decreased once the patients knew that they were heading home. His reading was not confined to the one ward because his presence had been requested in other wards once those patients became classed as convalescent. He read *Farewell my Lovely* in four different wards until in the end he could almost quote it by heart. He read several others books but the one he was asked to read over and over again was a collection of First World War poetry that was owned by one of the nurses. Men who had never read or heard poetry before were seen to be so moved by some of the poems that they unashamedly wept.

Jim liked to sit out on deck in the evening enjoying the cool run of air created by the ship's speed. The hospital ship was part of a convoy of several vessels with a screen of destroyers and cruisers. He was sitting there one night when one of the nurses came and sat alongside him. He'd seen her in the wards several times but had never spoken to her when she was off duty. She smiled as she sat down.

'Do you mind if I join you?' she asked.

'Please do, you're the nurse called Coral aren't you?'

'And you are Sergeant Crusoe.'

Jim laughed. 'You do know that's not my name don't you?' he said.

'No, what is it?'

'James Bullock, Jim to you.'

'Is it true what some of the nurses say about you shooting down a Japanese Zero with just a rifle?'

'Yes, it seems a long time ago now, but it is true.'

'Do you mind if I ask you a personal question, Jim?'

'No, go ahead.'

'Are you married or do you have a girlfriend?'

'That's two questions and the answer is no to both. If I did have either I'd have forgotten what they look like after all this time.'

'Why, how long have you been out here?'

'Six or seven years since I left England, I've almost forgotten what it looks like.'

Coral gasped. 'But that can't be true surely,' she said.

'My troop left England before the war with Germany began and I haven't been home since.'

'Where are they now, your troop?'

'Dead or captured, I buried some and some of your blokes. It tends to be kind of lonely when all you have for company are graves.'

'Is that why they called you Sergeant Crusoe?'

'Yes, that's it.'

Coral glanced at her watch. 'Duty calls,' she said. 'Tomorrow night out here again?'

He smiled up at her as she got to her

feet. 'Yes, I'll be here,' he said.

She was later the following night, so late in fact it was growing dark. Jim had almost given up on her and was about to go below when she arrived. It was obvious to him immediately that she was upset, she was quiet and withdrawn and at times close to tears.

'What's wrong, Coral?' Jim asked.

'I've been on the burns ward all day, it's horrible. The smell of burnt flesh is disgusting and the boys are in terrible pain. Even though they are drugged they still flinch when you change their dressings.'

'I haven't seen that ward.'

'No, and you wouldn't be allowed in if you did.'

She was quiet then for some minutes and Jim was wondering how to change the subject and cheer her up when she asked him to hug her.

'Please Jim, just one hug. I want to feel human again.'

He took her in his arms and held her close for a few minutes until he felt the tenseness go and she relaxed against him.

She lay there for a few minutes before loosening his grip and standing up.

'Dear God, Jim, you are a real tonic. I think I'll sleep now.'

He nodded and watched her go whilst wondering to himself whether he would sleep after such a close encounter with the opposite sex.

The following day started with a sombre announcement — the death of President Roosevelt. The announcement continued with the bald statement that he was to be succeeded by Harry S. Truman. 'The king is dead, long live the king,' thought Jim as he sat drinking coffee in the messroom. He looked around at fellow diners and apart from the odd one none of them seemed surprised by the message. Perhaps he'd been ill for some time, he thought.

Before he'd finished his coffee a second announcement got much more attention from everyone in the messroom. It said that the ship would be stopping for some hours whilst the engineers worked on a damaged bearing in the engineroom. Escorting destroyers would remain with

them until the repairs were finished but the bulk of the convoy would proceed without them. Stopping was a dangerous thing to do because there was the possibility that enemy submarines were in the area. The ship did have large red crosses on each side to indicate that it was a hospital ship but experience showed that such indicators had been ignored by fanatics in the past.

The silence when the engine stopped was unnerving. People walked quietly and talked in whispers fully aware that any undue noise could attract the attention of an unseen enemy vessel. Many of those off duty stood by the rails out on the deck and some of them carried lifejackets. Then when a series of loud clangs from the engineroom rang through the hull many silently added a prayer for good measure. It took five hours for the repair to be completed and there was an almost audible sigh of relief throughout the ship when the engine began to beat again. About two hours later another announcement informed them that the repairs had been temporary and that further work on the engines would be carried out on arrival in Pearl Harbour in a few days time.

That evening it was growing dark when Coral moved to Jim's side. She remained standing and took his hand.

'Ellis is on night duty,' she said.

'That's right,' replied Jim.

'Give me five minutes and meet me there.'

'Where?'

'Your bunk.'

She turned and walked quickly away. Jim sat stunned by her proposal for a couple of minutes before checking his watch and watching the second hand crawl round the dial. Could she have really said that? he thought.

Five minutes later he entered the darkened cabin and slid the bolt across the inside of the door. The reading lamp above the bunk clicked on revealing Coral lying naked in his bunk. He undressed with shaking hands and slid into the bunk beside her. There was little in the way of preliminaries, both desperately needing the comfort that the other could give.

Their initial lovemaking was urgent, almost desperate in nature but eventually, their need sated, they lay quietly in each others arms.

'Better?' Coral asked.

'I couldn't have dreamed of this,' Jim whispered.

'I did dream,' she replied. 'Now out you get and let me get dressed. You'd better get dressed as well and check the alleyway is clear before I leave.'

She dressed quickly and motioned him towards the door. He slid the bolt quietly back and inched the door open in order to listen before checking the alleyway. She pointed to the used condoms on the cabin floor and mouthed the words 'your problem' before easing her way past him. Her rubber-soled shoes barely made a sound as she hurried away and at the end of the alleyway she turned and blew him a silent kiss. A few minutes later Jim walked out onto the lee side and quietly dropped the condoms into the sea.

Later while he was dozing he remembered that he had asked her at one point the question 'Why me?' Her answer had been simple. 'You were kind to me when I desperately needed it and I felt your need at the same time.' When he turned over to sleep he realised that he could still smell her on his skin and on the bed-sheets. He slept well and late.

The news that the ship would be stopping in Pearl Harbour for repairs led to several calls for Jim to write more letters. He had to visit three different wards and as he was leaving the third with several sheets of paper in his hand he was handed another folded sheet by a nurse. He assumed it was the details of another letter request but when he finally opened it, it read, 'night shift next four nights, sorry.' There was no signature.

When the ship entered Pearl Harbour three days later her rails were lined with off-duty members of the crew, nursing staff and walking wounded. They gazed in silence at the wrecks of warships that still remained where they had been sunk by the sneak attack in nineteen-forty-two. Two tugs joined them and eased the ship alongside a jetty and a gangway was immediately slung into place. A dozen or so uniformed men and others in overalls stood impatiently waiting for the gangway to be secured. As soon as it was they hurried aboard. Jim stayed by the rail to watch the port activity and was surprised to hear his name announced on the tannoy.

'Sergeant James Bullock is requested to report to the commander's office immediately.'

When Jim got there the commander told him to collect his gear because he was leaving the ship.

'Where am I going, sir?' Jim asked.

'I do not know, Sergeant, but there is a car waiting for you on the jetty, you are urgently needed elsewhere.'

Jim saluted and turned to leave but turned back when the commander spoke again.

'By the way, Sergeant, your work amongst the patients has been noted and I shall be forwarding a report to your people. Thank you for your efforts on our behalf.'

'Thank you, sir,' replied Jim, saluting again.

He collected his gear and said goodbye to whoever he saw as he made his way to the gangway. One of the walking wounded who had listened to his readings stopped him and asked where he was going. Jim shrugged and said he did not know.

'You lucky buggers are going home,' he said. 'I'm told I'm needed urgently elsewhere. I don't like the sound of it.'

'Good luck, Sarge,' said the patient gripping his hand. 'We'll miss you.'

There were several official-looking cars on the jetty and Jim had no idea which one was waiting for him. He was about to work his way down the line asking at each one when a large Buick pulled out of line and stopped alongside him.

'Are you Sergeant Bullock?' asked the driver.

'That's me.'

'Hop in, Sarge, they're already waiting for you.'

'Who are?'

'The brass, you know the high flyers in the air force.'

'What do they want with me?'

'God knows, Sarge, I don't.'

A few minutes later the car pulled up in front of a large white building. There were armed sentries outside the main door and they sprang smartly to attention as Jim entered. A messenger was waiting for him and led him along a corridor and straight into a large office. There were four men in the room and they all stood when Jim entered. Jim was taken aback because all four men were senior officers. Jim started to salute but the most senior-looking man walked towards him and held out his hand. Jim took it and had his hand briskly shaken.

'Are you known as Sergeant Crusoe?' said the officer.

'I have been given that nickname, sir.'

'Did you witness an American aircraft shot down off Malaya?'

'Yes, sir.'

The officer pointed to a large aircraft recognition chart attached to the wall.

'Can you see the type of aircraft up there?'

Jim walked over to the chart.

'It had two engines,' he said as he

studied the chart.

'Like this one?' prompted the officer pointing to one outline.

'No, sir the cockpit looks wrong. It was more like that one up there.'

That caused a stir amongst the officers and Jim heard one say that the reports definitely said that it crashed in the sea.

'Can you give us anything else to help us identify it, Sergeant?'

'I can tell you the pilot's names — they were Abbott and Warren. I buried them.'

'Jesus, it is the one,' exclaimed the officer to his fellows. He turned back to Jim then and gestured to a chair. 'Sit down, Sergeant and tell us all you know.'

Jim did as requested and went over the story one more time. He was interrupted now and again by questions from one or the other of the officers.

'You said that you shot down the Zero, what with?'

'This,' replied Jim holding up his rifle. 'I killed the pilot because he was idiotic enough to come back at slow speed to gloat over the men he'd just killed. I hit him in the temple with my first shot.'

'Then what happened?'

'The plane's wing clipped the water and the whole thing cartwheeled into rocks and burst into flames.'

'Did you remove anything from our plane?'

'Yes, maps and a Very pistol.'

'Is the plane still there?'

'It was about a month ago. It was lying on the sand with the tailplane in the sea.'

'Are there any Japanese troops there?'

'Not when I left but they do visit now and again.'

'How did you get away from there?'

'Submarine pick-up.'

'Have you any idea of the depth of water off the beach?'

'No sir but there was a visit from a Japanese warship once, a vessel about the size of a small destroyer. The depth is shown on marine charts, we had one when we first went there.'

One of the officers spread a large-scale map of the Malay Peninsula on one of the desks and asked Jim to point out the island. Jim pointed it out but even on the large-scale map it looked minute.

While this was going on he could hear another officer on the telephone requesting marine charts of the area. A discussion broke out on the best way to get there and surface vessels and submarines were rejected in favour of going in by air. Jim heard B29s and PBYs mentioned but the terms meant nothing to him but from the nature of the discussion he gathered that speed was of the essence.

Eventually a corporal turned up bearing a selection of marine charts and Jim was able to point out the beach and the position of the wrecked aircraft.

'We could land a PBY there okay,' said one.

The senior man then took over.

'Okay, B29 from here to the Philippines and a PBY with escorts from there, agreed?'

There were nods all round.

'Good, I suggest four men with the sergeant here as guide. If you agree, Russ, go and get your men organised ready for an early morning departure.'

He turned to Jim.

'Have you flown before, Sergeant?'

'Yes, sir, on a brief flight.'

'Well your flight tomorrow will be long and boring I'm afraid. Oh, yes, before I forget, your people do know about this.'

'My people, sir?'

'The British military authorities here in Hawaii.'

'May I ask a question, sir?'

'Of course.'

'Could you arrange for those authorities to know that I haven't been paid since nineteen-forty-two?'

The officer burst out laughing before finally spluttering, 'Consider it done, Sergeant.'

'Thank you, sir.'

Jim was escorted across to an accommodation block alongside the airfield and allocated a room for the night. He was shown where the messroom was and joined the corporal who had escorted him in drinking a cup of coffee. The corporal introduced himself as Charlie, Chas to his friends, before asking if he'd heard correctly whilst standing waiting for Jim.

'Did you really ask the colonel to sort out your pay?'

'Sure, I'm getting fed up of being told that my people agree to things for me when the only pay I've had in three years is ten dollars. Anyway I didn't know he was a colonel.'

'Where are your officers?'

'I've no idea. I buried my last one three years ago.'

Chas finished his coffee, got to his feet and walked away chuckling about a sergeant who can get a colonel to sort out his pay. The last thing Jim heard was Chas saying, 'The guys will never believe it.'

24

I left it until eight o'clock that evening to dial the telephone number that I'd been given. At one time earlier in the day I'd considered ignoring Silver but when I thought just what he could do to Jim's friends I decided to go through with the call and the subsequent meeting. I wanted to see the man and tell him to his face that there was no way I was going to help him. Mind you, I must confess that I was curious to see just what he wanted of me.

The telephone rang only twice before it was picked up. Then a voice said, 'Who?'

'Luke Sharp,' I replied.

'Sutton Bank car park eleven a.m. Friday, come alone,' said the voice before the connection was cut.

I quickly noted down what I'd heard before going out to the car for the road atlas. When I got back Jim was reading the note.

'Are you going?' he asked.

'Yes, I think I'll be safe enough in a public car park at that time in the morning.'

'Probably,' he replied. 'The police will know where you are,' he continued pointing at the telephone. 'I'm going to that reunion on Thursday, I may stay overnight.'

'Do you need the car?'

'No, I'll get one from the garage; they usually have plenty of spare courtesy cars.'

I nodded and opened the atlas at the road map I would need. I knew Sutton Bank car park but I had never had to drive there from the village before so I had to sort out a route. By the time I looked up again Jim had gone back to his shed. I marked the page I wanted and put the atlas to one side knowing that I wouldn't need it for a couple of days then returned to my typing.

★ ★ ★

It was still dark the next morning when Jim was called. He had a quick shower, an

356

equally quick breakfast and was still finishing his coffee when the car arrived to collect him. The drive to the aircraft was conducted in silence with both the driver and Jim busy with their own thoughts. Virtually the only sign of activity on the airfield centred on the B29, the engines were ticking over with a low rumble and there were lights in the cockpit and in the open doorways. Jim was the last to arrive and he was helped aboard by one of the ground crew. The four members of the recovery party were already seated and Jim was directed to a seat beside them. All five were seated along one side of the plane with their backs to the inner fuselage. The co-pilot came down from the cockpit and checked that they were safely secured before takeoff.

'It's going to be a long flight fellahs so make yourselves as comfortable as you can. We'll have a fighter escort from here to halfway then we'll pick up another from Wake. The crew will get you food and drinks when they've got time. We'll be off in a minute.'

He moved back to his place in the cockpit as the outer door was slammed shut and secured. The engines increased in pitch and the plane gathered pace down the runway before lifting clear of the ground. The wheels bumped lightly twice then they were fully airborne and rising steadily into the dawn sky.

A day and a half later after two long and boring flights the PBY Catalina flew low over the bay that Jim knew so well. The pilots were checking for any underwater obstructions before making the landing. The aircraft made two slow runs over the water before finally coming into land on it. The pilot taxied his craft close into the shore so the five-man recovery party only had to wade into the shore. As far as Jim could see little had changed. There was more driftwood and the aircraft wreck had sunk a little further into the sand but other than that everything seemed the same.

The four men allocated the job of recovering the mystery object from the wreck hurried off carrying various tools. While that was going on the pilot turned the aircraft ready for a quick getaway and kept the engines turning over for the same purpose. Jim sat cross-legged on the sand with his rifle across his legs. He couldn't really understand why he was there; he'd told the officers all he knew before leaving Pearl Harbour and it was blatantly obvious that he was not needed now. Fifteen minutes after the landing the four men came staggering back along the beach bearing the item they'd removed from the wreck. Jim helped them to lift it into the plane and secure it in the cradle that had been specially fitted for it.

Suddenly before any of them had got themselves strapped into their seats again the engines roared into life and the plane surged forward. Jim and the rest scrambled to their seats to a chorus of urgent shouting from the crew. The Catalina bounced several times before finally lifting from the water and attempting to gain height. A crew member staggered past shouting as he did so.

'Hang on everybody, enemy ship coming at us.'

He'd barely finished when several holes

were punched through the fuselage and red-hot metal splinters whistled through the air inside. The man beside Jim screamed as one of the splinters found a home. The plane banked sharply as the pilot tried to throw the gunners on the ship off but a second stream of holes appeared and this time it was Jim's turn to scream. Something tore into his back and his arm and the pain hit him like a lightning strike. He heard another shout this time declaring that they were clear then a member of the crew scrambled towards him. A hand tore at his trousers followed by a sharp jab in his leg and he felt himself mentally floating towards oblivion. The last thing he heard was a distant voice shout, 'Two dead, two injured.'

He vaguely remembered being lifted from the aircraft but that was all he could remember for days. When he finally began to take some notice of his whereabouts he realised that he was onboard another hospital ship. For days he drifted in and out of consciousness and when he was awake he seemed unable to lift his head from the pillow. When he attempted to move his limbs felt extremely heavy and it seemed easier to simply close his eyes again and go back to sleep.

By the time he was told that he would be moving from the ship to a hospital on the shore the various drips and drains had been removed and apart from small dressings on his back and arm he was approaching bodily fitness. However, he could not make his limbs work properly and his head still felt like a ton weight on his shoulders. All he wanted to do was lie back and sleep, his body refused to respond as it used to. Nurses and doctors repeatedly told him that he was fit enough to walk but he couldn't manage it.

He remained in a hospital near San Diego for some weeks but didn't improve at all. Eventually a doctor told him that his war was over and he was being sent home. He travelled across America in a hospital train and across the Atlantic on a British ship with many other wartime casualties. He was only vaguely aware that some of his fellow passengers were freed prisoners of war. The fact that both the war in Europe and the one against Japan were over had completely passed him by. He remained in his half-awake state and was finally transferred to a convalescent hospital in his native Yorkshire in the hope that visits from friends and family would aid his recovery.

It was early in November nineteen-forty-five when he finally began the road to full recovery. An unexpected visitor proved to be the catalyst. Jim was seated by his bed when his visitor was shown in and initially he showed little interest in the stranger. His interest was kicked into action when the man held out his hand and introduced himself.

'My name is Fitzroy,' he said, 'Colonel Raymond Fitzroy.'

Jim took his hand and stared at the man in front of him.

'Fitzroy . . . Fitzroy,' muttered Jim uncertainly. 'Captain . . . not Colonel.'

'Captain Fitzroy was my son,' said the colonel.

'I buried him . . . I buried . . . ' Jim burst into tears at that point.

The colonel waited for the tears to

subside then asked another question.

'Where did you bury him, Sergeant?'

Jim wiped his eyes on his shirt sleeve then looked at his visitor again.

'What, what did you say?'

'Where did you bury Captain Fitzroy?'

'Beach . . . beach . . . island.' Jim shook his head and wiped his eyes again before descending into a bout of tears once more.

The ward sister came across then and led the visitor away.

'I'm sorry, colonel, I cannot allow you any more time today,' she said. 'Try again tomorrow.'

The colonel stayed in a nearby hotel and visited Jim twice a day for three days each time getting a little more from Jim. The doctor and nursing staff responsible for Jim's care watched as he appeared to come out of the lethargy that had held him for so long. On the third day Jim remembered Captain Fitzroy's notebook and harried the nursing staff until his pack was unearthed. The ward sister refused to let Jim have 'that dirty object' in the ward so he took it into the dayroom and opened it there. He was sitting holding the captain's notebook when the colonel arrived.

Colonel Fitzroy could see immediately that Jim was more alive, more capable of dealing with his questions but he allowed Jim to set the pace. The two men talked for almost three hours and as they talked Jim's confidence grew. He explained to the colonel how his son had died and how he had buried him on the narrow beach. In passing over the captain's wallet and notebook Jim told of how he had used the notebook to keep a record of the dead and missing soldiers.

'That may be the only record of those men,' said Jim. 'The army must be able to view it.'

'Yes, I understand, Sergeant. Although I am retired I have been in touch with a department in the War Office that deals with missing soldiers and they want to interview you. Would you be willing to talk to someone if I bring them in tomorrow?'

'Yes, sir.'

'Good, and remember, Sergeant, that

department may have news of some of your missing troop.'

After the Colonel left, Jim began to go through the contents of his pack refreshing his memory of the members of the troop that he knew were dead and others that were still missing. He opened Simmo's sketchbook and as he turned page after page the memories flooded back. He missed his lunch and one of the nurses discovered him in the middle of the afternoon still searching through the pack. She sat beside him and asked him how he felt.

'I'm beginning to feel alive again,' he replied.

'Good, I'll tell Doctor Pearson, he missed you when he did his rounds. Do you feel alive enough to read your mail?'

'Mail?'

'Yes, there are several letters that you've ignored for weeks.'

'Where are they?'

'In the cupboard by your bed.'

Jim looked up at her then and for the first time in weeks saw her as a woman rather than a nurse.

'What's your name?'

'I'm Susan, Sergeant.'

'I'm not a sergeant anymore. I'm Jim, James Bullock.'

'Then who is Sergeant Crusoe?'

'Dear God, has that name followed me here?'

'It's the name on some of your letters. Can you tell me about it?'

'I'll try,' he said.

He talked for fifteen minutes giving Susan a brief extract of what happened to him and how he came to be called Sergeant Crusoe. She sat quietly listening and raised a finger to her lips without Jim seeing her when a fellow nurse peered round the door behind him. They were finally interrupted when Doctor Pearson moved quietly into the room and sat beside them.

'How are you feeling, Sergeant?' the doctor asked.

Jim tapped the side of his head and said, 'I'm coming alive again up here, Doc.'

'Good, well don't overdo it. Come and

see me in the morning before the colonel gets here.'

'Yes, sir.'

Unbeknown to Jim, Doctor Pearson had discussed his case with Colonel Fitzroy when he'd seen the effect that the colonel's visits had on him. Later that day he talked to the nurse, Susan, and listened to all that she had gleaned in her exchanges with Jim that afternoon. Everyone concerned could see how he was suddenly coming out of the torpor that had beset him for so long but feared a setback if they rushed him too much.

That night the doctor feared that such a setback had occurred. Jim was found in the dayroom sobbing uncontrollably with a book and a letter in his hands. Despite the efforts of the night nurse he could not be consoled and eventually she called out the duty doctor. Seeing the state that Jim was in he led him back to his bed and gave him an injection. The nurse placed the book and the letter on Jim's side table and wondered how it had caused him so much anguish. Then she read the address on the envelope that they had come in. It read, *Acting Sergeant James Bullock (Sergeant Crusoe), C/O The War Office, London, England*. It had been the first item of mail that Jim had opened. The rest still lay unopened.

The following morning Jim was quiet and subdued at first but after eating a hearty breakfast he seemed to come round and sat quietly reading the letter that had upset him so much the previous evening. As soon as he read the night nurse's report Doctor Pearson came to see him.

'I hear that you had a bad time last night, Jim. Can you tell me about it?'

'It was this, Doc, a simple little letter that means so much,' said Jim handing the letter over. 'Read it, Doc, and look at the flyleaf of the book.'

San Diego, July 1945.
Hi Jim,

We were all sorry to hear that you'd gone back to the war. The boys asked me to send you the enclosed book. It has done the rounds of the wards and has been signed by all those you helped, including me.

Love Coral,
Farewell my Lovely.

The book carried fifty-four signatures but it was the one at the top of the page that had really tipped the balance emotionally for Jim the night before, it was Todd's and appended to it were the words 'I can see, Sarge, I can see.'

'Every one of those men was seriously injured and I read that book about five times in different wards aboard the hospital ship,' said Jim. 'Todd started it by asking me to write a letter to his mother and his girl. I wrote and read for my supper, Doc.'

'What were you doing aboard there?'

'Recovering from malaria.'

'There's nothing in your record about malaria, Jim.'

'No, that came before I was injured. I had three or four bouts while I was stranded. The last time was just after I was rescued by the submarine.'

'I'd like to sit in when the colonel

comes this morning, do you mind?'

'No, Doc, I don't mind at all.'

★   ★   ★

I was still sitting reading over what I'd typed when Jim came into the room.

'Have you still got that copy of *Farewell my Lovely*?' I asked.

'Try the bookcase,' he said.

It was still there, some of the signatures had faded but they were all still legible.

25

When Colonel Fitzroy arrived he brought with him a woman in civilian clothes who he introduced as Miss Williams. Doctor Pearson arranged for the four of them to assemble in a staff common room equipped with comfortable armchairs and side tables. It was the doctor who started the day's proceedings by stating that if at any time he thought that Jim was in trouble he'd bring the meeting to a premature close. He then handed over to the colonel.

'Sergeant Bullock, Miss Williams has a record of your troop up until you sailed from Kota Bahru. What we would like you to do is tell us in your own words what happened to you after that time,' said the colonel.

Jim talked steadily explaining how Captain Fitzroy decided that the small island was of little use to them and how they moved on to the big one. No one interrupted him until he came to the departure of the first boat with the injured men. He listed all those in the boat although he couldn't remember all their names.

'There were the injured men, Sergeant Browning and the radio operator, the other radio operator, one of the drivers and two of the beach crew and of course the boat's crew, one of the radio men was called Bill but I can't remember his mate's name.'

'That checks with my list,' said Miss Williams, 'most of them reached Australia.'

Jim looked startled. 'How . . . when?' he exclaimed.

'They were picked up by a merchant ship and landed in Darwin. Apparently after leaving you they lost the boat's propeller and drifted for nearly two weeks. Sergeant Browning died, the rest eventually recovered.'

'Where are they now?'

'I'm afraid I don't have that information, sorry,' she said.

Jim sat in a stunned silence for a short

while before looking up and smiling.

'My mate Simmo's still alive,' he exclaimed.

'He was, Sergeant, we don't know if he still is,' cautioned the colonel. 'Can you carry on?'

When Jim listed those in the second boat Miss Williams intervened.

'Go through the list again please, Sergeant,' she said.

'Well of the original troop there was Captain Fitzroy and Fred the medic, then there was the last of the drivers, the interpreter and two of the camp crew,' said Jim.

'You said the last of the drivers, surely there were three of them,' she said.

'Oh yes, that's right there were. We buried Tim Simons on the beach. He died of a fever, probably malaria.'

'What happened to that boat?' She asked.

Jim went over the horror of the attack describing how the aircraft had destroyed the boat then returned and machine-gunned those in the water. After his halting account of his attempt to save Captain Fitzroy, Doctor Pearson called for a break and one of the nursing staff brought in refreshments.

In order to refresh his memory Jim had been using the sketches in Simmo's pad in order to put names to faces. Whilst they were busy with the refreshments Miss Williams asked to see it and Jim passed it over to her. Ignoring her cup of tea she thumbed through the pages asking Jim about the faces and events depicted. When she reached the page showing Jim and Sylvia dancing she asked Jim who it was.

'That's Sylvia, one of the passengers,' he replied.

'And the man?' she asked.'

'Me.'

She smiled and raised an eyebrow at him but made no further comment. On a later page Simmo had drawn head and shoulder impressions of most of the original troop and that helped Jim identify most of them. When it came to Dai, George and four of the others Jim's response changed. Everyone immediately registered the fact that here was something that they hadn't touched on so far.

'Those six and two of the beach crew were killed or captured by the Japanese while I was attempting to save Captain Fitzroy,' he said in a harsh tone.

'Killed or captured?' repeated the colonel.

Jim tried twice to answer him before finally getting the words out in an even harsher tone.

'A Japanese warship got to the beach before I returned. Dai had been shot several times whilst George had been beheaded. The others were missing.'

There was a stunned silence then. Jim's face was drawn and white and there was a hint of a tear in his eyes.

Doctor Pearson looked at the colonel and shook his head but before he could say anything Jim started again.

'The next time that ship came I killed the bastard with the sword and half a dozen of his men,' he said, his voice shaking with emotion. 'Then the buggers bombed me, thought they had me but I'm still here.'

He was silent for a while and picked up his cup with a visibly shaking hand but managed to drink without spilling his tea. That seemed to calm him and he looked across at Miss Williams.

'Sorry, Miss, I didn't mean to swear,' he said.

She smiled back at him. 'I've heard worse, Sergeant, it goes with the job.'

'I think that will do for today,' Doctor Pearson said in a quiet tone.

'What about the commendations?' Miss Williams asked.

'Leave them and the rest until tomorrow, you can see that Jim's upset, I don't want him having another bad night.'

The following day Jim went through all the many events that happened to him while he was alone on the island without any interruption from the others. When he came to the arrival of the Australian major and the two Americans, Miss Williams spoke for the first time that day.

'I was beginning to wonder how you got away from the island,' she said.

'When we left on the submarine I never guessed that I'd go back twice more,' Jim replied.

'We have information on those return

visits from both the Australian army and the Americans. In addition we have received three commendations from those same sources,' she continued.

'Commendations?'

'Yes, the first is for your actions in destroying a Japanese aircraft and for looking after the two dead American fliers. The second for your part in the action when one of the Americans was injured and the third for your help in leading the American party to their downed aircraft, when you were injured. There is also a letter of gratitude from the staff of a certain hospital ship. You've been a busy man, Sergeant.'

'Too busy to look after your own health,' said Doctor Pearson.

'Everybody keeps calling me Sergeant but I was only acting in that capacity,' muttered Jim.

'You were promoted in the field and that promotion has since been confirmed. Your pay should reflect that.' Miss Williams smiled as she spoke. 'We also have messages from Australia and from a certain Air Force colonel asking us to sort your pay out.'

'Good grief, he actually did pass on the message,' said Jim. 'How do you know all this, Miss Williams?'

'I'm actually a serving officer, Sergeant, but we thought it would be better if I left the uniform in the hotel. We didn't want you put off by officialdom.'

'What will happen to me now?'

'That is up to the doctor, when he declares you fit we'll be informed and I'll contact you again. In the meantime decide if you want to stay in the army. You are currently on the list for demobilisation.'

'Thank you, you've given me a lot to think about.'

After they'd all gone Jim went back to the cupboard beside his bed. Taking out the bundle of letters he walked down to the day room and found a quiet corner to settle in while he went through his mail. Three were short but chatty letters from his sister dated over three years ago, letters that had failed to reach him because of the onset of the Pacific war. The fourth bore American stamps and proved to be from Coral. She had heard that he had been injured and wished him a swift recovery and congratulated him on his being recommended for a medal. The recommendation was news to him and he smiled at the thought of him wearing an American medal. He decided she'd got the wrong information from somewhere.

Two letters remained and both were in official-looking brown envelopes. The first was from a solicitor in York and the name of the firm sounded familiar. He couldn't place it at first until he thought of the death of his old employer. The writer asked him to contact them when he returned from the war. They had news that may be of advantage to him. He lay that letter aside and opened the final one. The news it contained came as an almost physical blow, his sister and her family had been killed in an air raid three years earlier. The letter dropped to the floor as his sobs resounded around the room. Susan, the nurse, was alerted by another patient and came in to sit beside him. She made no attempt to speak but he picked up the letter and passed it to her. She quickly read it then took his hand in hers.

'I'm sorry, Jim, we didn't know about this,' she said.

'That was my only family and I never got to say goodbye.'

'I know how you feel, Jim, I lost my husband on D-Day. He never got to see our daughter.'

'I'm sorry, Susan, when things like this happen you tend to think you're the only one feeling hurt, you forget others have had the same experience.'

After Susan returned to her duties in the ward Jim thought about the contents of his letters. His sister and her family were buried in York, the solicitor was also in York and the army barracks where he could collect his pay was also there. He had to go there so he went to see the doctor for permission to leave the hospital.

'I'm not sure you should go yet, Sergeant. You haven't been out of the hospital since you arrived. I'd like you to go out to Driffield or Beverley to see how you manage first. How would you feel if I arranged for such a visit first?'

'Okay, Doc, I would like to see the outside world again.'

'Tomorrow?'

'Yes, the sooner the better. I do have a problem though, I haven't any outdoor clothes.'

'I'll give the Red Cross lady a ring, she'll bring something in for you. She's used to us calling for such assistance.'

The following day Jim was driven into Driffield wearing his newly acquired civilian clothes. His driver was Susan the nurse, she was to be his escort on his first day out. On the way she began to prepare him for what to expect as a civilian if he chose to leave the army. There were things that he would need such as a civilian identity card and ration books and so on. When they reached the town Susan took his arm as they strolled along looking in shop windows. They had a cup of tea in a small café and Susan asked how he felt.

'I feel unbalanced,' he said.

'Unbalanced?'

'Yes, it's the first time I been out without a rifle for years. I miss it.'

'Well if you want something to carry we could go and get my daughter. I live here with my mother. She looks after Sally while I'm at work.'

Jim put down his cup and smiled across the table at her. 'Yes, I'd like that,' he said.

So for the next two hours Jim, Susan and her daughter strolled around the sunny but chilly streets of Driffield. When it was time to return to the hospital Jim asked if he could drive the car but Susan said no.

'Sorry, Jim, it's the only car that the hospital owns and it's my responsibility. I had to almost sign my life away to get the loan of it today,' she said.

The next day Jim ventured out alone taking the local bus into Beverley. He walked round the town rebuilding both strength in his body and confidence in himself. That day taught him that he had a lot to do to regain his strength and it also showed him how the war had changed life in England. He came across women doing jobs that before the war were primarily for the male population and queues outside food shops that he'd never noticed before the war. Because of what he saw that day he decided that he wasn't quite ready to venture out into the world on his own. For the next two weeks he went out either by bus or train to towns in the vicinity continuing his programme of strength and confidence building. It wasn't until he went by train into Hull that he realised that there was work for him in the post-war world. The city was a wreck. Everywhere he went he saw damaged buildings, great gaps where buildings had been completely wiped out and piles of rubble awaiting clearance. The city was in dire need of builders of every kind and that included surveyors. He considered himself to be employable as a surveyor's assistant.

Jim spent Christmas 1945 in the hospital although he had Christmas dinner with Susan and her family in Driffield. He planned to leave the hospital on the second day of January and to go to York to sort out his affairs. He had already arranged an appointment with the solicitor and had decided to leave the army. Despite the fact that he didn't have a job he hoped that his back pay would keep him going until he had somewhere to live and work.

When he boarded the bus to York he still had not been discharged by the hospital but he felt his first call had to be at the army barracks. Having lived in York he knew his way around the city so en route to the barracks he visited the cemetery where his sister and her family were buried. The grave bore only a simple wooden cemetery marker but he was assured that the whole family were buried together. He stood before it for ten minutes silently remembering his sister before walking away dry-eyed.

On his arrival at the barracks he was directed to the admin office where he was initially greeted by a sergeant who asked him to wait while he checked if the adjutant was available. Ten minutes later he was escorted to the adjutant's office. Major Wiseman, the adjutant, greeted him while a smile.

'It's good to meet you at last, Sergeant,

I've heard a lot about you. What is your medical status now?'

'I'm still waiting my final clearance, sir. I hope it will be this month.'

'Have you decided whether you want to stay in the army?'

'I've decided to become a civilian again, sir.'

'Well you can't go just yet; there are a number of things to sort out including your pay.'

'What else is there?'

'Have you still got your uniform?'

'No, sir, my last uniform issue was in Singapore three or four years ago; since then I've worn mainly American army issue. I came back in a hospital ship.'

'Yes, of course, you're virtually the only army unit not to surrender to the Japanese.'

'Can one man be called a unit?'

'In your case yes, according to the Americans. They want to give you a medal and some sort of commendation. You'll have to go to London once your medical clearance comes through. Have you anywhere to stay tonight?'

'No, but I'm sure I can find some-where.'

'Right, I'll get the office to issue you a month's pay today then when you come back tomorrow I'll arrange for the balance to be paid. You'll have to draw a uniform as well.'

'Uniform, why?'

'You are still in the army, Sergeant and we want you looking your best for the Americans.'

'But I'll have to hand it back when I'm demobbed.'

'That's true, but then we'll give you a nice shiny civilian suit.'

Twenty minutes later Jim walked out of the barracks with a month's pay in his pocket. He knew he wasn't far from the solicitor's office so he decided to call there even though he hadn't made an appointment. He showed his letter to the receptionist and she took it through to an inner office. She returned within a minute and showed him through to see the solicitor.

'Good morning, Mr Bullock, it's good to see you again. You were in the army if I remember correctly.'

'Yes sir, technically I still am. I'm waiting for medical clearance.'

'So you will be leaving the army in the near future?'

'Yes, sir.'

'What will you do?'

'I'm hoping to get work with a surveyor.'

'I see, well we'd better get down to business. Do you remember Mrs Raven?'

'Yes, she was Mister Withers' housekeeper.'

'That's correct. After his death the property was sold and she went to live in her mother's old home. Now she has died and she's left you the old cottage. It is in a terrible state but with work it could be habitable again.'

'But I don't understand — why hasn't she left it to her family?'

He smiled. 'What she called her family were three cats and an old dog. She wasn't even married even though she used the married title.'

'Good grief, so I was shooting rabbits and pigeons to feed her cats.'

'Well, with rationing as it is you may have to resort to that again to feed yourself. Now, the cottage is in the village of Hutton Cranswick so if you will sign for the keys and the deeds our business is concluded.'

'Thank you, sir.'

Jim signed and accepted the keys to his property and tucked the deeds into his pocket.

'Can I sell this place if I don't want to live in it?'

'Yes, of course. You're the owner.'

Jim walked out of the office in a daze, he owned a cottage. No-one in his family had done that before. He knew of a hotel by the railway station and he decided to make that his base for the night. Having no luggage he was asked to pay for his night's accommodation in advance. He wanted to buy things like a change of underwear but as he was still a soldier he did not have a civilian clothing card and therefore had to manage with just what he was wearing.

It was after he'd eaten his evening meal that the events of the day took an even more startling turn. He was sitting in the lounge drinking his first pint of beer and listening to music provided by a trio of elderly musicians when he felt a tap on the shoulder and a female voice said, 'May I have this dance?' He looked round and saw the smiling face of Sylvia, the woman he had danced with on the voyage out from England.

26

When Jim awoke the following morning Sylvia had gone. Her scent lingered on the pillow beside him but he knew she was on her way to a new life in America. He relaxed in a hot bath until the water began to cool then strolled down to the restaurant where he enjoyed what the hotel called a hearty breakfast.

He felt like singing as he walked through the chill morning air. A sharp frost had left its mark on the gardens and trees with icicles hanging here and there from buildings and fences. Despite the cold he managed to remain cheerful until he reached the barracks. He greeted the guard at the gate with a cheerful good morning and smiled back at his retort.

'Whose bed were you in last night?'

Jim merely moved his hands in the shape of an hourglass before walking on to the admin office. Two hours later with his back pay in his inside pocket and a kitbag holding his new uniform on his shoulder he walked past the same guard.

'You're not smiling now,' said the guard.

'I will be tonight,' Jim retorted. However he knew that he'd be spending his evening sewing sergeant's stripes and other insignia onto his new uniform instead of renewing his acquaintance with Sylvia.

It took him two days to bring the uniform up to the required standard and a further day to achieve the necessary gloss on the boots. When he was finally satisfied he walked around in the boots trying to work some flexibility into the leather. He even wore them inside the hospital but in order to deaden the sound he wore a pair of thick socks over the top of them. It looked ridiculous but he was more interested in comfort than smartness at that time.

At the end of that week he went to see Doctor Pearson to ask for medical clearance. They talked for about fifteen minutes about Jim's plans for his future and whether he felt confident about living alone and coping with everyday events. The doctor seemed perfectly happy with Jim's response until he asked about the cottage that Jim was planning to live in.

'What is it like?' asked the doctor.

'I haven't actually seen it yet,' replied Jim.

'So you don't know if it is habitable?'

'No, but I'm sure I can manage.'

'It's the middle of winter, Jim, the house hasn't been lived in for years and you are proposing to live there. Go and look at it this weekend and come back and see me on Monday. In the meantime I'll get in touch with the major in York and tell him that you are fit enough to travel to London.'

'Are you giving me medical clearance?'

'Not yet. If you come back with a favourable report on the cottage I'll consider it. I may suggest that you continue living here while you knock the place into shape. After several bouts of malaria I cannot condone you moving into a cold, damp cottage in mid-winter.'

The following day Jim caught the train from Driffield to Hutton Cranswick. The weather was cold and grey with occasional short, sharp snow showers. At the station he asked the way to the cottage. At the first sight of his proposed new home his heart sank. The windows were boarded up and the garden was so overgrown that he had great difficulty at first reaching the front door. Weeds hung from the gutters and the garden fence had collapsed across the path. He fought his way to the door and when he inserted and turned the key the lock screamed in protest. It was pitch dark inside and he had to leave the door ajar to let in some light. In the kitchen he discovered a candle and using a cup as a candle holder he toured the place by candlelight.

He was pleasantly surprised to find that it was dry inside and that it was still fully furnished. Although it was described as a cottage there were three sizeable rooms downstairs, one being the living kitchen and three upstairs. There was no bathroom but there was running water in the kitchen. He discovered two oil lamps and several more candles but no sign of electric lighting. The only heating appeared to be coal fires. The hearth in the living-room was thick with bird droppings and twigs indicating that birds were nesting in the chimney. He knew that if he attempted to light a fire the room would soon fill with smoke so he abandoned that idea. Taking one of the oil lamps towards the door so he could see what he was doing he felt the swish of fuel inside. He lifted off the glass funnel, trimmed the wick and lit it and the room came to life. There was dust everywhere and cobwebs hung in corners and ceiling edges.

'Are you moving in?' said a woman's voice from the doorway.

Jim moved over to the door and found a middle-aged woman dressed in an old army greatcoat standing there.

'I'm hoping to move in soon but I've got to get out of the army first. I may be coming to clean the place up as and when I can get free days.'

'Do you need any help?'

'The first thing I need is a chimney sweep, is there one in the village?'

The woman suddenly shot out her

hand and shook his.

'I'm Doris, I live across the road. The chimney sweep is Dave Morris, he lives up the street. I used to clean for the old dear that lived here.'

'Mrs Raven?'

'Yes, and for her mother when she was alive. I could clean the place up for you and get the sweep in. I've also got two young lads who would clear the garden.'

'Come in, Doris, you are beginning to interest me. How much would it cost to clean the place up?'

Doris looked around the room, peering up at the cobwebs and running her fingers through the dust. She walked over the fireplace and looked down at the bird litter in the hearth.

'Can't do anything till Dave's done the chimneys, he'll want ten bob. It'll take me two or three days to give it a good clean, say one pound for me. If you want the garden clearing it'll take them days, say five bob each for the lads. I make that two pounds altogether — is that okay?'

'How soon can you start?'

'Tomorrow.'

She picked up the lamp and walked through into the kitchen. Peering into the cupboard under the sink she muttered to herself, 'Carbolic, donkey stone and a new scrubbing brush,' then looking up at Jim said, 'I'll need two bob for stores.'

'How much do you need in advance?' Jim asked.

'Two bob for the stores, ten bob for Dave — he's a tight bugger; he won't work until he sees the money — and five bob for me.'

The pair sat at the kitchen table and Jim laid out the cash. Then he suddenly thought about the key, he only had the one and was reluctant to leave it but Doris produced her own and held it up for him to see.

'I've had it for years. The old lady liked me to have one just in case she keeled over at night. Half the time we never use keys but there're some Eytie prisoners still knocking about so it's best not to tempt them.'

Jim told her that he would be back in three or four days and left her to it. He knew he had to go to London so he went back to the hospital to get that trip organised. The doctor gave him permission to use the hospital telephone so he rang the London number that he'd been given. It turned out to be the American Embassy and he spoke to the military attaché. The following day he was onboard the first train for London via Hull and Doncaster. It was the first time that he'd worn his new uniform in public.

On his arrival at the embassy Jim was shown into a waiting room full of highly polished ornate furniture and gleaming brass fittings. There were four others waiting, two civilians and two American military personnel. When the inner door was thrown open they all got to their feet but the air force colonel who entered made straight for Jim. He thrust out his hand and shook Jim's with some vigour.

'It's great to see you, Sergeant, how's the wound?'

'Fine now, sir.'

'Great, now did you get your pay?'

'Yes, thank you, every penny.'

They walked together down a corridor on carpet so thick that Jim thought that his boots would disappear into it until they reached another door. Jim was asked to wait while the colonel went inside. He didn't have to wait long because the door was thrown open within a minute and he was ushered inside. Five men in various uniforms stood rigidly to attention facing him and they all raised their hands in salute. Jim looked round in confusion before he realised that they were saluting him. He quickly returned the salute and everyone relaxed. A military photographer appeared and stood waiting with a camera. He seemed intent on taking opportunistic pictures because the camera clicked several times whilst Jim was answering questions thrown at him by the assembled officers. Finally Jim was presented with two commendations on vellum, one from the army and the other from the air force. The army one came with a medal whilst the air force presented him with a Purple Heart, the award for those wounded in battle. More photographs followed before Jim was allowed to escape. An American car was laid on to take him back to King's Cross station and Jim's medals etc were in the driver's care.

At the station a long queue of people stood waiting for taxis and Jim's driver deliberately pulled up in front of them. He then made a show of opening the door for Jim and giving him a smart salute before presenting him with a leather briefcase.

'Your medals, sir,' he said, passing over the briefcase before saluting again. Jim returned the salute with a smile and accepted the briefcase.

Half an hour later on the train Jim peered into the case. He knew instantly that there was more inside than he had thought. A third commendation was accompanied by a photograph framed in light-coloured wood and he took it out to investigate. It was picture of a rifle, his rifle, hung on a wall and beneath it were the words: *This rifle was used by Sergeant James Bullock, British Army, also known as Sergeant Crusoe, to shoot down a Japanese Zero.*

Jim was drinking a tepid cup of tea

when the ticket collector came along checking tickets. Jim handed his over and the collector examined it before asking where Jim would be changing trains.

'Doncaster and Hull,' replied Jim.

'Sorry, Sarge, this train does not stop at Doncaster. You'll have to get off at York and catch the milk train back via Beverley in the morning.'

'How did I make that mistake?'

'We're half an hour late, your train is behind us.'

Jim spent that night in the hotel he'd used earlier but that time he slept alone. In the morning he caught the train to Beverley where he had to make a final change. However, the train from Beverley to Driffield stopped at Hutton Cranswick so he decided to see how Doris was getting on.

He watched the train steam away from the station before turning and walking down the street. Several people nodded to him and wished him good morning and one old-timer stopped and shook his hand. When he approached the cottage he couldn't believe his eyes, it had been transformed. The wooden boards had gone from the windows and the glass gleamed, smoke was rising from one chimney and a larger plume of smoke rose from a fire in the garden. The fence was back in place and the path to the door was clear. The front doorstep had been scrubbed and its front edge showed the yellow glow of donkey stone application. He was scrabbling in his pocket for the key when the front door opened and Doris said, 'Welcome home, sir.'

'Good morning, Doris, forget the sir business. I'm Jim. Jim Bullock.'

'I haven't finished inside yet, I still have a couple of rooms to do.'

'That's okay, Doris, as you can see I'm not out of the army yet.' He nodded towards the fire. 'I see you got the chimneys swept fairly quickly.'

'Aye, well Dave was short of beer money so he was down here like a shot. I needed the kitchen stove for hot water for the scrubbing. Yon electric man says you can get a water heater if you have the electric.'

'Electric man?'

'Aye, the village has got electricity, you can get it connected to the house for nothing. Electric man comes from the shop in Driffield.'

Doris led him from room to room showing him what she'd done and making various suggestions for improvements he might like to make once he'd moved in. Together they agreed to add a further pound to her money provided she lit a fire in the house every day until he took up residence.

On the last short train journey to Driffield he decided to investigate getting the electricity supply connected. He talked to the people at the electricity place and got quotes for electric water heaters for the kitchen and for a bathroom upstairs, a thing that didn't exist in his new home at that time. He planned to have a bathroom installed as soon as he could afford one and to that end talked over the possibilities with a plumber. Once again he got quotes for a fully fitted bathroom.

He returned to the hospital tired and hungry only to find the place almost empty. Many of the patients appeared to have been spirited away while he had been in London. He dined in an almost empty messroom and he was joined there by Susan, the nurse.

'What's happened, Susan, where is everyone?' he asked.

'The powers that be are rationalizing us.'

'What does that mean?'

'It means that there too many similar hospitals and not enough patients. The war's over and there are no new patients coming in. We are being closed down.'

'Will you be out of work?'

'Oh I expect I'll find something somewhere. The trouble is there are more and more soldiers like you being demobbed and they all want jobs. My younger brothers have both come home and really there isn't room for us all.'

'How do you mean?'

'Not enough rooms, not enough beds. We keep falling over each other.'

'May I ask a personal question, Susan?'

'Try me.'

'Does your little girl remember her dad?'

'No, he was dead before she was born. Even I struggle to remember his face now.'

'Would I be out of order if I asked you to marry me?'

Susan looked completely stunned and sat open-mouthed so Jim continued.

'I know we're not in love but I thought companionship might be enough initially. We could comfort each other and your little one would have a father figure.'

'But . . . but it's so unexpected. Where would we live?'

'My house in Hutton Cranswick, you could help me modernise it.'

'Modernise it?'

'Yes I'm getting electricity installed and I want to put in a bathroom.'

'Oh, Jim, stop, please stop. You're too much, let me think.'

Susan sat for a few minutes then got to her feet and paced up and down. Eventually she resumed her seat and reached across to grip his hands in hers.

'You're a lovely man, Jim, may I think it over?'

'Of course but I'd like you to know that

this isn't some spur of the moment thing. I was planning to leave it till later but this hospital move has made me ask now.'

Susan stood up and squeezed his shoulder. 'Tomorrow, Jim, I'll let you know then.' She started to walk away then stopped and turned back. 'I nearly forgot, Doctor Pearson would like to see you.'

The doctor's office door was open and he looked up as Jim approached.

'Come in, Jim, have a seat.'

'Am I your last patient, Doc?'

'No, young Private Clarke is still with us. The poor little devil is still crying and shaking and Staff Sergeant White is still here. We thought he was on the mend but he almost strangled an orderly last week, said he was a German in disguise.'

'Can you clear me, Doc?'

'I can and I will. You're to report to Catterick next Monday for demob. How's the house?'

'Clean and warm and I'm getting electricity installed. Is it okay if I stay here until Monday?'

'Sure, just inform the catering staff.'

That night Jim sat poring over the

quotations from the electricity people and those from the plumber. His back pay had hardly been touched so he could see that he could afford to install both the water heaters and the bathroom but that it would leave him little to live on if he didn't find a job quickly. Then there would be the cost of a wedding if Susan said yes. He went to bed still wondering what to do.

He was still eating his breakfast when Susan found him the next morning. She sat opposite him at the table, picked up his cup of tea and took a sip.

'Come on, lazybones, I've got the car. Let's go and see our house,' she said.

Jim sat open-mouthed before stuttering, 'Do . . . you mean marriage?'

'Yes, on one condition.'

'What's that?'

'We'll be man and wife from day one.'

Jim smiled. 'Agreed,' he said.

27

Whilst Jim was away in Catterick going through the demob procedure Susan was supervising the installation of the electricity with help of her brother Joe, an army trained electrician. In fact Joe did quite a bit of the work himself thus keeping down the bill. As a result of his handiwork he was offered the chance to work for the electricity board, an offer he readily accepted.

Although the registry office wedding was three weeks away Jim and Susan lived together as man and wife from the day he returned in his demob suit. My mother, their only child, was born exactly one year from that day. Susan's first daughter, Alice, and my mother were inseparable. It took Jim a month to find a job as a survey assistant to a firm of surveyors in Beverley. He worked for that firm for almost ten years and during that time he met the farmer, Graham Fairbrother and his wife.

The survey that Jim conducted on Graham's farm involved three new fields that Graham wished to buy. During the survey Jim was astounded by the number of wild deer he saw. When he happened to mention that fact to Graham he learned that a licence was required to cull them. Jim obtained a licence then went to the police for gun licences. Once he had those he bought himself a rifle and shotgun and began to reduce the deer on the farm to manageable levels.

My mother met and married my father in 1966 and two years later I put in an appearance. I was their only child. My father worked for an international charity and although we had a home in Beverley we would spend months overseas every year. However, when I was old enough to go to school I was left in Beverley in Alice's care. Alice never married. In fact for some years it was as if I had two mothers, Alice for half the year and mother for the rest. During that time I would see Grandad Jim and Grandmother Susan three or four times a year, usually during the school holidays.

I was twenty-five when I got married and my wife and I went off on a six-week touring holiday through the continent. That was a marvellous period and we returned home six weeks later suntanned, happy and practically broke. The police were waiting for us. During our absence a terrible motoring accident had claimed the lives of my parents, Grandmother and Alice. Grandfather Jim was in a depressed state and refused to see me when I called.

It was Jim's doctor who told me how it happened. Apparently the five of them had been to a show in Scarborough and were on their way home. Jim was driving. On a section of unlit road they came upon several vehicles stopped with their hazard warning lights on. There were also the blue flashing lights of police cars. When Jim lowered the window they could all hear the screams of injured animals. A traffic policeman moved down the line of vehicles looking for someone who could handle a hand gun. Jim went with him to find two badly injured cows kicking and screaming in the road and a very shaken vet trying to put them out of their misery.

He'd already fired twice and missed and only had four shots left. He was shaking when Jim took the gun from him and immediately moved behind the first injured cow. Its legs were thrashing about wildly but Jim was safe behind it. His headshot killed it instantly and the sound of the shot seemed to stun the second injured beast. Jim killed it with his first shot. It was then that the horrible crunch and scream of distorted metal came from the back of the column of vehicles. A lorry laden with concrete blocks had driven at an estimated fifty miles an hour into Jim's car completely crushing it and the four people inside. Jim had to be restrained by two policemen when he attempted to attack the lorry driver.

Eight weeks later at the lorry driver's trial I saw Jim again. He looked haggard and distraught. The driver pleaded guilty to causing death by careless driving so no evidence was called. Jim stood up before a sentence was passed and shouted at the judge.

'Careless driving! That man is guilty of four murders.'

'Sit down or I'll charge you with contempt,' retorted the judge.

Jim stormed to the front of the court and cried, 'If I'm guilty of contempt then this court is guilty of contemptuous justice.'

He shook off the attentions of two court officials and stormed out leaving the court buzzing. It took the judge some minutes to restore order and pass sentence.

Two days later one of the tabloids revealed that the lorry driver had left his glasses at home and without them he was as blind as the proverbial bat. He could read a number plate only when it was ten feet from him. Eighteen months later he was released from prison and although still banned from driving took his lorry out on the road. Several weeks later he missed a turning at night and drove into a river. His load of concrete blocks shifted over the cab preventing his escape. He drowned.

I suppose I buried myself in work after the trial, building up my corporate travel business. For five years I grafted away behind the scenes while my wife met the actual customers. When I think back now I only had myself to blame for the divorce because I put so much into the business that I had little energy to spare after work. She wanted the month of the honeymoon to continue but I was too busy working. In the end I lost her and the business.

★ ★ ★

Jim had already left for his reunion when I left to meet Silver. He had wished me luck the night before because he was leaving in the early morning, hours before me. When I drove into the Sutton Bank car park there were several family cars already there but I saw no sign of Silver's. I sat and waited for ten minutes before his car turned in and parked alongside mine. His driver backed in tight up to my car, so tight that I couldn't open my driver's door. The big ugly brute got out of Silver's car and moved into the seat alongside me. He began checking me for weapons but I had used my common sense and left the handgun at home despite Jim's urgings. Once big and ugly was satisfied that I wasn't armed he left but not before telling me to lower my window. In the other car Silver did the same. It was like looking into a mirror.

'Good morning, Luke,' he said.

'I prefer Mr Sharp,' I replied.

'You're angry.'

'Naturally, you attacked my friends.'

'That was a mistake, it will not happen again while you're working for me.'

'I have no intention of working for you.'

'Now, Mr Sharp, you haven't heard my proposal yet. There's five grand if you visit my barber then ten grand for each stand-in appearance.'

'So you want me to stand up and be shot at for ten grand a time, no thank you.'

'You'd be protected.'

'What would you be doing while I'm your stand-in?'

'Conducting my business in private.'

'No thank you Mr Silver, goodbye.'

I started my engine and pulled carefully away as he snarled, 'You fool.'

Big and ugly moved to stop me but I

caught his knee and set him stumbling backwards. /After that I drove out of the car park and turned towards home. I kept my eyes on the rear-view mirror half expecting to see Silver's car come after me. It turned out onto the road but took the opposite route down Sutton Bank.

I hadn't had much stomach for breakfast that morning so I was beginning to feel rather hungry as I drove. There was a café in Malton that I'd visited before so I decided to stop there and get myself a meal. After I'd eaten I wandered round the town for a while window shopping before finally heading for home. I think I used that town walk to calm myself down because I was still rather uptight over the earlier meeting.

The first thing I saw when I got back was Jim's borrowed car badly parked outside the house. I parked behind it and went inside wondering why I was feeling uneasy. Jim's coat was slung over a chair which was unusual because I'd never seen him do that before. I went through to the shed but that was locked so I came back in to see if I could find him. He was collapsed across his bed still fully clothed and breathing as if gasping for breath. I felt his forehead and realised that he had a temperature. I rang for the doctor before undressing him and tucking him up in bed. He never woke despite my ministrations. His skin was hot and dry at first but while I was waiting for the doctor to turn up he began to shiver quite violently. I pulled a couple of blankets over him.

Doc Wilson, his old friend and occasional drinking partner, took one look at him and said, 'malaria'. While he was taking his temperature Jim opened his eyes and muttered 'no hospitals' before groaning and closing his eyes again. The doctor motioned me outside and later joined me at the foot of the stairs.

'Where has he been?' he asked.

'He told me he was going to a reunion.'

'I told him the last time this happened that his body could not stand another bout. Stay with him while I collect some medication. I won't be long.'

I rang the garage and asked them to

pick up the loan car before going back upstairs. Jim had thrown off the blankets and was shivering again so I pulled them back over him. He began to mutter occasional words that I remembered from the tapes. He mentioned Simmo's name a couple of times and Fred's. He kept saying sorry to Susan over and over again. He was still saying that when the doctor returned and shooed me out of the room. A few minutes later the doorbell rang and I answered it to find a nurse standing there carrying the metal frame for a drip.

'The doctor sent for me,' she said.

I showed her where to go then put the kettle on for a cup of tea. When it boiled I changed my mind and opened a can of beer instead. I'd nearly finished it when the doctor came back down.

'He's in a bad way, Luke. To borrow one of your grandfather's sayings, his temperature is up and down like a whore's drawers.'

'He kept saying sorry to Susan, do you know why?'

'The car crash, he blamed himself for all those deaths. He once told me that if he'd stayed in the car he'd have seen the lorry coming and got the car out of the way. He went back into his post war depression for months after the trial.'

'He wouldn't see me.'

'I know, he wouldn't see me for weeks either. He went out at night and bought supplies at a late night shop somewhere. The poor old bugger couldn't stop blaming himself.'

'Will he be okay?'

'I don't know, his system is weak, he may not pull through this time.'

'Is the nurse staying?'

'Yes she'll be here all night. You will have to relieve her now and again so she can eat and so on. I'll look in again in a couple of hours.'

I was dozing in a fireside chair about eleven o'clock when the nurse came down.

'He wants to see you,' she said.

When I got to the bedside he looked to be asleep but he opened his eyes and looked at me.

'You're a good lad, Luke. Look after my guns.' He closed his eyes again then gripped my hand. I could barely hear what he said then but I'm sure he said, 'I wasted a bullet.'

He didn't speak again and he died twenty minutes later. I heard the doctor behind me say, 'Who am I going to drink with now?'

The following morning I was wandering around trying to make myself some breakfast when the phone rang. At first I tried to ignore it but it kept ringing so I answered it.

'You missed all the fun,' said the familiar voice of Sergeant Cooper.

'What fun?'

'Silver going up in smoke just after you left him.'

'What do you mean?'

'The vigilantes got him with a grenade launcher. The whole car went up in smoke.'

'Thanks for letting me know but I can't rejoice at the moment, Jim died last night.'

'Oh Christ, I'm sorry. Let me know when the funeral is.'

Doc Wilson helped me with all the

various paperwork and organisation for the funeral. In fact he showed me where Jim kept his will and various insurance papers. He even contacted the solicitor for me. Not only did he know where Jim kept the will his signature was on it as a witness. Jim left me everything. As far as the funeral was concerned he wanted a simple memorial service at the crematorium at Octon. That was arranged for ten days after his death.

On the day after he died a letter with an American postmark turned up so I opened it. It turned out to be a renewal notice for the veteran's newspaper that he received every month. There was an email address so I sent a message to say that Jim had died and therefore to cancel the order. That evening I got a reply asking if they could post an obituary notice at no cost to me so I gave them the go ahead. They wanted dates and funeral details so I gave them all they asked for.

Cards and letters of condolence began to arrive almost daily mostly from local people but also from America. The American names meant nothing until I opened that signed book again and crosschecked them. The name on every American card corresponded with a signature in the book. Simmo's card from New Zealand was the last to arrive.

About two or three days before the funeral I remembered what Jim had asked me to do, to look after his guns. When I opened the gun cabinet it was immediately obvious that Jim had put his rifle away in a hurry. It wasn't racked properly and it hadn't been cleaned. While I was cleaning it I tried to think just when it had been used last. Then I began to wonder if he'd used it on the reunion day. After I finished and racked the gun correctly I went to check the coat he'd worn that day. I remembered hanging it in the hall where it usually hung. In the right-hand pocket I found a spent cartridge case. It must have been a strange reunion, I thought.

28

Jim had already specified in his will the type of funeral he wanted so I did my best to follow what he requested. He wanted a celebration of his life — big band music, no dark clothing and no sky pilot. I had to have that last term explained to me — no churchman. I decided that I would attempt to give a potted history of his life from all that I'd learned from the tapes. Graham Fairbrother had asked to say a few words as had the doctor so the order of service was fluid to say the least.

Ours was the only funeral that morning and that was fortunate because we overran the timing somewhat. The crematorium was packed and many of the people there I'd not seen before. The coffin was brought in to the strains of the tune, 'When the Saints Go Marching In' and two flags were laid across it, those of the United Kingdom and the USA. That was something I hadn't arranged. People clapped or sang to the music so it was more like a revivalist meeting than a funeral at first.

I had originally given myself ten minutes to present a potted history of Jim's life but I was the first to overrun time wise. It was obvious that many there knew nothing of Jim's wartime exploits and his three year private battle with the Japanese came as a surprise to many. When I finally stepped down and handed over to Graham and the doctor there was a loud round of applause.

There was a surprise for me and everyone else after the doctor stepped down having bemoaned the loss of his drinking partner. Two grey-haired, elegantly dressed ladies stood up and walked to the front, both wanting to say a few words. I stood aside and let them have their say. The first lady looked around the packed room before speaking.

'My friend and I have come from America to say goodbye to a very dear friend,' she said. 'My name is Sylvia, I first met Jim before the war. We danced together on the boat deck of the P & O liner that took him to Malaya. He was a poor dancer, a great friend and briefly my lover. He restored my faith in myself when I was at a low ebb. A wonderful man.'

Her friend stepped forward then.

'Jim was a patient of mine when I first met him, he was suffering from malaria. My name is Coral and I was a nurse on a hospital ship. He was first a patient, then a colleague and finally very briefly my lover. He had and still does have many American friends.'

She stepped down and walked over to the coffin, briefly brushed her lips over its surface the stood back and said in a low voice, 'Farewell my lovely.'

Once more there was applause but this time it was deafening. As the two women resumed their seats one more person walked to the front. He looked round the room and everyone could see the tears in his eyes.

'I'm Simmo,' he said. 'I've just come over from New Zealand to say goodbye to the best mate I ever had. You've got to be mates when you're taking leeches from each other's backsides. Goodbye mate.'

He came to attention and saluted the coffin before returning to his seat.

When the coffin finally slid through the final curtain it did so to the strains of 'Moonlight Serenade.'

Afterwards many of us assembled in the adjacent refreshment room where tea, coffee and sandwiches were laid on. The two American ladies said they would like to see where Jim had lived and as they hadn't a great deal of time to spare the doctor agreed to take them while I stayed on with the other guests. Simmo came over and handed me a brown envelope.

'I thought you might like this,' he said. 'It's a copy of my sketchbook, the one Jim saved for me.'

I opened it and looked through the pictures and as I did so I could relate to the events that I'd listened to on the tapes. It was a wonderful gift and I thanked him for it. When I asked if he was staying he said no, he was intending to see family that he hadn't seen for years.

People drifted away gradually until I

thought I was the last one there, I wasn't. Sergeant Cooper appeared beside me munching a sandwich.

'Some surprises there,' he mumbled through his sandwich.

'Were you here for the whole thing?' I asked.

'Certainly, I was tucked away at the back. Have you got time to listen to me for a few minutes?'

I nodded.

'That day when Silver died, I was there watching over you.'

'Thanks.'

'When Silver's car started down the hill there was a big van behind it. About halfway down that first section before that big bend Silver's car started to move from side to side. I thought they'd seen what was coming from that van but now I think differently.'

'Go on.'

'Well those vigilantes in the van fired off their grenade launcher through their missing windscreen just as Silver's car reached the bend. The car went over the edge as it exploded.'

'I thought that thing was supposed to be armoured?'

'It was but the glass was bullet-proof, it couldn't stand up to a grenade launcher.'

'I take it they were all killed.'

He pointed back over his shoulder with his thumb. 'Cremated, all three of them.'

'Did those vigilantes get away?'

'Sure, they abandoned the van and the launcher in that lay-by halfway down the hill and disappeared in the shambles that followed.'

'How did they know about the meeting?'

Cooper shrugged his shoulders. 'Someone must have let something slip,' he said with a half grin.

I waited because I felt he had something else to say.

'I saw the car the following day. Inside there was nothing left, the armour plating had contained the fire quite well. The tyres were okay though except for one. Someone had put two bullets through one of the front tyres.'

He held out his hand and opened it to reveal a spent cartridge. He gave it to me.

'I think your grandfather was looking after you as well,' he said. 'The grenade launcher wasn't needed, that car could never have got round that bend with the front tyre wrecked.'

He held out his hand and shook mine. 'Goodbye, Luke, it's been nice knowing you. I'll disconnect the phone when I get back.'

Those two matching cartridge cases are sitting on the desk in front of me as I type this. I can also hear Jim's last words: 'I wasted a bullet.' My assumption was that he was talking about a Japanese Zero but he was actually telling me about Silver's front tyre.

THE END

STORM EVIL

John Robb

A terrible storm sweeps across a vast desert of North Africa. Five legionnaires and a captain on a training course are caught in it and take refuge in a ruined temple. Into the temple, too, come four Arabs laden with hate for the Legion captain. Then a beautiful aviator arrives — the estranged wife of the officer. When darkness falls, and the storm rages outside, the Arabs take a slow and terrible vengeance against the captain. Death strikes suddenly, often, and in a grotesque form . . .

ROOKIE COP

Richard A. Lupoff

America, June 1940. Nick Train has
given up his dreams of a boxing
championship after a brief and unsuc-
cessful career in the ring. When one of
his pals takes the examination for the
police academy, Nick decides to join
him. But what started out as a whim
turns into a dangerous challenge, as
Nick plays a precarious double game
of collector for the mob and mole for
a shadowy enforcement body . . . Will
the rookie cop's luck hold?

THE DEVIL'S DANCE

V. J. Banis

When Chris leaves New York for a vacation with her half-sister Pam, who is staying at a Tennessee country mansion, she discovers that the remote backwater is the site of a centuries-old feud raging between the Andrewses and the Melungeons; and Chris's elderly host, Mrs. Andrews, lives in fear. Danger lurks everywhere, from the deceptively tranquil countryside to the darkly handsome, yet mysterious, Gabe who hides amid the shadows. And when events take a more sinister turn, it seems that the curse of the Melungeons is hungry for more victims . . .

FIND THE LADY

Norman Firth

When gangster Mike Spagliotti is found shot through the head inside his locked New York hotel suite, it is a perplexing problem for Detective-Inspector Flannel. And when newspaper reporter Anita Curzon begins to interfere, Flannel's temper does not improve . . . In *The Egyptian Tomb* Tony Gilmour and his friends Ron and Alan travel to Egypt to investigate the suspicious death of Ron's father — but they are dogged by enemies who will stop at nothing to ensure that no one discovers the secret of the tomb of Ko Len Tep!